THE EMERALD ENCHANTRESS

The Silver Order
Book 3

by Ella Leon

ARE YOU SIGNED UP FOR DRAGONBLADE'S BLOG?

You'll get the latest news and information on exclusive giveaways, exclusive excerpts, coming releases, sales, free books, cover reveals and more.

Check out our complete list of authors, too!

No spam, no junk. That's a promise!

Sign Up Here

www.dragonbladepublishing.com

Dearest Reader;

Thank you for your support of a small press. At Dragonblade Publishing, we strive to bring you the highest quality Historical Romance from some of the best authors in the business. Without your support, there is no 'us', so we sincerely hope you adore these stories and find some new favorite authors along the way.

Happy Reading!

CEO, Dragonblade Publishing

Additional Dragonblade books by Author Ella Leon

The Silver Order Series
The Sapphire Heiress (Book 1)
The Crystal Alchemist (Book 2)
The Emerald Enchantress (Book 3)

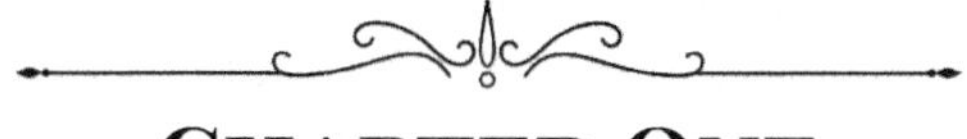

CHAPTER ONE

Healer

London, 1910

AMARA ABBOTT, COUNTESS of Webb, braced herself against a pillar. The bastard wasn't giving up. He was still after her. In the crowded ballroom, there was absolutely no escape.

She couldn't let him get anywhere near. If he asked her to dance, she'd have to say *yes* or make some excuse and endure an entire conversation. She couldn't just say *no* and walk away. That was a rule she'd always hated. As if Englishmen weren't entitled to enough.

The man, a viscount, she believed, had pestered her all evening. She had put up with him and all the others long enough. For three London seasons, to be precise. Three. But enough was enough. In spite of her mother's efforts, she was never going to find a match.

It wasn't as if suitors didn't notice her. It was simply a different sort of notice. The lascivious kind any decent lady would have been expected to reject. And yet the so-called gentlemen of London were always so surprised when she did.

Of course none of them even remotely considered the possibility of marriage. Not with her background. Apparently, it was something few of high rank could see past. They wanted her as a mistress and nothing more. A fact her mother refused to acknowledge.

Fortune and titles were supposed to make one popular in

society. Especially when one had both. She was the exception. Despite being a countess, she was too unusual, too "exotic," they called her.

She had failed before she had ever even had a chance. The guilt was hard to escape. She had a responsibility to her estate.

Even a transactional marriage, which was her duty as a peeress in her own right, was no longer in the cards.

Attending tonight's ball had been nothing more than a farce. As much as she wanted to leave, her lady's maid and chaperone would never let her. From across the ballroom, Granger was searching for her too.

Perhaps she could slip off somewhere darker and more secluded like the gardens, but no. She couldn't make that mistake again. A year ago, she had barely escaped the stonewalls and arbors with her corset intact. Since then, she rarely, if ever, entered any areas that weren't crowded with people. Even empty halls with their curtained window alcoves were risky. They gave men too many ideas.

She peered over the edge of the pillar, hoping her unyielding suitor had given up. Instead, narrowing, dark-brown eyes caught hers. He panted, raking back his gray mop of hair. He was only twenty or so paces away. Amara cursed, taking off across the ballroom. Anywhere it was most crowded so he couldn't get through so quickly. If she had to run in circles all night, she would.

Her cheeks would be flush enough that her mother might actually believe she'd had a full dance card. It might even lift her spirits.

Earlier that week, her mother had taken a turn for the worse. The poor woman could barely open her eyes to see before Amara had left, but she had managed to smile. It was the only reason Amara had forced herself to come out tonight and endure all the stares. More than anything in the world, more perhaps than getting well, her mother wanted this. She wanted to see Amara galivanting amongst high society and, better yet, married off to an English gentleman who matched her late father's rank or higher.

Amara didn't have the heart to tell her the truth.

The crowd suddenly opened and she ran so fast that when a black jacket stepped out and blocked her path, she couldn't stop. She crashed into what felt like a solid wall of steel.

"Excuse me," she apologized profusely. She was mortified. Then he turned around.

It was Darren Pierce. He loomed over her, impossibly tall and broad-shouldered. But of all the men in the ballroom, she detested him the most. Even if there was something about his face she liked, that didn't make him a good or decent person. No matter how brilliantly his blue eyes gleamed, a wonderfully steely contrast to his rich-brown hair. He was far from it.

"What's the—" He broke off, his playful smile dropping. He straightened, somehow standing even taller. He must have caught sight of the man closing in behind her.

"Excuse me." She tried to move around him, but the crowd had closed in again. If she could just get past, she might still be able to—

"Lady Webb." The viscount gripped her arm and heaved a breath. "I was wondering if you'd care to dance."

There was no hint of malice, no indication of a chase. But the bastard knew she'd been avoiding him. He just didn't care.

"I'm afraid she's already promised a dance to me." Mr. Pierce stepped between them.

The viscount stared him down, almost as if to assess if he was worth the fight. Appearing to think better of it, he clenched his jaw and moved away. She supposed Mr. Pierce was the lesser evil of the two. At the very least easier to escape.

"Don't worry," he whispered. "We don't actually have to dance. I don't like it much myself. I prefer conversation." He led her away to a more secluded corner of the ballroom where they could more easily hear each other.

"You did that on purpose."

"Did what on purpose?"

"Blocked my path."

He crossed his arms and widened his stance in false and exaggerated outrage. "I think what you mean to say is 'thank you.'"

She sighed. This was the last man to whom she wanted to feel indebted, much less thank. She turned away and looked out at the crowd. Somehow, in that small span of time, the room had filled up even more. And yet there was no one she recognized. No one, therefore, to escape to.

"Running from your suitors is no way to catch one."

"They're not *my* suitors." She bristled, flicking her eyes upwards. "You couldn't even call them 'gentlemen.'"

"Are there more on the chase?" He made a show of looking around. "You best hide, then." He turned to a large candelabra and pinched six of the twelve of the candles, casting them into dull darkness. "Allow me to assist."

She caught a hint of slurring in his words then. A little wobble in his steps as he pinched the last candle.

"Heavens, you're drunk, aren't you?" How hadn't she noticed before?

"Not quite, my lady. But almost." He waved over a footman and grabbed another champagne glass from the tray. He handed her one too, though she barely sipped it.

"Spirits are the half reason I attend these events."

"And the other reason?" She didn't know why she even bothered asking.

"To assist troubled damsels such as yourself, of course."

"Well, I don't want your help."

She pulled the glass out of his hand and placed it back on a passing footman's tray, along with her own. Her mind was as altered as it needed to be and so was his.

In spite of the move, he smiled, the sharp angles of his face traced by faint candlelight.

"I quite understand why you're running, you know. The men here are bores and a half."

"Including you."

He laughed and brushed a hand through his hair. "Boorish, maybe but never a bore. My father doesn't allow me the time. You know how much the Silver Order demands of me."

Thanks to her late father's membership, she did. The Silver Order was one of many secret societies in London. And Theodore Pierce, Mr. Darren Pierce's father, was chair. They were the scholarly, head-in-a-book sort. They just didn't study the usual topics. Mr. Pierce was well-versed in Latin and Shakespeare, of course, but preferred other more unusual topics, like the study of energy, meditation, and universal consciousness. Hardly the topics polite society approved. Rules Mr. Pierce didn't care to follow. Neither had her father, for that matter.

"Those earrings." He tilted his head and leaned in. "What are they?"

He always took an interest in her jewelry, particularly the gemstones. He had the oddest fascination with crystals. Or maybe it was just an excuse for him to get close.

"Garnets." Amara stepped back. "They're not my favorite. Too much like the color of blood."

"Then why wear them?"

"My mother wanted me to. They belong to the estate. My father's mother wore them last."

Mentioning Earl Webb aloud made her throat tighten. He'd been gone only a year now. First his accident and now her mother's poor health. Some people said it was losing him that had made her mother sick. Whatever the reason, her mother couldn't leave her alone in the world. She *had* to get better.

"How's your mother?" Mr. Pierce asked, like he was reading her thoughts, his face pinched with worry, nothing mocking or false about it.

"Ill," Amara said tersely.

"You don't want to talk about it?"

Amara shook her head. She knew all too well that he'd lost his mother some years back. To draw any comparisons would be too painful to bear.

"I can imagine it—" Mr. Pierce started, but Amara cut him off.

"Just because your father and my father once shared an association, that doesn't mean we have to continue the connection."

Amara had told him this before. He still happened to attend all the same society balls, dinner parties, and soirees that she did. If she didn't know any better, she might even think he was beginning to like her in the same useless way the other men did. He might have been younger, taller, and objectively good-looking, but he was still like the rest.

"They didn't just *share an association.*" Mr. Pierce crossed his arms. "They were friends."

In her mind, it was *his* father's fault the earl was dead in the first place. Theodore Pierce had always been sending the earl on expeditions, a hobby her father had loved more than anything. If the elder Mr. Pierce wasn't around to give the earl's travels endless funding and purpose, would her father have gone as often or at all? Would he have died looking for rare amethysts in South America, a thousand miles from home?

"My father mourned your father deeply," Mr. Pierce said. "So did I."

Amara shrugged. Because he, too, was a member of the Order, he was just as guilty.

"He should have never left home in the first place," Amara said. "If it weren't for your father—"

"Sins of the father… Is that why you insist on hating me? You know, if it weren't for my father, yours would have never met your mother."

He was right. Amara hated that he was right.

"It was your father's choice to become one of our most loyal crystal hunters."

Whatever that meant. An occupation she didn't like to talk about. She hoped no one had heard him. She had it bad enough.

Mr. Pierce went on, undeterred. "He wanted to take you with

him one day."

Amara huffed. She couldn't picture it. At the same time, she couldn't picture herself here among all these painted peacocks, either. She didn't belong anywhere.

She found Granger in the crowd, her pale eyes watching her. When they locked gazes, the young lady's maid didn't wave Amara over to hurry up and find a suitable dance partner. In her eyes, Mr. Pierce *was* the suitable dance partner. Anyone was.

"The way I see it, you have two choices," her dance partner said. "Stand here and have a conversation with me. Or find your next dance partner amongst this sea of bores."

He was an unabashed flirt. But at least he had yet to try to sneak her out into the gardens. Sadly, he was the best she could hope for.

"Fine," she grumbled.

For the rest of the evening, they talked while Granger lingered nearby, playing with her fan.

At least Amara was giving her something positive to report.

CHAPTER TWO
The Visitor

AMARA WAS HOME by midnight. A reasonable enough hour to show that she'd made at least some meaningful connections. Also late enough she wouldn't have to provide her mother with an evening summary until morning.

She moved extra quiet on the staircase. Oddly, all the sconces were still lit.

"Hmm." Granger hummed. "I thought your mother would be asleep by now."

Amara nodded. Had something happened while she'd been gone? She quickened her steps, not caring about silence this time.

In her room, her mother wasn't alone. Someone was there, standing over her sleeping mother's fragile form like the grim reaper. When she stepped out of the shadows, her skin was brown like her mother's. Almost immediately, Amara recognized her face. Even though she'd never met this woman before, it was strikingly obvious that they were related.

Amara waved Granger off.

"Hello there," Amara began.

Her visitor wore wide, white sleeves and a plain, black skirt. Unlike the fashions here, the skirt was flat with no ruffles. It was made out of one layer of some thin linen material too. Whatever it was, it would hardly hold up on the streets of London. Amara swung the door the rest of the way open. She had never met any of her mother's relatives. Not once.

"You're Amara?"

The woman spoke Tagalog, a language Amara only spoke with her mother. Most people didn't even know she could speak it. For the first time in her life, she spoke the language to someone new. It felt so odd but wonderful too.

The woman rushed over and took up both her hands. "Do you know who I am?"

"I think so. You're my…"

"Call me 'Lola.'"

In Tagalog, it meant *grandmother*.

She motioned Amara into the hallway and slowly shut the door behind her.

"What are you doing here?" Amara asked in disbelief.

"Your mother begged me in her letters not to come. But I refused to stay away."

"When did you arrive?" Amara asked. It couldn't have been more than a few hours ago. "You need to rest."

"No." Lola shook her head ardently. "It is nothing. First I had to see if I could cure her."

"Not even the best doctors in London can."

Lola clucked her tongue.

"I see your mother hasn't told you anything about me? About us?"

Amara bit her lip. Her mother always tried so hard to fit in here. So did she.

Lola heaved a heavy sigh, frustrated, apparently, with Amara's ignorance.

"I'm a healer. So was my mother before me and her mother before that. For centuries. A long and most distinguished bloodline. Your mother has told you the legends, hasn't she?"

"She's told me a few."

Amara always loved listening to her mother's stories. Maybe it was because she told them to her before bed, but they were always so soothing.

"They're not just tales, you know. They're truth."

Amara felt herself sway. She touched her temples, trying to steady herself. "Mother failed to mention that."

"First—where is your hearth?"

"I'll take you," Amara said, somewhat in a daze. By this time, she had expected to be in bed. Instead, Amara was leading her lola, whom she had never met before tonight, down the stairs into the kitchen.

The woman immediately started rummaging through the cupboards, sniffing the teas, herbs, and spices. She took something out from a bag that hung at her hip.

Lola gathered a mix of spices and herbs, though Amara couldn't tell which. She assumed enough to put the kettle on.

"We didn't choose this talent of ours. We were chosen. By the diwata. Do you know what those are?" She narrowed her eyes.

"Strange, little beings that dwell in the mountains and protect them," Amara said. "With supernatural abilities, right? They call them 'fairies' here, I think."

"It's important to know that they aren't all sweet and well-intentioned. Only sometimes. They certainly don't give anything away for free. A trade was made. The most precious thing a person could give. Not jewels, gold, or baskets of cocoa, but a loved one. To gain, one must always sacrifice."

"A sacrifice? For what?"

"A talent. With nature's tools, particularly those hidden beneath the trees, we could heal anyone we want, no matter how serious the illness. We became renowned for it, sought after. People would travel for miles and miles." Lola tilted her head. "Until eventually, it turned into a curse. We had to go into hiding. We had no choice but to limit our talents and use them only in the rarest of circumstances. One day, we'd leave the islands altogether. At least your mother did."

Amara nodded. It was the same story her mother had told her. She wanted to believe it. Maybe she was just a cynic, but it seemed only too convenient that her mother had never gotten the chance to prove her abilities.

Lola scrunched her nose. With her silence, Lola could sense Amara's skepticism. The truth was Amara knew so little of that culture, only what her mother had told her. She hadn't been immersed in it. She had grown up like any other English lady. Aside from a ghost story or two, English high society was too modern to believe in things like magic.

"You don't believe it, do you?" Lola confirmed. "You never have."

"I never got any proof."

"Are you so sure about that?"

"When I was a child, Mother applied plenty of odd herbs to my scrapes and cuts, of course. Sure, they healed, but not overnight or anything."

"Our gift doesn't always work fast, you know. But your cuts, they never got infected did they?"

"Thanks to the herbs."

"Maybe. Maybe not. You shouldn't get caught up on such details."

"If only Father had had an accident here," Amara said. It was something she had considered often. "Do you think Mother could have healed him?"

"Of course." She reached out and touched Amara's hand. "You must let him go, dear. A dark aura hovers over you. Enough to steal the light from everything you touch. Whatever gift you've inherited from your mother has diminished, I can tell. It doesn't help that you don't use it."

Amara turned away, though it was hard to pretend she didn't care.

"I didn't say it was gone completely. Just faded a little. There're still so many people you can help. Most of all, your mother."

"I thought you said *you* could cure her."

"I said I would try. But alas…the gift fades with age."

Was it really possible she had such a gift? Amara wanted to believe it. A gift like that could solve everything. Maybe the Philippines had special herbs that worked better than the medicine did here. Maybe there was a science behind them Lola or everyone else just didn't understand.

"Then I will try," Amara finally agreed. "Just tell me how."

"No. No. Unfortunately, you must go back."

"'Back'?"

"Yes, if you want to save her, you have to return back home and bring back the right gemstones."

Amara gulped. "You want me to cross the sea all the way to the islands just for some gemstones?" Just the thought of traveling... The long sea journey in God-knew-what weather terrified her. Her father had told her enough stories from his expeditions. Not just of wild storms, but of unfathomable sea creatures that sounded more like monsters. They waited hidden underwater just waiting for a ship to pass so it could strike.

She could never forget the giant squid her father had told her about once. How it had tried to bring the ship down into the depths of the sea, wrapping its tentacles along the railing like twine. The only way they could free themselves had been stabbing and shooting at its eyes. Unlike its tentacles, those couldn't be replaced.

The tale sounded especially fantastical as an adult.

"Green ones. Esmerelda. I don't know what you call it here. You place the stones in the water like tea. Then drink."

"Can't I just buy them or something similar somewhere in Town? We have a jeweler—"

"No," Lola said flatly, starting to get frustrated. "Not these stones. These ones are special."

"You really think that will work? Do you really think that will cure her?"

"Of course!" Lola huffed. "You know nothing of our ways, do you?"

Lola shook her head, making Amara feel ashamed for it.

"Her illness is not so bad yet. But she is weak and I expect her condition will only worsen."

"The doctors call it 'tuberculosis.'" Amara said the word in English. "They told me she could have years. But not beyond three."

"You need to help her," Lola insisted.

"What if there isn't enough time? What if she dies?"

"Death is not near." Lola held up her hand as though waiting to sense it. "Not yet."

"Can't *you* go back home and get it?"

What if she was wrong and her mother only had days or weeks left? If she died when she was away, she'd miss her last days.

"It's not so easy. If it were, I would have brought them back myself. One must travel through jungle to get them. Harsh jungle, no less."

"You could have told someone the way."

"You forget, my dear, how valuable these gems are. They can heal anything and so they are a secret we must protect."

"You've used them before?"

How much could she trust this woman? She was her lola, yes. But up until today, a complete stranger. Now she was telling her she had to travel thousands of miles for some crystals that could supposedly cure any ailment?

"I've handled a few of them. Their potency does not last. And they only work in our hands."

"I don't know…"

"You must go. It is your fate. What do they call it here? Your *destiny,*" she said in English before switching back to Tagalog. "I can feel it in my bones."

She came close again, tracing Amara's every facial feature with her eyes, sensing again something she couldn't see.

"You're different than your mother, you know. Your ability is much stronger than hers ever was. All you must do is release it. Perhaps that is more important."

No, Amara wanted to protest, *nothing could be more important than my mother's recovery.* If this journey could come anywhere close to accomplishing that, perhaps she should agree.

"Sit down." Lola motioned Amara to the stool alongside the long, oak table. Amara couldn't remember the last time she'd sat in the kitchen. It had been years. This late at night, it was completely empty.

"You're sure I have time before the illness takes her?" Amara didn't like thinking of her mother's death, but she needed to be sure.

"It is a risk. But a small one. The bigger risk is doing nothing," Lola said almost philosophically.

"But who will take care of Mother while I'm gone?" Amara asked.

"I will, of course. In a house as grand as this, you have servants too, don't you?"

Amara nodded. That was the convenience of having money and an estate. At the same time, even the best, most expensive medicines couldn't cure her. Maybe she did need something from home. This might very well be her mother's only chance.

Amara dropped her head down, smelling onions on the wooden table. This was all too much. She hadn't even the time to take off her shawl. The smell of cigar smoke was still in her hair and the faint wisp of Mr. Pierce's cologne. He was always scented with the same cedar and moss blend. Something that reminded her of a forest. All from an evening that felt miles away.

"Amara? Concentrate. We must book you passage quickly. When you arrive you will stay in my home. Your cousin Selene is awaiting you." Lola pulled the kettle from the hearth and poured it into a teacup. She didn't bother straining the ingredients. Did she not know they had a strainer? Without servants to assist her, Amara had no idea where it was. She wanted to look, but she was too overcome with the journey ahead to play host.

"It would be best if you left before the end of the month," Lola went on. "The sooner, the better. Money, I assume, will be of no concern?"

"I will have to talk with Mother first. And Granger, my lady's maid. I'll need her to accompany me."

Had she really just agreed to go?

"For your sake, I pray that she is willing. The journey will not be an easy one. Here." She handed Amara a cup. "Drink this. I will join you in a moment."

Amara looked down at it. Whatever was in it had completely dissolved. She'd expected tea. Rather, it was chocolate with a hint of spice.

"What is this?"

Lola raised a brow. "You haven't had chocolate like this, have you? It's from home. Far better than anything you've had here, I can promise you that."

She was right. Amara had had chocolate before, but this was by far the richest. Greedily, she took another sip. Calmness washed over her.

"Drink up. You're going to need your rest. Tomorrow, we'll make the arrangements."

"Don't worry. I'll have Granger take care of it."

"You'll at least have to pack your things."

"Granger will do that too."

Lola put her hands on her hips, not much different than her mother. For a second, it almost made Amara laugh. "What will *you* have to do?"

"I'll have to handle the seasickness."

"You've never been on a boat, I imagine."

"Not once."

Maybe Lola could see the fear in her eyes. She put a hand on Amara's shoulder. "You come from sterner stock than you think. Soon, you will know."

Amara was really going to do it. For the first time, she was going to see her mother's home, the place she had only dreamed about after a night of her mother's storytelling.

"You said I have a cousin. What about other family? Aunts

and uncles?"

"You have two of each. Best keep them out of this. Until your mother is healed, involve only Selene."

Amara felt her heart drop. She looked away. She'd never had much family, least of all on her mother's side. She'd always been curious to meet them, to see how they might be alike.

"But what if I want to meet them?"

"There will be another time for meet-and-greets. When your mother is well."

"Is this that big of a secret?" she asked, though if it was all true, she could see why.

"Of course."

But she wanted to meet them. She could only imagine how vastly different her mother's relatives would be from the stiff, upper-lipped relatives on her father's side. They didn't pay many visits, not even for an afternoon. It was like she and her mother hadn't any family at all.

This townhouse, and their country estate, for that matter, always felt so cold and empty. To have Lola here, making herself right at home, the house suddenly felt warm and cozy.

Lola prepared a second cup of cocoa, pulling out another piece of chocolate wrapped tightly in parchment.

It didn't seem to matter how different this house or the whole country probably was to her, or that, as mother of the dowager countess, she ought not to have been acting a servant. She moved around the kitchen hearth with such skill, Amara almost felt like a guest. Usually, she was. The kitchen, after all, belonged to the servants. The room didn't have the carpets, the scrolled furniture, or the cushions of the dining and drawing rooms, and yet it emanated comfort nonetheless. Here, they were surrounded by the glow of copper pots and a thousand shades of tan stone. At the end of the long, wooden table, the hearth took up almost an entire wall. Even though it was not her place, Amara rather liked it.

"Do you have a man yet?" Lola asked, snatching her right out of her ease and back into the frigid drawing rooms of the ton.

"Not quite."

"Not one?"

Amara shrugged.

Lola sat down across from her and sipped. Something flickered across her face, something sad. But in an instant, it was gone. She was difficult to read again.

"It can't be easy for you here," Lola said.

That was an understatement.

"It's better for you even so."

Amara chewed her lip. "I'm not so sure about that."

She immediately recalled the odd and malicious looks she received at parties, even from those who were supposed to be her friends. She remembered every single one.

"I am. This trip will be but a blip on a long and prosperous road ahead. But the islands are still part of your soul. They always will be." She stared at the table. "Try not to forget that."

"No one here lets me," Amara grumbled.

"It's a small price to pay, I suppose. You mustn't forget…you are a lady, an English noblewoman. You've been bestowed a title, haven't you?"

Amara nodded. "My father's estate allows daughters to inherit by writ in the absence of a son. Some of our ancestors were Scottish." Nonetheless, her father had never made her feel like anything less than for not being born a man. He'd been more than glad to have her inherit. The estate's entail was one of his greatest gifts. Tagalog from her mother was perhaps an even grander gift, especially now. Her mother might only use it to talk badly about the servants, but without it, Amara wouldn't have been able to talk to her grandmother. Or anyone else on the islands, for that matter.

"There's a whole other part to you you don't even know. There were days I feared you might never know." Lola gripped her hand. "The journey will be difficult. You'll have to transfer onto at least two different ships and perhaps stay overnight at various ports. And that is just to get to Manila. When you arrive, you'll have to make your way…" Lola looked about the room, making sure they were alone. "To the cave."

"A cave?" Amara swallowed just as softly. When she thought of caves, precious jewels didn't come to mind, only bats. "But my mother will be saved when I come back?" Even if it were a mere fifty-fifty shot, Amara knew she had to take it. If she did nothing and she died, there would always be that possibility and Amara would never be able to forgive herself.

"Oh, yes." Lola smiled. "I will tell you how to get to the cave, but the directions must be committed to memory and never written down."

"Why? What if I get lost? After a long sea journey, what if I forget?" Amara asked, growing more panicked.

"Then you must remind yourself every day. Run through it every night before you go to sleep. Because the cave must never get into anyone else's hands but ours. It must stay a secret to our family forever. That was the deal."

"'The deal'?"

"With the diwata, of course. Using this medicine, we've helped people. For centuries. We were proud to, but, as I told you, word began to spread faster and faster."

"What happened?" Amara wanted to know everything.

"When I was a child, healing requests flooded in, more than we could handle. Then our house was broken into." She paused, as if to let that sink in. "We feared the cave would be found out, that the outside world would take the emeralds and break them up. So we kept our gift quiet from then on. So did your father."

"He took it to the grave," Amara said. Even if it was just the kind of thing his crystal-loving benefactors, the Silver Order, hoped to find. After funding his travels, the Pierces probably thought they were entitled to any otherworldly information the earl had found.

"He wanted to protect your mother. But now you must. And that means getting to the cave."

Amara nodded, fully accepting her fate as her lola gave careful directions toward her newfound destiny.

CHAPTER THREE
The Crystal Hunter

DARREN STUMBLED UP the stairs, the effects of the evening still with him. He just needed to make it into bed. A simple task that was proving to be quite the challenge at the moment. On the second-floor landing, he launched himself into a painting, effectively unhooking it from its hanger.

He acted quickly, catching it before it could clatter loudly down the stairs. *Curses, that was a close one.* There were a few scuffs, but it didn't look too badly damaged. The scene depicted a small skiff caught in a storm. The last remains of a shipwreck. Fitting. He sniffed.

His life felt like a shipwreck these days and there was no way to turn back or correct course. He was trapped in a storm that was entirely his father.

This past year, his father had gotten progressively worse. He didn't just lose his temper over the smallest thing—he was constantly challenging men to fists at dawn. Darren never bothered to watch. It took far too long before his father decided his honor was satisfied.

Darren had seen the injuries, though: the bloody faces and his father's bruised knuckles. He had heard them too, out on the lawn and sometimes even down the halls. Everyone was whispering about it.

No matter how hard Darren tried, his father couldn't be

reasoned with. Whenever Darren confronted his father about his anger, they came to blows.

It will pass, he used to tell himself. But it hadn't. Far from it.

Darren had some sympathy. When his mother had died, he too had wanted to punch the world to dust. He, too, had wanted to inflict pain that matched what was in his heart. Over time, Darren had willed it away, but his father hadn't.

Social engagements beyond the purview of the Order were the only way to escape. But the more social engagements he used to fill his time, the more he drank, the more he started to wonder about the point of it all.

He placed the painting down gently and made a mental note to hang it up later. Or maybe a servant might take notice of it and fix it for him. As long as his father didn't find it. *God save him.*

He braced himself on a piece of molding and got to his feet again. His room seemed so far away. He kept tight to the wall until he caught himself on his bedroom door. It swung wide open, nearly throwing him to the floor. That wasn't a good sign. He always closed it. Barely hanging on to the doorknob, he cursed.

"Father." He hung his head. "You know you needn't wait up for me."

His father burst up and papers flew from his desk. He had no doubt been rummaging through them. The man didn't mince words—with both hands, he picked Darren up by the collar and threw him against the wall.

Darren didn't fight back anymore. That only made things worse for both of them. It was better to just be his punching bag.

But he was already starting to reconsider. The collision had nearly knocked the air out of him, but at least the wall wasn't paneled. A badly angled piece of molding might have knocked him out cold.

"I'm starting to deeply dislike this drinking habit of yours."

Darren said nothing. When his father was this angry, it was best not to make excuses, just to take what was coming. If he was lucky, he'd only get hit once. But from the sounds of it, another long lecture about expectations and duties was in the cards.

"You missed another one of our meetings this evening. One you were obliged to attend."

It isn't fair, he wanted to groan like a child. He hadn't chosen this lot in life, but because he was his father's son, his path had been already carved out for him centuries ago, just like their old furniture. He couldn't go off and make his own path, not with all he was to inherit.

He'd looked forward to it once. Back before his father had erupted with madness at every opportunity. All it made him want to do was run.

"Tell me why," his father demanded. "Why do you insist upon being absent so often?"

His father knew why. At the last meeting, his father had grabbed one of their members and knocked him to the ground. All because the man had been "disagreeable." While he had paid the man off to not make a fuss, Darren wasn't sure how much more anyone would take.

"I don't understand it." His father's face shifted, going from stern and intimidating to suddenly quite grave.

"You used to love taking part in these studies. They fascinated you just as much as they fascinated me. You grasped the subjects well. And yet that is where it ends for you. You have no interest in continuing your studies, performing new research, or coming up with any new theories. And research, spending hours in the laboratory, that is the lifeblood of the Order."

His father huffed out an angry breath. "Is this what you want to do with your life? Spend your nights schmoozing about? Drinking until you can barely walk? That life is not for a Pierce. You owe your ancestors more than that."

Darren closed his eyes to avoid rolling them so blatantly in front of his father. That would only serve to get him backhanded. Once his father brought up his ancestors, he was in for the long haul. Couldn't he wait until Darren was sober?

"You know you have other responsibilities besides your studies. Perhaps you should start attending to them instead." His father kicked the bottom of his boot, jolting him.

"Like what?"

"Like fieldwork. Bringing home worthwhile specimens for study. Our members need something new to excite them."

Darren sat up. Was he trying to get rid of him? The only person who questioned him and his ill temper? Maybe it was a good thing. Anything to get away. "Where will you have me go? Antarctica?" Not even that seemed far enough.

"The Philippine Islands. It will be our second expedition there in more than two decades."

"Since we commissioned Lord Webb. The late earl."

"You were just a child then, but I see you remember…" His father raised his brows. "He was tasked with finding a cave brimming with gems. So many, you could pick them up off the ground. That's at least what the ancient legends claimed."

"But he didn't find them, did he?"

"Yes, well. He came back with a wife and nothing else. Or so he said. For years, I've thought otherwise." His father folded his hands behind his back and began to pace the small confines of his room. "He has a daughter, you know, the countess."

"You can't be considering bringing her into this." Darren stood, suddenly sober, his heart racing. He didn't want her anywhere near his fly-off-the-handle father.

"If Lord Webb had any secrets he wanted to keep from us, they died with him," Darren argued. "He wouldn't have bothered to tell anyone, let alone his daughter."

Why was his father so suspicious? Lady Webb, as far as he could tell, was one of the few decent women in nobility. She could actually carry a decent conversation and wasn't at all self-serving. What was he planning?

His father kicked his boot again. "Then why is it that she's recently booked passage to islands? To the same exact place we sent her father on expedition? The project that supposedly turned up nothing."

"Maybe she's just going over to visit some relatives."

"In the middle of her *third* London season?"

Even Darren had to admit that was unlikely, especially when, if she wanted an heir to her father's estate, her need for a husband was rather dire.

"As it happens, her mother is sick," his father said. "The gems, you know, are believed to have healing properties. She wouldn't just leave her sick mother for a pleasure cruise."

The month-or-so-long journey was far from what Darren considered a pleasure cruise. Why hadn't she told him she was going on this long trip when he'd seen her just the other evening? Then he remembered. She hated him.

"Lord Webb *lied* to me when I thought we were friends." His father clenched a fist, looking for a second like he was going to bust another hole in the wall. "I won't let him get away with it. You have to follow her."

"What? I can't just follow her. She'll think I'm mad!"

"I want those gems, Darren. You have no idea what the legends say, do you?"

"Let me guess, they're powerful?" he drawled, exhausted with all of this.

"They can heal anyone from anything." His father threw his hands out excitedly. "Some believe they can even reverse death."

Darren rubbed his temples. Reverse death? His father wasn't going to let this go.

"Once you've found them, you'll send word and I'll send more men."

"But, Father—"

"Your playboy days are over." His father crossed his arms, a signal that meant he was not to be bargained with. Even the way he cleared his throat had a ring of authority. "I rather think you'll enjoy the adventure. Maybe then you won't be so listless."

"Father—"

"You'll have to resort to more than just your charm and

pretty words, you know," his father said, his face as still and serious as stone. "You must stop at nothing to discover the location of these emeralds, and I mean *nothing*. You'll even need to consider violence. They're important."

Darren didn't like what his father was implying.

"How important?" More important than someone's life? He might have asked if it weren't so damn obvious. If there was anyone's life he wanted to protect, it was Lady Webb's. Since her father's death, she only had her mother. No brothers or even uncles.

"Important enough that if you fail, I'll send one of my men to finish the task."

"Not just some brute like that Marx." His violent tendencies were even worse than his father's. That was probably why his father had hired him, to fill in when his fists got tired.

"Had to fire him days ago, I'm afraid," his father returned. "But I have other men who share a similar temperament."

Darren groaned. He knew then that not only did he have to go, he needed to succeed. He couldn't allow anyone like Marx to come near the countess.

Darren got up and walked around the bed. He only stopped when he was inches away so they stood nose to nose, like rivals. These last few years, as Darren had gotten older and closer of age to replace him, that was how it had been. Not just for him, but for every Pierce. Darren wondered if it had been the same with his father's father.

"No need," Darren simply said. "I shan't fail you. And you'll be glad to be rid of me."

"Assemble a team of at least two other men." His father folded his arms behind his back, talking like this was some kind of military operation. "You'll need the added strength. And not those alley dogs you insist on keeping."

"They're not *dogs*. They're my best men."

His father rolled his eyes. "Loyal, perhaps, but not quite as skilled as you'll need. Or smart. It won't be an easy task. I'm trying to prepare you."

No, he was trying to tell him what to do. An order he planned to ignore. Along with many others. He didn't want to be like his father and do awful things for the so-called "good of the Order."

Darren raked a hand through his hair.

The sudden thought of a long sea journey alongside Lady Webb excited him for a moment. He doubted he'd get any sleep now. He'd be thinking of all the possibilities long into the morning.

Darren motioned to the door, anything to get his father out of his room.

"You leave by the end of the week," his father said.

"You already booked the tickets?" Darren was a man in his prime and his father still got to make all his decisions for him. Even the ones he hadn't yet agreed to.

"Goodbye." His father bowed his head. "And happy travels."

The way he'd said it almost sounded like it was the last time they'd see each other. Was he really just trying to be rid of him? His father hated men who questioned him. He knew that much.

Darren tried to look on the bright side. If he failed, he could at least warn Lady Webb of the danger. But as it stood, he was just as much her enemy.

Countess Webb hated him enough. But now she was really going to loathe him.

CHAPTER FOUR

The Storm

Amara gripped both sides of the boarding bridge. She was shaking and she wasn't even on the ship yet. That didn't bode well, did it? All morning, she'd kept her eye out for bad omens. No strange animals had crossed her path, no birds had flown in an unfavorable direction. Yet.

She just didn't like heights and she couldn't ignore that the only thing separating her from the ocean below was a thin plank of wood. She already made the mistake of looking down. She squeezed her eyes shut so as not to do it again. Everything would be fine, she told herself.

Lola had given her a good luck amulet or an "agima," she'd called it. Made of solid gold, it had carvings Amara couldn't read. Something her family had held on to for generations. She pulled it out from her pocket and rubbed it between her fingers, praying it would give Granger and herself strength for the journey ahead.

They'd have adjoining rooms and she would be a good enough chaperone. They might not have been close in station, but they were close in age and friendship. Granger was merely three years her senior and the kind of beauty that would have been snatched up at once had she had a dowry.

When Amara finally landed on deck, the floor shifted ever so slightly. Amara's breath caught in her throat. Almost immediately, she lost her balance. In her panic, the amulet slipped from her hands, pinging onto the floor.

Amara froze in her tracks. It was too crowded to see where it had gone, but if she didn't move soon, the people behind her would be angry at best. At worst, she'd get trampled on.

"Granger!" she shouted. "Wait!"

Amara crouched down. Losing her amulet couldn't have been a good omen, not at all.

She weaved between passengers, who huffed and nudged into her. She couldn't lose the amulet within the first hour of having it. Not something that had been in her family for generations, a distinguished line that could very well go farther back than her father's. Judging from the thickness of the gold, her mother's side had accumulated generations of wealth too. Why hadn't she told her? Had she really expected her to become completely English?

Whatever the reason, she had a duty now. She had to keep things like the amulet safe. She couldn't give up until she found it. Down on her knees, she didn't care how the crowd jostled her.

She almost fell on her face when it came in and out of view between skirts. She leaped forward to get it, but before she could grasp it, a hand fell over it.

"That's mine!" she shouted with some panic. Whoever this was, she couldn't be sure they'd give it back. It was solid gold, after all.

When she looked up, her eyes almost didn't register who it was. Standing before her, eyes gleaming, was Darren Pierce. On this ship, headed as far as Bombay.

She gasped almost as much in annoyance as in surprise.

"What in the world are you doing here?" She stood and snatched the amulet out from his hands.

"Traveling, of course," he answered innocuously.

"Are you sure you're on the right ship?" This couldn't have been a coincidence.

"*Evangeline* will take us through Gibraltar and across the Mediterranean, through the Suez Canal down the Red Sea and into the Indian Ocean...no?"

"Yes, but…"

"And where are you headed?"

Something told her he already knew. "Manila."

"Are you visiting family?"

"Not exactly. I mean…" Amara panicked. The truth had almost slipped. How could she have been so stupid?

"I must go." Amara pushed ahead of him between lines of bodies. Leaving was so much easier than lying.

She was in a state of shock. She couldn't believe that for at least two weeks, they'd be trapped on this ship together. No matter his destination.

Nothing seemed to make sense. How could he have known she was boarding this very ship on this very day? She hadn't spoken a word of it to anyone.

He couldn't have known, not unless the Order was involved in some way. If they were, she had far bigger problems at hand. The last thing she wanted was to attract the attention of the Order. They were more powerful and wealthier than any secret society of the day had a right to be. Though its members were a strictly guarded secret, they had prominent members in all aspects of government. Mr. Pierce's father, the one who served as a leader to them all, had terrified her as a child. Even her father had bent the knee to him and the man didn't even have a title.

They weren't supposed to know about the emeralds. No one was.

"Come on now," Granger shouted, already put out. "While I'm young."

Amara moved ahead. The ship was getting busy. But as they got closer to their accommodations on the upper decks, the crowds thinned out and the roar dissipated.

Their rooms were on the edge of the ship, its doors overlooking the glistening sea. Despite the storm roiling inside her, the sky was perfect and calm. The type of day that couldn't last.

She had never been on a steamship before, let alone one this size. Every year, they were getting bigger and more impressive.

She should have been taking in more of the ship, eager to see all their rooms ahead. But when Granger opened the door, she could barely focus. All she could think about was Lola's warning. She had to keep everything about this trip a secret. She couldn't allow for another slip. With Mr. Pierce, she feared that wouldn't be easy. There was something about his eyes. If she gazed into them too long, they made her feel foolish and weak.

"Was that Mr. Darren Pierce I saw?" Granger asked with suspicion as she pulled in the trunks that awaited just beside the doors.

"Never mind him."

Amara needed to focus instead on their new living situation. On the other side of the living room was Granger's quarters. Even though this was supposed to be the ship's best accommodations, the room was tight with mahogany chairs that matched the French-trim walls. With two bedrooms and its own private bath, it was close enough to what Amara was used to.

"If he asks, we can't tell him—or frankly, anyone else, for that matter—that we're looking for a cure for my mother. He can't know."

Granger already knew too much as it was, but there was no avoiding it. And Amara hated lying.

"Then I shan't say a word." Granger flipped open Amara's trunk with a bang.

Amara could tell she was a little irritated by all the secrecy. Probably how it cast Granger's loyalty into question. Still, Amara wondered. Could she really trust her? She'd been working as her lady's maid since her debut three years ago. Amara had paid her extra for the trip, but just how much loyalty could that buy?

"I doubt we've seen the last of him," Granger said. "Not with the way he looks at you. Do you want me to make the usual excuses?"

Amara knew she had to say *yes*, but part of her wanted to say *no*. Part of her actually wanted to see him again. On the massive *Evangeline*, he was something familiar when everything else was so uncertain. The skies were clear today, but what about tomorrow?

"I think I can handle him, thank you."

All she had to do was lie. She could do that, couldn't she? It was perfectly reasonable to say she was visiting family. But what if he asked questions? Like how could she leave her mother when she was so sick? What if he could tell she was lying?

Lola hadn't been explicit about what would happen to the emeralds if others found out. She needn't have been. Amara already knew. It would be like everything else the British touched. They'd auction them to the highest bidder. It didn't matter to whom the things belonged. They'd end up on someone's finger or wrist or in some nobleman's vault.

Although Amara and her family could use the gems however they pleased, Lola had made it clear that the cave didn't truly belong to them. It belonged to the diwata.

If her family let others know about the cave, when they had been sworn to secrecy, Lord knew what the curses might befall her and her family. She wasn't about to take the risk. She had come this far.

☾

As AMARA HAD predicted, the perfect weather didn't hold. When Granger shook her awake, the whole world seemed to be teetering on a precipice.

"Milady…you have to see this!" Granger said with wide eyes, her hand clutching her dressing gown. Amara threw hers on too.

"What is it? Some kind of hurricane?" Immediately, she feared the worst.

Given the way the ship rocked back and forth, it might very well have been. Her stomach twisted and turned with each sway. Just like on the boarding dock, she struggled to catch her balance.

"Not yet. Come look." Granger opened the door to a grayness that had become the vast, open sea. Amara had just stepped out when the wind practically threw her into the railing. She yelped. The metal bar was like ice. Somehow, since the time they'd boarded the ship, the temperature had dropped some thirty degrees. And far out along the horizon, across a distance impossible to measure, was a line of storm clouds and heavy streaks of rain. From that distance, the streaks appeared still and almost peaceful, but it was only a trick of the eye. Out there, the sea was churning. Even from a great distance, the ship was feeling the effects, teetering back and forth like a rocking chair. Amara leaned against the railing trying to stay steady.

"What time is it?" Amara asked.

"Almost 7 A.M." Grainger looked at her watch. "London time."

"Where's the sun?"

Somewhere along the horizon there should have been at least some light, but blacked out by clouds, it was dark enough to be evening.

Amara gripped the railing tighter. She didn't know much about storms or the ocean or ships, but whatever was to come looked powerful in the most terrifying and awe-inspiring way.

"How long until it reaches us?"

"A few hours," someone shouted, a deckhand passing through. "You both best remain in your rooms. Cap'n's orders."

He didn't address her with the usual deference for a countess. Few ever did. It didn't seem to matter how finely she dressed; people still mistook her for a governess or companion. She didn't get it. They must have assumed the clothes were hand-me-downs.

But the longer she held on to the title, the sooner things would change. Or so she thought. Instead, it only happened more often. Though she preferred the deference, she never had the gumption to demand it. Least of all now. Being on a ship wasn't the same as being in England. There was a whole different set of rules. Here, she was just another traveler.

"Her ladyship, the Countess Webb," Granger said, taking it upon herself to correct the man, "requires breakfast. We haven't—"

"Her ladyship and yourself would be far better off not eating." The tall and thin yet broad-shouldered crewman handed Granger two buckets. His face was tight with worry, not just for them, but likely for himself too. "Even a sailor with the sturdiest sea legs will need a bucket for what's ahead. Believe you me."

"He's right," Amara said. "We would be safer inside. Perhaps we can try to sleep through it."

But that seemed unlikely. Amara just didn't want to say it. When Granger gripped her hand, there was a slight shake to it.

"I'm sure it will pass over us quickly." Amara wrapped her arm around her, unsure which of them needed the comfort more. At least they had each other.

As the day carried on, the storm closed in and the sea got more restless. In less than an hour, the storm was beating on their door, loudly proclaiming its arrival. The ship listed back and forth, not fast but steady and at intense angles. Only the beds were screwed into the ground. In the sitting room, everything else—the desk, chairs, and sofa—scraped against the floor and banged into the opposite wall.

"Granger?"

"Just hold on to the bed, my lady!" she shouted from her quarters. "It will pass."

Amara held on as best she could, her body slamming into the detailed wooden post. It was so slick with lacquer, she could barely keep her grip. Any reprieve in movement was short, barely offering her time to take a breath.

Eventually, it was Granger who ran for the bucket first. Then Amara. The cold metal edge dug into her fingers. Like the deckhand had said, she was glad she hadn't eaten much. The bucket could only hold so much, especially with the sway. Even with what little came up, some still smacked to the ground. The sour smell was awful, and so was the spinning. Everything was awful. She hadn't been on the boat for more than a day. If things continued like this, how could she possibly survive the rest of the trip? Or was she already doomed to fail?

This is nothing, she tried to tell herself, *nothing compared to the pain my mother is going through.* If Amara had to go through hell to get a cure for her mother's sickness, she would. And hell this was, indeed.

She closed her eyes, hyper-focused on the sound of waves crashing, the rain pelting and furniture sliding across the floor. Mixed in was a banging noise. It had to have been the rowboats hitting the side of the ship, except it sounded so close. Right next to her, in fact. She lifted her head from the bucket and wiped her mouth with her hand.

The door shook with each bang.

Granger and Amara both looked at each other, the same question in their eyes. Who in the world?

Granger braced herself against the wall. The pounding continued as she worked her way to the door.

The moment she twisted the knob, the door flew open and pounded twice against the wall. As if on cue, the ship stilled, just long enough for Amara to make out Mr. Pierce, soaking wet from the rain. What was he doing here? How had he found her room? The questions were on the tip of her tongue when the ship listed again. It happened so fast, she didn't have the chance to grab anything. She couldn't have even if she'd wanted to. It was almost as if her arms had turned into jelly. They were useless when the ship threw her hard into the molded walls. The room was spinning again. This time, too fast.

Her vision was tunneling.

She blinked and glimpsed Mr. Pierce catching himself on the frame of the door. Before everything went black, he called out her name.

CHAPTER FIVE
Proposition

"THIS IS MOST untoward." Lady Webb's maid continued to complain.

All Darren had wanted to do was to help and this is what he'd gotten? He couldn't believe his ill luck that her old-fashioned maid hadn't been knocked out instead. Then he and Lady Webb could have been alone. Unless another giant wave came and knocked her out too, he was stuck with the servant. Lord, he almost wished for one.

He gathered Lady Webb up from the floor. His hair dripped onto her face as her limbs swayed with the ship. His arms ached as he lowered her gently into bed. The maid wasn't far behind. She was practically breathing down his neck.

"I do have some medical training." Darren grunted. "Think of me as your local doctor."

She ignored him. "Young men don't belong in the bedrooms of young ladies! And certainly not when they're in this sort of condition. When she wakes, she'll be mortified. She'll have my—" The maid stopped abruptly and dry-heaved in a nearby bucket.

He was glad the storm had hit when it had. Breakfast had not yet been served, saving the guests and crew from a far worse mess. The day ahead would still be messy, but perhaps a little less so. Lady Webb was the only lucky one. Save for a bit of a headache, she'd likely sleep through the rest of the storm.

He was fighting nausea himself. It helped to stay distracted.

"We should take her to the infirmary," the maid went on.

"They'll be busy enough, believe me."

"But she is a countess." She huffed.

"What is your name?" Darren asked.

"Cassie Granger. *Miss* Cassie Granger."

"Miss Granger, do yourself a favor and take this." Darren tossed her one of his homemade lozenges. He unwrapped the wax paper and popped one in his mouth too.

"Where did you get this?" She marveled at its swirling S-stamp and bright-copper color. "One of those back-alley London apothecaries?"

"I'm something of an apothecary myself, actually." More like an alchemist, actually, but he would never admit to that, least of all to this supercilious maidservant. It brought on too many questions, not to mention the negative connotations of witchcraft and the like. It was the entire reason the Silver Order found it useful to stay anonymous.

Unlike much of the Order's concoctions, the ingredients were simple. A bit of chamomile, ginger, lemon, and sugar. What made it effective was the fact that it was magnetized. The chamomile, specifically.

"Not bad at all." Miss Granger hummed.

Darren brushed a hand through his hair and shook off the excess moisture from his fingers.

The maid handed him a towel, although grudgingly. "You are acquainted with the countess," she said.

Was she asking him a question? He wasn't sure.

"We run in the same circles..." he answered.

"She asked me to fight off your attentions, I'll have you know. There has to be a reason."

He snickered. "Do you think it's my looks?"

Granger cast her eyes down to her feet, not daring to look him in the eye. "Perhaps it's something you've done."

Darren sighed. "Things were different once. When we were

children, before her father died, we actually got along quite well."

God save him, why was he even entertaining this conversation? He much preferred to be rid of her. But there was no way in hell she'd leave the countess alone with him. Devil that he supposedly was.

"Lord Webb and my father were the greatest of friends," he said.

"He was? With Earl Webb?" She gasped in evident disbelief. As if it was impossible for Lord Webb to be familiar with anyone who wasn't noble.

"Indeed. His father and mine shared a great many interests. Exploring, mostly. Finding treasures in far-off places. Whenever the earl paid visits, Lady Amara—that is, Lady Webb now—and I would spend the day together."

It wasn't like they had never been alone together. They had always been alone when they'd roamed the estate and nearby woods. She knew all of their secrets too. Things she hadn't much liked talking about as she'd grown older, especially within so-called polite society.

"The late earl would have wanted me to take care of her," Darren went on. "To watch over her. When someone dies and you make them a promise, you can't turn your back on it. You understand that, don't you?"

It was a lie, yes, but he felt responsible for Lady Webb nonetheless. At least he wanted to be.

Miss Granger crossed her arms.

He held his hand up as if he were taking an oath. "I shall think of the countess as my ward and nothing more."

"You are too young to be her caretaker. It's ridiculous. No one would believe it. That's far from acceptable in any circle."

"Then what would you suggest I do? What will keep her reputation intact?"

"'Reputation'?" Miss Granger grasped the bedpost, pressing her body against it as the ship swayed yet again. "What need has she for a reputation? So she can marry? Fat chance of that happening. She may have money and a title, but she's long ruined. The gossips like to make up their own stories, you see. To my lady, they've been particularly cruel."

He had overheard some of the stories too. Affairs with one duke or another. He'd never believed for a second that they had been true. The women who lived that bold sort of lifestyle had a different way about them. One that he was familiar with—in passing. But not Lady Webb. She wasn't like that in the least.

"Then what on earth are you so concerned about?"

"I still have a duty to protect her honor, sir. She has had to endure enough harassment from men who are merely interested in a mistress."

Just the idea of other men approaching her with such intentions made his hands curl into tight fists. He wasn't a thing like them.

"I don't like what you're implying."

"Do you think I'm stupid?" she barked at him, her eyes intense. "I've seen the way you look at her. I might be a simple maid, but I know that look."

He had a look? Not even Darren himself had been aware of this. Though he knew very well he'd thought about it... He shook his head, releasing the lascivious thought.

"You're mistaken," he said with false outrage.

Though the maid's eyes narrowed, he knew he had at least some of her trust. Enough not to call the bridge, anyway. Or maybe she was just smart enough to realize he was their only hope.

"She's a good young lady, you know. Just shy and awfully unsure of herself. Even if she weren't, well...that wouldn't be enough, would it?" Miss Granger mused. "She was doomed from the start."

Darren knew very well that Miss Granger was right. Frankly, he was glad for it. Otherwise, Countess Webb would have married to continue her estate's line years ago. Those fools. Just being herself should have been enough. She was smart. It was the one trait she wasn't afraid to show. Like her father, she had the spirit of adventure within her. She wouldn't have taken this trip otherwise.

"Or maybe she doesn't want to mold herself into whatever society wants her to become," he said.

"And what's that?" Grainger's brow crinkled.

"A novelty. They're all play actors, who you know. Every single person in society acts as though they're so much more than they really are. The countess, on the other hand, doesn't much care to pretend anything."

"You think you know her so well?"

"Perhaps not so much recently. Not since her father's death." He hesitated to admit it because deep down, he knew that was the very root of the matter Miss Granger had been trying to get at from the start.

Ever since the death of Earl Webb, Darren had struggled to continue his friendship with the earl's daughter. It didn't matter that the death was determined to be accidental. She still blamed his father for it and by connection him too.

Even though he'd made it a point to go to many of the same engagements, their encounters had always been so short-lived, not to mention bitter. The last time they had spoken at that ball had been the longest amount of time they had talked in months.

No matter what he did or said, she refused to change her mind about him. Her father traveled not because of his father or the Order, but because he'd loved it. There was no denying that.

Darren looked down at her still face, studying the features that no one in London could match. The fullness of her lips and the curve of her chin. Despite all that he said, his thoughts were far from pure.

If only the maid knew that her first instinct had been right. When it came to Lady Webb, he wanted everything that was base and improper. He had wanted it for years.

Darren couldn't help himself. Lying there with her dark hair loose around her shoulders, the countess brought to mind

Sleeping Beauty and Snow White all at once. He got lost for a moment. He traced a finger down Lady Webb's hand and suddenly, he was full of everything Miss Granger had accused him of. In a way he had never been full of anything before. He swallowed—hard. Miss Granger stomped her foot in protest.

He snapped his hand back and held them up again in surrender.

"Since she is unable to remind you, I shall. Whatever feelings you have for the countess are unrequited, Mr. Pierce."

The maid took entirely too much pleasure from the words. He grit back his anger. It wouldn't do. At a minimum, he didn't want to be enemies. He wanted to be allies.

"I am offering my assistance," Darren said one more time. "Not just for today, but for the duration of the trip. Nothing more."

His father would have preferred to become enemies with the earl's family. Darren would show him. There were far better alternatives than violence.

"It's not for me to decide," Miss Granger said. "She's the one you'll have to convince."

Darren looked down again at Lady Webb. He saw it written on her face, nothing but a challenge soon to come.

CHAPTER SIX
The Blue Crystal

AMARA WOKE TO something cold and heavy on her forehead. Fearful it was some kind of bug, she swiped it off, sending the object thudding to the floor and a scent of lavender wafting through the air.

"What in the world—" She snapped upright. A small crystal, of all things, a blue one, twinkled in the glow of the lamps. The extra shine was undoubtedly from oil.

"Countess?" Someone hovered near her.

"Darren?" she said, regressing to the way she'd once addressed him as a child. She cleared her throat. "I mean, Mr. Pierce."

She finally remembered. In the middle of the storm, he had appeared at their door, out of nowhere. Just like this. She should have known. Who else would have placed a calming crystal atop her forehead? Like her lola, and perhaps like herself, he believed some crystals had special properties. She wondered where the stone was from, the caves of South America? Peru?

She rubbed her face, noting now the ship was still. It felt like a different world entirely. "How did you find my room?"

"We paid someone off for that information a week ago…" He shrugged off the ridiculous comment like it was nothing. "Made sure to obtain the cabin right beneath yours too."

Had he really just admitted that? Amara sat up. "Are you mad?"

"I don't think so."

"Why would you do that?"

He picked up the crystal from the ground. "I just wanted to make sure you were well."

"No, truly."

"Look, it's simple, really. I know this journey will be a difficult one. I just want to help make it easier. So I'm at your service. Really, I am."

God, he sounded like some servant. What was his aim?

Granger approached from the other side of the room. "You ought to be honest, don't you think?"

"Yes." Amara straightened. She wiped at the corners of her lips, grateful she didn't feel any sort of drool or crust. Though she was certain her breath was awful. She covered her mouth. "First, do you have any water?"

Granger brought over a glass. "I just filled a pitcher."

Amara drank greedily, catching the droplets at the corner of her lips.

"Well?" She was losing her patience with him when maybe she should have been grateful. Was it really true? Had he really come to help her? To travel thousands of miles by sea? No. There had to have been something much more selfish behind his presence here. Something related to the Order. Something sinister. If the Order was involved, it would undoubtedly be sinister.

"All right. I suppose now's as good a time as any. My father sent me here to follow you." He bowed his head a little, his hair dry and shaggy. "But it's true. I really do want to help you."

It was more forthcoming than she'd expected.

"Why?" she asked, dumbfounded and worried all at once.

"Do you remember the trip my father funded before you were born? The one where your father met your mother?"

Amara nodded. It was the one trip her father had told her about most.

"And you do know the purpose of the trip was to bring back—"

"Spoils." She cut him off. "Like in war. You wanted him to take something. To steal."

"In a manner of speaking." Mr. Pierce took her now-empty cup and refilled it, handing it back to her. He was quite the gentleman with her. But behind his eyes, she could tell he was hiding something.

"Your father claims he found nothing," he went on. "But my father… He believes otherwise."

Amara cleared her throat. She didn't like where this was going. "I can't believe you would betray your father like this."

"Of course I would. He's been a bastard these days—excuse my language—not just to me, but to everyone."

Amara supposed this was true. "Still. You're leaving something out."

"Not at all."

"You can't pretend you have more loyalty to me than your own father."

"If you want my loyalty, you can have it."

Amara quirked her brow. Whatever did he mean?

"We need not be enemies on this trip," he said. "I was telling Miss Granger we could be allies."

"How?" Amara looked to Granger, but she kept her gaze down. God knew what they had been talking about while she'd been asleep.

"I could protect you. The sea can be a dangerous place. Surely, you already know this."

Amara couldn't deny that he was right. That she was very much afraid of what lay ahead, but she couldn't let him see that. She only hardened her exterior further and crossed her arms.

"Are you really so sure that I'm in danger?"

"Because of what you're after, yes."

He said this like he already knew. But how? "How could you know—"

"I know the kind of thing your father once spent his life searching for. And furthermore, I know the type of projects my father funds. You know it too."

Amara had fought so long to keep her father's activities a secret, particularly from society. She turned to Granger. Now she knew too.

"You ought to consider it," Granger said with a shrug.

"And in exchange?" She couldn't just accept without knowing what he wanted in return.

"Just a few of the emeralds."

The demand made her heart skip a beat. He spoke about the gems so casually when they shouldn't even have existed.

"It wouldn't just be a few emeralds, though. You would also know their location. Undoubtedly, you'd return for more."

"On my honor, I would not. All we want is to study them."

"Yes, that crystal alchemy nonsense." She huffed. She had heard her father speak of it on more than one occasion. Just another one of the many unusual subjects the Order had its hand in. Even though her mother had never made mention of it, Lola had made her realize it was something that her ancestors might have had a hand in too.

"It's a promise I know I can keep," he said.

But it wasn't one she was willing to accept. She'd be a fool to. Anyway, she had other promises with which to concern herself. Particularly the one she had made to Lola. She had to keep the cave secret.

"I'm sorry. But no." Amara forced herself to smile. "I could never come to trust you. Not a man with your interests."

Men of his kind were the reason her father was dead.

Mr. Pierce's face visibly dropped. When he spoke, his voice rose with anger. "Can I ask why? Why do you insist upon making me the object of this undeserved loathing?"

"Because aligning with the Order would kill me just as it killed my father. Accident or not. You'd exploit the islands too."

The words hurt him, she could tell that much.

"I can never change your mind on that, can I?"

Amara said nothing.

"But the danger you face is real," he said. "I promise you that."

Amara chewed her lip. If she continued to say *no* to his offer, what would he do then? Continue to follow her? She'd spend the whole damn trip trying to evade him.

"I just want to make sure you can bring those emeralds home to your mother. That's why you want them, yes?"

It wasn't just that. Amara was responsible for so much more.

More than he would ever have an obligation to her, Mr. Pierce had an obligation to the Order. He was to inherit the Silver Order, after all. So therefore, he and his father had the same goals. Maybe he was just as dangerous.

"I've heard rumors about your father," she said. "They say he uses his fists more than his mouth."

Mr. Pierce stood up, his jaw tight. "I'm well aware of the rumors, Countess. I resent his ways as much as you do. But I'm not like him. I swear to you I'll do my best to avoid violence. On my honor."

Still seated, she was eye level with the crystal he squeezed in his hand. She recognized it then, the way he held it between his thumb and forefinger. It was his lucky one. He'd had it since childhood.

"The best I can offer you is a day's more thought. Until then, it's best you go." She crossed the short distance to the door and opened it to a now calm and settled sea. As the ship shifted ever so slightly, her stomach flipped. Her head throbbed too. Maybe that crystal had been helping.

"Very well." Mr. Pierce took the hint well enough. "I pray you'll get your answer to me by tomorrow's dinner. Meet me in the dining hall, will you? For dinner? Together?"

"That will depend upon my decision, don't you think?"

Mr. Pierce ignored her bitter question. "Until then, you can keep this." He placed the gem in his hand on her nightstand.

"Fine." She conceded, feeling slightly sorry for her words earlier.

"Countess, miss." Mr. Pierce nodded a goodbye as he passed into the cool morning air. As he walked farther down the deck, two more men followed after him seemingly out of nowhere. His own guards. The ones who could be Amara's too if she wished it.

She shut the door and locked it. She almost wanted to put a chair against the door too, but even that wouldn't have felt like enough.

CHAPTER SEVEN

A Stranger in Spain

B Y THE NEXT morning, Amara was awoken by a whistle that signaled port. They had reached Spain. It wasn't a big milestone so far on their month-or-so-long journey, but it was a milestone nonetheless.

The blue crystal on her nightstand reminded her that she still had a decision to make. That was probably why he had left it in the first place. She thought her mind would be clearer in the morning. But here she was, as torn as ever.

Mr. Pierce's protection would add significantly to their chances of success, and therefore her mother's survival. But if she accepted, the sanctity of the cave depended on a promise she wasn't quite so sure she could trust. And what of this danger Mr. Pierce spoke of? So far, she sensed none of it. Sure, that storm was hardly a good start. Nevertheless, Granger and she had handled it fine. She was mortified more than anything: for throwing up, for her state of undress, and for awkwardly collapsing. *I shouldn't care,* she told herself. *Not for the likes of him.*

Amara stepped out of her rooms and looked out over the railing again. This time at the chaos of port. Dozens of passengers departed the ship for a day's excursion while the crew carried cargo aboard in massive crates.

Beyond the melee, the stone buildings were tightly packed and made of plaster instead of stone. Unlike the wooden roofs of

London, these ones were terracotta. Beneath the gentle morning sun, they were quite striking. The city was different from London in every way. The caws of diving sparrows demanded her attention, calling her to explore. She ached to try the local cuisine and shop the markets. She could practically smell the slightest hint of them from there. But Mr. Pierce's warning had struck enough fear in her heart to keep her aboard. Watching from the deck was much safer.

Her only source of entertainment was a stroll on the deck. With Granger in tow, she looped around the ship twice until she faced south, the direction of the journey ahead.

After they made it through the Strait of Gibraltar, they'd cruise east straight across the calm Mediterranean Sea. Instead of steamers made of iron, she tried to picture older boats of wood and their great, billowing sails. The danger of the seas had been even greater back then. The modern boats of today were sturdier, but like the sailors of the past, they faced the same threats. There was no knowing what could have been dwelling in a sea so wide and vast. And there was no knowing when the next storm could strike.

She could almost understand why the ancients had sacrificed virgins for good weather. Praying for blue skies hardly seemed enough. Maybe she just needed a good pair of *sea legs*, or so the deckhands called it. Granger sighed loudly not far behind. She had clearly grown tired of Amara's sulking and Amara had grown tired of Granger's comments about Mr. Pierce. They weren't all bad. In fact, they were surprisingly positive. So much so, she was starting to think Granger actually liked him.

"He's not terrible-looking… Some might even say he's handsome."

"His looks matter little to me," Amara replied. Her mother's life did—that, and the promise she had made. She had an equally important duty to both.

"What will you decide?"

"I don't know. I don't want to rush. I have to consider all the variables."

Amara pulled the shawl around her tighter. The normally warm sea breeze had taken on a sudden chill. She could still feel Granger's eyes on her, trying to figure out what was going on in her head. Not even she knew.

They worked their way back to their rooms. As much as the salty sea air soothed her, she felt exposed on the southern decks. Compared to the vastness of sea, the *Evangeline* and herself within it felt so tiny and insignificant.

While the possibilities of danger were ripe, so was all that she might see and experience. But not if she remained cooped up on this ship. Though her heart held plenty of fear, she had to at least remind herself of that. And that with Mr. Pierce, she would experience all the more. She wouldn't be so afraid of land to stay on board. When she wrote home to her mother and Lola, her letter filled with nothing but bright and happy words wouldn't be a lie.

Granger opened the cabin door for her. Amara hadn't taken a single step when an arm yanked her inside. Another hand muffled her scream. Before Granger could escape, someone had grabbed her and pulled her in too.

Their rooms were chaos. In addition to their captors, a third man was tearing through their things. The closet door was wide open and her clothes were strewn all about.

These men were Filipino, speaking Tagalog so fast, Amara couldn't understand. All dressed as English gentlemen, they had likely been following them since London. A thought that chilled her more than icy sea wind.

Naturally, she recognized none of them. Though part of her wanted to. They were among the very few Filipinos with whom she had ever crossed paths. But clearly, they didn't mean well.

In her captor's tight grasp, Granger was shivering. Amara couldn't think of her own fear, only Granger's. She hadn't asked to be taken halfway across the world and put into this situation. They were both in entirely new territory. A ship at sea was nothing like the ballrooms of London. Her biggest enemy then had been the gossips and the philanderers who'd tried to corner her unchaperoned. Amara didn't know what to do, just that she had to fight, even if she didn't know how.

For Granger's sake, Amara couldn't crumble. In the face of these scoundrels, she had to be brave. She didn't dare show them an ounce of fear.

She struggled, her exclamations muffled against the man's hand. Just as she thought to bite him, his hand dropped. The relief was short-lived. With the same hand, he gripped her throat, the tightness of his grasp taking her breath away. At any moment, she might faint. But where would that leave Granger? She had to think of something fast. Playing dumb would not work with these men. She had to play it smart.

Among all the words they exchanged, she had caught one: map.

"How do you know of it?" she demanded back in Tagalog.

"You speak the language?" her captor said in Tagalog with surprise.

"We were told that might be the case," another one of the men said. "Remember?"

"By whom?" Amara demanded, but they didn't answer.

"The map belongs to us," her captor explained. "Like so many things, it was stolen."

"That's a lie," she blurted out, though she hadn't meant to. The map didn't exist, as far as she knew. She certainly didn't have such a thing.

The man just laughed.

"Where is it?" he demanded again in English.

"I don't have what you're after," she returned. "But I know where it is."

The men looked at each other.

Though the man didn't completely let her go, she felt his grip loosen an inch. Granger whimpered.

"I already gave it up…" Amara swallowed, though she was barely able to. "I was forced to."

"To whom?" The man responded in perfect-though-accented English.

"He's…traveling alone. He's our…our guide. Well, he was."

"What is his name?"

Amara hesitated.

"What…is…his…name?" Her captor demanded louder.

"Darren Pierce." Somehow, the admission felt like a betrayal.

"Pierce, you say? He was supposed to have booked passage, but we haven't sighted him." He shoved back a stringy strand of black hair, the rest of it pulled back in a low and refined ponytail.

Mr. Pierce was better at playing incognito than she'd thought. She supposed it went hand in hand with being a member of the Order. He was only seen when he wanted to be. But this was more than some sleight-of-hand parlor trick he showed her in a ballroom. She was impressed; she couldn't help herself.

"A man like him, I'm not surprised you were forced to hand it over." The brute looked at her with a sudden flash of sympathy.

"Where is he?" the other one demanded, looking much less sympathetic.

"You're in luck." She twisted slightly, testing his grip in vain. It was as strong as ever. "He's on the ship."

"Then it's as we feared. You take us to him." The man let go of her completely and pushed her forward. "Now."

The other man said something in Tagalog, but in a dialect she couldn't understand. Something that sounded like a warning.

The man sheathed a blade Amara hadn't known he'd had. It was so much worse than she'd thought. Mr. Pierce was right, damn him. This journey was dangerous. She didn't know who these men were or how they could possibly know about this supposed map. But danger had arrived nonetheless.

"Tie her up." The man looked back at Granger. "Gag her."

"Don't," Amara shouted as one of the men led Granger off into the bedroom.

"We can't have her informing the bridge, can we?" her captor said.

Half out the door, Amara watched as one of the men tied Granger to the bed by the wrists while another wrapped a cloth around her mouth. Amara winced. For all she knew, that might very well be her fate as well. Especially if Mr. Pierce didn't answer the door. What if he had gone to shore like all the other passengers? Or what if he was in the dining hall? Or someplace else on the ship?

"Now let's go say *hello*." The man grabbed Amara's arm again.

With the two other men trailing behind them, she couldn't be sure what might happen. There would be a fight, she knew that, but she wasn't entirely convinced that the outcome would necessarily be in Mr. Pierce's favor. These men had knives and it was three against three. Those were pretty even odds. There was no knowing what these men were capable of or what other weapons they might have had.

"Don't drag your feet," her captor demanded. "I just want to clear up your little story."

With most travelers touring the city, there was not a soul in sight—no one she could shout to, no one who could save her even if she tried. Beside the vast emptiness of sea, they marched straight down to the end of the deck and down the stairs to Mr. Pierce's room. The one directly beneath hers. As much as she resented it, she was glad to have him near. What other option would she have? Her trip might have been over before it had even begun.

Her captor knocked and waited patiently. As if he were simply calling on someone for tea. There was some commotion inside before Mr. Pierce answered. She couldn't believe her relief when he poked his head out the door. His hair askew and with one eye open, he was only half-awake. They had woken him up from a nap.

There wasn't any time to warn him, not even with a telling glare. Her captor kicked the door in.

The horrible crack of Mr. Pierce's nose made her cry out. It was all her captor needed to get inside. Darren Pierce was done for. She was done for. They were all done for.

The inside of his room was not what she'd expected. It wasn't empty. Mr. Pierce's guards stood tucked into the corners of the room, their weapons drawn. While Mr. Pierce only had on a thin, collared shirt—now stained with drops of blood—his men were fully dressed. She realized then. The moment that knock had come, they had come up with a ruse. Making it seem as though Mr. Pierce had not only been alone, but caught off guard and sleepy. Now with his own pistol drawn, he seemed anything but. Even with blood dripping down his chin. They had been prepared.

"Why, Countess," Mr. Pierce said rather casually, as if his nose weren't busted open, "do come in."

"Don't move," Mr. Pierce's guard echoed, his weapon pointed straight at her captor. "Or it will be the death of you."

"'Traveling alone,' eh?" Amara's captor hissed in her ear in Tagalog. "Liar."

Just then, the two other Filipinos took off running down the deck. With a tilt of Mr. Pierce's head, his guards ran after them, leaving behind just Mr. Pierce, Amara, and her captor.

Mr. Pierce shut the door behind them. He didn't need to ask the man to release Amara. The man was smart enough to know when he'd lost. He stepped back. Amara's relief was instant. Mr. Pierce wasn't satisfied with that, however.

In one swift movement, he pressed his forearm across the man's neck and forced him back against the wall. Her captor's knife pinged to the wooden floor. While startled, Amara had enough wits about her to swoop down and pick it up. She tucked it, hilt first, into her sleeve. For good measure, Amara took a step back too.

Every line in Mr. Pierce's arm tensed. He had promised to avoid violence, but it was already proving necessary. Just for the way that man had grabbed her, for the fear he put in Granger. She couldn't deny that she wanted her captor to suffer.

"She led you straight into a trap." Mr. Pierce laughed. "Not bad, Countess." Then with far more seriousness and power, he shouted for the man to get to his knees.

Her captor dropped down. Amara could see his face better now, his eyes too. Compared to earlier, he wasn't nearly as intimidating. He was just a person, one of her own. Lord knew why he wanted to do this, what lies he had been fed.

"There are more men waiting for me on the ship," he said to Mr. Pierce. "Kill me and—"

"Shut up and tell me what you scared this nice, young lady for."

Scared? Amara resented the word. But as prideful as she was, she couldn't deny that she had been, in fact, scared. More than she had ever been in her life.

"The map," the man answered.

"The map? To where?"

"The emerald cave. You may be from the West, but you know all about the emerald cave, don't you, *Silver Order member?*"

Mr. Pierce tipped his head to the side. "How do you know about the Order?"

The man just shrugged. "You have it, don't you?"

"That is privileged information."

Her heart stilled, reminded again that he knew far too much about the emeralds.

"It doesn't belong in your hands," the man said.

A knock sounded at the door, a rhythm that Amara could tell was some kind of code. When Mr. Pierce quickly opened it, the two guards dragged in the two other Filipino men. Neither of them had a single scratch. They weren't bleeding, anyway.

"Countess," Mr. Pierce said, "you best leave."

"No!" Amara shouted. She wanted them punished, but she couldn't bear to see the only Filipinos she had ever met outside her own family killed. It was a strange situation, indeed. "They're just doing what they believe to be right."

Maybe they didn't understand who she was.

"The location of the cave is my secret and my secret alone," she tried to inform him, though perhaps foolishly. "These men will agree." She looked at them pointedly. "Yes?"

"These men will lie," Mr. Pierce spit. "You'll regret releasing them, I promise you."

"Why do you want this map?" Amara asked them, even if she knew it existed only in her and her lola's mind.

"To destroy it," her captor answered.

Amara crossed her arms. It wouldn't have been such a bad thing, considering what British men like Mr. Pierce might do with it. Maybe this man wasn't her enemy at all.

"Who put you up to this?" Mr. Pierce demanded.

"No one." Her captor turned to Mr. Pierce. "When people like you come and steal from our home, we take action."

Mr. Pierce sniffed. "You really expect me to believe that you're somehow able to access our plans and agenda?"

The captor just smiled. "Your little organization is not as impenetrable as you think. Even if you kill us all, our mission will continue on. You will stop nothing."

"Perhaps we should oblige." One of Mr. Pierce's guards cocked his weapon.

"No!" Amara shouted. "Don't."

The guards turned to Mr. Pierce, who paused for a moment in thought. His face calmed, his anger diminishing.

"We should spare their lives," Amara argued. "If we hand them over to the authorities as common thieves, they won't be able to follow us."

"I don't know…" Mr. Pierce debated.

"These men were only trying to protect their home and its belongings. Isn't that right, sirs?"

Reluctantly, all three nodded. Though it could very well have been a lie.

Amara looked to Mr. Pierce with satisfaction. She couldn't have violence play out this early in her trip. Mr. Pierce's nose and that storm already seemed a bad enough omen. She swiped a napkin from atop the round, wooden table.

"Take this." She handed Mr. Pierce the rag. His face reddened. She didn't get it. Was he really too sheepish to put the rag to use? It was an expression so rare on him, someone so full of confidence and bravado, it almost made her smile.

"You're right." He pressed it to his face. "Of course you're right. Violence in this case is unnecessary. Thank you."

"We haven't left port yet, have we?" Amara asked. "Let them go and make sure they don't board again."

"We'll inform the captain, then." Mr. Pierce backed off. "We'll report them as common thieves, just as you said. Their stay with the local authorities should keep them off our heels long enough. They won't catch up."

"But not without getting more information out of them first," his guard quickly put in.

Mr. Pierce turned to Amara. Since she'd arrived, he'd looked so different. His hair wasn't combed back as it usually was at society parties. Instead, it had fallen down to delicately frame his face. A look that should have made him seem disheveled, but somehow didn't.

"Now *this*, I will have you leave for," he said.

Amara wanted to protest. There was still so much she wanted to ask these men too. But all she could think of was her poor maid, tied up in her room.

She had to go. No matter how much she wanted to stay and discover what these men knew.

Mr. Pierce motioned to his guard with a tilt of his head. "Go with her."

Amara hesitated again. But for an entirely different reason. Despite herself, she worried about Mr. Pierce now. Would he be safe with one less guard? She didn't care for his sake, but for her own, she told herself. He was her only form of protection.

"Let's go," the guard commented.

Amara nodded, taking one last glance at Mr. Pierce and wondering why her heart suddenly squeezed. "Of course."

CHAPTER EIGHT

The Deal

SOMEONE ELSE KNEW. Darren didn't know how, but someone knew. Not just about the emeralds, but about *them*. He wasn't sure if he believed what that man had said. As much as he wanted to get the truth out of him, torture wasn't in the cards on a passenger ship like this. Even if he took him to the deepest bowels of the *Evangeline*—which he had considered—the risk of being heard was too high. He was just glad they hadn't hurt the countess. Lord knew what he might have had to do then.

He had come here prepared for everything, but the look in her eye with that blade at her neck... The horrible emptiness deep in the pit of his stomach had been wholly unexpected. A piece of it was still there lingering, even now when she was safe. There was so much that could have happened.

Thank God Lady Webb had been able to get to him when she had. *Thank God.*

He cursed himself for not keeping a better eye on her. He'd checked on her room often, but clearly not often enough. He should have taken shifts with his men, watching her door. If he had, one of them would have seen those men heading toward her room.

As Lady Webb had requested, they reported and delivered the men to the local authorities before they left port. His guards had tried threats, but the assailants still hadn't revealed much about why they'd been there or who they might have been working for. Unlike Darren, his guards wanted to resort to torture. It just wasn't practical. There was no way to know if their violence would yield honest answers or false ones.

It veered far too close to the sort of stratagem his father might have employed, and he refused to be anything like his father.

His father only preferred violence because it made him feel powerful.

And the Silver Order was all about power, not mercy or humanity. No wonder his father had lost so much of his.

He was glad the countess had reminded him of his vow. Something about her face, her words, the sound of her voice when she'd handed him that napkin sapped his impulses and more importantly, his anger. More often than not, that was where his urge for violence originated.

His father had once told him anger was an emotion too wild and uncontrolled to be useful. More likely, it would yield disaster. A piece of advice his father had clearly forgotten over the years. Since his wife's death, he'd forgotten a lot of things.

Of course violence wasn't necessary. Not this early in their trip. It would have been nice to have more information, but he was committed to remaining a gentleman. In fact, it was already starting to anger his men. They had argued about the incident long after they'd left port.

"You're paying us to protect you and that woman," Miller said back in their quarters. He smoothed down his brown, almost-black beard. "You have to let us do that."

"Don't forget the maid." Drake stood over them all, the largest and broadest of the three. "Just because she's a member of the servant class don't mean we should forget her."

"If we keep treating our enemies so kindly, word will get around," Miller roared. "I've spent my life making a reputation for myself. If someone even *tries* to inflict harm on those I've been employed to protect—"

"It's not like we let those men go free," Darren argued back. "Drake turned those men in to the authorities."

"These aren't just your father's ways." Miller thrust out a hand. "They're *our* ways. Those men deserved punishment."

"Which is it? Were we to torture them as punishment or to get answers? Because, in my mind, all torture leads to is lies."

"We can't afford to look weak." Miller crossed his arms.

"We're going to give this a try nonetheless." If they didn't like it, he would replace them. Darren almost said as much but held his tongue. That sort of sentiment wouldn't do anyone any good right now.

Fact was, Miller and Drake were his closest friends and frankly, the only people he truly trusted. He'd known them since he'd been sent away to school. Back when they'd both snatched his belongings and saved his life all in the same day.

He didn't know how long they had been following him that day so many years ago, not until he'd gotten lost and nearly strolled right down a street overrun by plague. Even if they had been only watching him to steal his bookbag, they hadn't had the heart to let him die.

He had been so grateful he'd bought them lunch. Even though they'd still stolen his bookbag by the end of the day, he'd returned to the same part of town the next day with a small stock of food. All that he could carry. They had been cautious of him at first, even offering him back his bookbag. But Darren hadn't wanted it. He'd only wanted to be friends. They were different than his other friends, who never seemed to forget who his father was. Even if he was just another nob to Drake and Miller, they still treated him as an equal.

Darren continued to bring them food and other necessities whenever he could get away. Eventually, the boys had begun to feel sorry for their misdeeds against him. In exchange for the food, they'd insisted on telling him things, little bits of knowledge that only the people who lived on the streets could really benefit from. Since it was all they'd had to offer and seemed to assuage their guilt, Darren had graciously accepted.

He'd learned things like which baker burned the most bread that had to be tossed, how to follow cats for the freshest scraps, and the wealthy men to run from even if they offered you gold. Enough to soften Darren to their situation. They'd been orphans. If Darren hadn't tried to help them, who would?

When winter had come, he'd taken them home, stowing them away in his carriage house like stray dogs.

His father had learned of them by March and, to Darren's surprise, had quickly agreed to give them training in the guard. He'd said people like them, who had no one else, were the most loyal. Darren, however, had never seen it like that. He had always cared more about their friendship. They were never just his guards. It was why they so freely and often challenged him. They were just saying what they thought was best. *So I ought to listen,* he told himself.

"You hope to woo the countess, is that it?" Drake raised a brow.

Darren released a puff of breath. "What do you know about wooing anyone, Drake?"

"I know plenty." Drake straightened, his chin raised in indignation. "I know that, for one, there comes a time in every man's life when it becomes quite necessary. More than anything else, in fact. When you must have her."

Had he really been so obvious?

"It couldn't have come at a worse time," Darren yielded.

"You're different around her," Miller said. "You play the part better."

"What part?" Darren sneered, not liking where this was going.

"Heir to the Chair, of course."

But it was more than that. Everything he did seemed to hold more meaning.

"Perhaps it's the best card I have to play," Darren said. "I don't exactly have a title like those other nobs, do I?"

"How can you say that?" Miller consoled, albeit in a some-what mocking tone. "You have your wealth. Not to mention a handsome face…"

They all laughed.

"She doesn't care a wit about any of that," Darren said. "She's simply trying to save her mother."

"But you do mean to help her," Drake said, surprisingly en-couraging when it came to such matters. Now Darren felt bad for even considering getting rid of them. He had just been angry. But not like his father. Never like his father. He had handled himself better than that man ever could.

"If you do, she'll have to show some appreciation," Drake finished, puckering his lips and rubbing his hands over his body like a goon.

Darren rolled his eyes.

"Now we know your true mission," Miller put in.

"Perhaps." Darren crossed his arms. "I don't care a farthing for the emeralds. With any luck, my father will bore of trying to obtain them." Though Darren doubted it. Not when vendetta was involved.

Miller and Drake exchanged a glance. They knew it too.

"If my father gets involved…I won't risk the countess getting stuck in the crosshairs," he said, the mood suddenly turning serious.

"He hasn't mentioned that bastard Marx, has he?" Miller asked.

"My father had him sacked, actually."

"About damn time." Drake sighed.

Having trained with the man in the guard, Drake and Miller knew him well. He had once been the Order's most ruthless killer. The kind who had been born into violence, far worse off than Drake and Miller, with a childhood that had been the stuff of nightmares. It was said he had killed his first man at age seven.

"What did he do?" Miller asked.

"I don't think I want to know," Darren answered. "Took it

too far, no doubt."

"I can only imagine." Drake sniffed. "Serves him right."

"I'm sure your father means to replace him," Miller said.

"He did say he had other men with his sort of tendencies," Darren suddenly remembered.

Miller swore.

"My father has the tendency to overreact, doesn't he?" he asked without needing confirmation. "Especially when he thinks he's been wronged."

"By Lord Webb, not the countess herself," Drake said for the record.

"If I refuse to suffer for my father's sins, then neither should she."

"No matter what your father demands?" Miller questioned.

"It's not the only order of his I plan to refuse."

"Then say nothing else," Miller said with definitiveness to his voice. "There's still a chance it might not come to that."

To speak any more on the matter would have been treason. Like in England as a whole, treason in the Order was among the worst crimes. Even the slightest hint of treason was met with swift punishment and little mercy. The fact that he was Heir to the Chair didn't matter. The most mercy they could hope for was a quick death. Something they might not need to risk just yet.

Miller was right: it was best to stop these discussions now and for good. They had already reached an unspoken understanding.

"Should be smooth sailing for the next several days, boys," Darren said, changing the subject. "Tomorrow, we'll begin our trek across the Mediterranean."

"Does that mean all is well and good with the countess?" Miller asked. "Has she agreed?"

With all that had happened, Darren had nearly forgotten. The countess was well past the deadline for her to choose or reject his promise of protection. But she had to make a decision. He felt a bit foolish that he still had yet to do so.

"I, um, I shall secure that now," he said gruffly.

He turned to leave the cabin. When his men got up to follow, he waved them away.

"He wants his alone time," Drake whispered to Miller.

Rather, Darren was just trying to give them a break. After a day like today, they needed it. Furthermore, dealing with the stubborn countess he was sweet on was *his* burden. Lord knew it wouldn't be easy.

He knocked on her door. He couldn't help feeling a little disappointed that he'd been forced to do this. Part of him had expected her to come to him entirely of her own volition, begging for his protection. It would have been nice for a change. A moment he would have savored.

"Mr. Pierce." She opened the door and leaned out, looking across the deck, clearly suspicious of something—what, he didn't know. "Best come in."

She let him into the sitting room without challenge. Perhaps that was something. He was welcome, at least.

Miss Granger was cleaning the floors. No doubt now that he had arrived, she would be taking her time, eavesdropping on every detail and filling the countess's head with her take on the matter. He tried to ignore her, tried to pretend that it was just him and the countess. Just like when they were as children. Alone.

Lady Webb motioned him to a small settee that creaked beneath his weight.

"Would you like something to eat?" she began politely, taking a seat across from him. She didn't wait for him to answer. "Granger, would you mind getting us a tray of something? Whatever is available is fine."

"Are you sure, milady?" Miss Granger asked.

"Of course I'm sure," the countess said stiffly.

Miss Granger leaned the mop against the wall with a slight grumble. Finally, they were going to be alone. Though this time, they wouldn't be exploring the woods of his father's estate or harvesting flowers in her father's greenhouse.

Of course she could trust him. They had been friends once, he wanted to remind her. It wasn't like he wasn't going to try anything. At least without her consent. No one of the ton need ever know.

"I thought you said you could offer me protection," she said the moment Granger had shut the door behind her.

"I-I—" Darren stammered, caught off guard by her sudden indignation. He cleared his throat. Where was his Heir of the Chair bravado now? Drake had no idea what the hell he was talking about. Usually, he was quicker than this.

"You didn't even know those men were on board."

Darren didn't like what she was implying. Yes, he should have had someone keeping watch, but if she was going to agree to accept his protection, he couldn't admit to that.

"Perhaps if I had been allowed to stay nearer to you…"

"You were right below me. How come you didn't at least hear them? They were here, in this very room, Mr. Pierce. For God-knows-how-long before they attacked me."

"I suppose I thought it was just you and Granger getting back from your walk." He bit down. He hated that he hadn't heard. He had been a fool to stop paying close attention—was that what she wanted to hear?

"So you *were* keeping an eye on me. And still, I nearly died."

She was absolutely brutal. Maybe worse than his father.

"Are you always this oblivious?" Lady Webb stood and paced around the room. "Even if I were to accept your earlier proposition, would you even be capable of fulfilling your end? Because, I must tell you, I have my doubts."

"I would… I-I…" Again, he stammered like a fool. He needed to get control of himself. Damn it, if he could face down his violent, loose-cannon of a father, he could face her.

"For instance, have you trained? You and your men have revolvers, yes, but do you truly know how to use them?"

"I thought you despised violence."

"It should be avoided at all costs, but just in case, I fear it may be necessary."

"I assure you, it will be."

"I've come to terms with that, but still. There are things that can be done."

"Such as?"

"Instead of killing someone, you could injure them instead. Shoot them in the arm or in the foot, but that requires skill, doesn't it?

She wasn't going to make this easy.

"Like most gentlemen of the ton, I've spent my summers hunting and shooting."

"So you've shot fowl. What about an actual man? It's quite different, I'm sure."

"I'm an excellent shot."

"So you *have* killed."

"No, but I'm an excellent shot nonetheless." He considered lying, but she was smart enough—she'd probably find him out. He couldn't believe he had to convince her that he was capable. He hadn't expected this.

"I've had training, of course. Just like the two men in my guard. Protecting you won't just involve shooting a revolver. If it comes to hand-to-hand combat, I shall be ready for that too. We succeeded enough in your rescue, didn't we?"

The countess scoffed. "I suppose."

From where he was sitting, he could see into her sleeping quarters. Her bed was neatly made. On her nightstand was the crystal he had left her. That alone made him smile. Next to it, a book was opened facedown. He nearly sat up to see what she was reading. It was one of the things he had been trained to do no matter the situation: to take in his surroundings. What she read might help reveal about her mood. Was it a Gothic? A romance? An adventure like the Robinson Crusoe one that he'd quite enjoyed? How might she have liked it? But they hadn't the time to talk of such frivolity. Though part of him ached to know.

He noted the bracelet that sat on the nightstand as well, along with a couple of rings. Neither of which she had bothered to put back on. He wondered what that meant. Maybe she was ready to put aside finer things for the difficulties not far down the road. At some point, they'd have to make their way through jungle to find the cave. Their destination was easy to forget in staterooms like this one. Those ruffians yesterday had served as a stark reminder.

Ever since, she seemed to touch her lucky amulet, tucked under her bodice, more than ever. As if that might activate it somehow. It was clearly some family heirloom, given the strange symbols he'd noticed that first day at sea. He was almost certain it was a sort of protection. Unnecessary with him around, he wanted to tell her. A job he was going to take far more seriously. Starting at once, he would set up a schedule and make sure she was being watched at all hours.

"How do we know other men won't come for us?" she asked.

"We don't."

Despite her indignation earlier, her face betrayed fear now and true vulnerability. "There could still be dangerous men on board and at every stop. And I have a feeling it's all your fault."

"*My* fault?" He stood now. "For those men? The emeralds are just that powerful. Of course they're sought after. They have been for generations. Perhaps longer than the Order has even been around."

"But those men knew about the Order. You and all your other members—your father too probably—guided them straight to a secret my family has kept for generations."

"Don't forget *your* father."

She shot daggers at him. The statement that was to follow would surely be venomous.

"Instead of you, maybe I should join up with them. At least then I'd know my family's belongings wouldn't end up in the British Museum."

The words were worse than venom. They were bullets.

He shook his head. "When they got whatever it is they want, they'd kill you without a moment's hesitation."

She reeled and he immediately regretted his words. Even if they were true, he and Lady Webb couldn't continue on like this, constantly bickering. He forced himself to remember that she did, in fact, trust him. Even if she refused to admit it. She would never dare be alone with him if she really thought him a danger. She just wanted some reassurance. Unfortunately, he was giving her the opposite. He decided to lay it out straight.

"Next moment I get, I'll send a letter on the ship's wireless. I'll report those men to my father. We'll get to the bottom of it, I promise."

"Really, I thought your members were better at keeping secrets." She sucked in a breath and released it. "Our secrets are just as important as yours, you know."

"I shall remind my father. Perhaps we did mess up." He decided it was in his interest to concede even if he couldn't be sure either way. "Nonetheless, you're safer with me and you know it."

"Do you think there's more of them already aboard, like that ruffian said?"

"You can't take everything he said for truth. The man would have said anything not to be killed."

"I suppose you're right." She turned away from him, facing the wall to disguise whatever it was she was feeling. Even as a child, she had done this, shielding herself from him whenever she'd felt the slightest bit exposed.

"It won't happen again. I promise you this. I never travel without my pistol." He tapped the metal that sat atop his ribcage. "And I'll never leave your side…outside your staterooms, that is. Satisfied?"

"I suppose."

She walked forward into her sleeping quarters, grabbing something from the nightstand and turning back to him.

"But I want it known you're my guard." She held out his favorite crystal, waiting for him to take it. As if holding on to it would have meant there was something between them. But that wasn't why he'd given it to her.

"Keep it. I gave it to you for—"

"It doesn't matter." She took a breath. "There shall be no embellishments, no claims that we are anything more. I might not have much of a reputation to speak of, but I do have my honor."

"In case you should ever marry." Darren took the stone grudgingly and shoved it into his pocket.

She sniffed. "Not likely. Rather, I think it should only serve to complicate things if we… It's just better this way."

"Complicate things"? Things are already complicated, he thought. But that wouldn't stop him from winning her over. No matter how difficult, he was still going to try.

"In exchange—" she started.

At that, Darren couldn't help leaning forward.

"I'll give you three emeralds of no nominal size."

He sank. He didn't know what he'd expected. But like he'd admitted to his men, he didn't give a damn about the emeralds. It was her he wanted. He just didn't know how to ask for as much without sounding like a complete heathen. Perhaps if he won her over the right way, he wouldn't need to.

"But I want one promise," she went on. "You'll allow me to travel to the cave alone. You won't follow me in. If we make it that far." She cast her eyes down.

After what had happened so early into the journey, he wasn't surprised that she was beginning to lose hope.

"We're going to make it." Darren caught her eyes and stilled her in her steps. "And we're going to make your mother better."

"Then just a few gems is agreeable to you?"

"I only ever wanted a few for study." He shrugged, saying nothing of the crude things he really wanted, much less the revenge he feared his father wanted too.

"Really?" She crossed her arms, clearly unsure if she believed him. Perhaps part of her knew. "That's worth risking your life for?"

"The Order has risked more for less."

"Like my father once did," she put in.

Darren sighed at the belabored point. She wouldn't let him forget it. Ever. He fought to change the subject at once.

"Whatever my past, it is you who is in my debt. Not the other way around," he said. "You are still alive, aren't you?"

"Yes, w-well…" Apparently, it was her turn to stumble. "I did mean to thank you for all that."

"Don't worry. That's all I wanted." He smiled at the lie. "A simple thank you. Nothing more."

She blushed. "Also for not hurting those men, for submitting them to the proper authorities. I doubt your men made it easy on you."

"I want to spill as little blood as possible on our trip." He was different from his father. At some point, he would convince her of that.

"Will you trust me to do this?" He held out his hand.

"I think if—"

"No." He kept his hand out steadfast. "It's a yes or no question, I'm afraid."

He preferred to keep things simple. Either she trusted him to protect her or she didn't. He had made his mistakes with those Filipino men, but in the end, she had survived them unscathed. In the end, she had come to him for help. So he had no doubt what her answer would be. He was just forcing her to say it. Out loud.

She pursed her lips then gently grasped his hand.

"Very well," she said. "My life is in your hands. I haven't much of a choice, do I?"

"Either way, I shan't let you down." He stepped back, breaking the contact, and looked about the room.

"Now, show me this map."

"'Map'?"

"The one that leads to the emerald cave? The one those men were after?" *What they were willing to kill for*, he almost said. But he didn't want to remind her that she could have been killed. From now on, he didn't want her to feel anything but safe.

"'Map'?" Lady Webb chewed her lip. "There is no map."

Disappointment dropped through him. "No map? Then how—"

"I have it all up here." She pointed to her head.

"I see," he said, pondering the fact for a moment. She truly had it memorized? It was, after all, the safest method. "Then tell me."

"I'm afraid that wasn't part of our agreement." She crossed her arms. "I shall lead you to the cave, not tell you how to get there on your own."

He supposed she was right.

"You've gotten far enough for one day, don't you think?"

He snickered.

"Yes, well…" He stood up. "I shall check back soon. There will be no more strolls, at least not without my supervision. Agreed?"

Darren cringed at the words. He probably sounded like her mother or a strict chaperone.

Lady Webb just pressed her lips together and sighed. "Very well."

At a loss for any other words, he left quickly, suddenly feeling the need to jump overboard. He wasn't sure if he'd ever change her feelings for him. At least he'd have more opportunities to try.

CHAPTER NINE
Training

A MARA COULDN'T BELIEVE what she had just agreed to. The man she could trust least in this world was supposed to protect her. She had put her life in his hands.

The horrible image of her father broken and bleeding atop a rock flashed across her vision. The Order hadn't been able to save her father, so why did she think it could save her?

She had only just come to terms with his death. For months, she'd still expected to see him when she'd woken in the morning. In her sleep, she would allow herself to forget. That was why she'd spent so much time in bed. Deep sleep was the only place she could be blissfully unaware.

But she was done being so self-indulgent. As her mother's health worsened, she simply hadn't the time to waste. More than sadness, anger burned in her gut. She missed him badly and for some reason he'd been taken away. Why? For what purpose? A few amethysts? They weren't worth her father's life. Just the *idea* enraged her. Nothing, not even Mr. Pierce's blue crystal could soothe her.

Not long after Mr. Pierce had left, Granger returned to the room more sour than usual. She had a tray in hand. Seeing him gone, she dropped it on the low table and began to eat one of the little sandwiches herself.

"Well?" she pressed. "What did you agree on?"

"He'll help watch over us."

Granger sighed. "I thought so. There's no avoiding it, not after those men. I have to say I'm relieved."

"Good." That helped settle Amara's turbulent mind. She still blamed herself for what had happened to the poor innocent maid. Amara couldn't have that happen again. The last thing she wanted was to lose the trust of her companion.

"I'm sorry, Granger. I hate myself for what they did to you. You know you're more than just a servant to me."

She wished she could say it would never happen again, that Mr. Pierce and his guards would protect her, but it was a promise she couldn't make.

"I hadn't expected this journey to turn out so terribly dangerous." Amara frowned. "I thought—foolishly, I thought the jungle would be the hardest part."

"Oh, don't you worry about me. I'm hardy, I am. We'll get through this. Maybe I'll end up with one of those emeralds myself."

"I know you don't actually believe they'll work—"

"No, I don't. I don't think they'll give your mother another day."

She had said this often enough before they'd left for sea. And still, she had come.

"Then why agree to accompany me? I at least thought you'd put up some resistance. You agreed rather quickly."

"Oh, knowing what I do now, I don't think I'd change my mind, either. Adventure is what I wanted. So few people in my class get the opportunity, you know. And I've always wanted to see the world. Haven't you?"

"I suppose I was curious."

"The only problem is that we're not much prepared." Granger twisted her hands together.

"We aren't. But perhaps we can do something about that." Amara got up quickly. "Come with me."

AMARA AND GRANGER followed Mr. Pierce and his guards across the open deck. There was some alacrity to his step. To her surprise, he had agreed to Amara's request for some training without much convincing.

She had expected to argue. But he said it all himself: he couldn't deny the possibility that Amara and Granger may one day need to fend for themselves. There was always the possibility that Mr. Pierce and his guards might all be killed.

Amara had swallowed hard at the brash statement. But it was true. Even if on the horizon there was no hint of ominous storms to come.

The weather had much improved in the past day and she had been itching to spend more time outside their accommodations. Though perhaps it was a bit too sunny.

Halfway through the Mediterranean, the sun seemed stronger. Using her lace parasol, Amara did her best to shield herself from the ocean's glare. Granger fanned herself. Mr. Pierce and his guards, however, weren't bothered in the least. Mr. Pierce held down his hat and turned his face up to the sky, basking in the glow.

"You know," he said, looking back down and out into the sea, "you shouldn't have left your room without having Miss Granger inform me first. Remember?"

He was right. Instead of enjoying this sunny weather, they all should have been on edge.

"I suppose I didn't think it was necessary at the time," she replied.

"Everything I tell you is necessary. You need to trust that. Or better yet, you need to trust *me*."

Amara bit her lip. He was right. Already, she was putting them all in jeopardy.

"Fine," she agreed.

"It is absolutely imperative to remain unseen whenever possible. It's the best way to avoid being followed."

Mr. Pierce stopped at the end of the deck and turned around. Here, they had plenty of space, more than either of their rooms, anyway.

The sun darted off the water. The whole world seemed to open up. The sea before them was so vast and consuming, it was slightly overwhelming.

The ship rumbled beneath her feet and she could almost feel the bow cutting across the water, closer to their future destination. Unlike in Spain, she was determined to get off the ship for a short excursion in Malta. With Mr. Pierce and his guard, she might actually have the courage to do so.

"You might want to try dressing less lavishly," one of the guards put in. Mr. Miller, she remembered from their earlier introduction. "Bright red, even if it's just the trim on your dress—it stands out."

"I'm afraid that's the point. Most of the time, anyway." She liked the fact that her dresses made her stand out. It was the only thing that helped display her status. It wouldn't be easy giving them up. God knew what people would say or do when she was dressed in anything less.

"Well, if you want to be inconspicuous, muted colors are best, particularly gray or black," Mr. Pierce said. "Sorry, Countess."

"But all my clothes are like this." Amara looked down at her fine, silk gown. She'd chosen it specifically because it was looser and allowed for more movement than her other gowns. She hadn't known color was such an important factor to staying safe.

"You can borrow my gowns," Granger offered. Though her clothing would likely be a little big, Amara didn't care. She'd always thought her own were a little tight. If plain, Granger's would at least be comfortable.

"How are you with knives?" Mr. Pierce asked.

Granger visibly gulped.

"I don't imagine you've used a knife beyond the dinner table?" Mr. Pierce produced one deftly seemingly from midair.

Granger *ooh*ed and *ahh*ed while Amara rolled her eyes. Clearly, it had to come from the inside of his jacket.

"I thought you were going to teach us how to protect ourselves, not magic tricks." Amara crossed her arms.

"Call it whatever you want. If you produce a blade without your opponent realizing, you can cut him all the easier," Mr. Pierce said.

Mr. Miller stepped up behind him and Mr. Pierce immediately twisted around.

"Dear Lord," Granger mumbled. "They're going to demonstrate."

The blade in Mr. Miller's hand glinted as if in warning. Amara stepped back, praying they didn't hurt themselves. Mr. Drake stood several feet back, explaining away the friendly spar to concerned passersby. Most of them, finely dressed for afternoon tea, actually stopped to watch. Though she doubted the young ladies were actually interested in the sport. Behind their fans, they were merely ogling the men.

Mr. Pierce removed his hat and jacket, revealing a muscled set of shoulders. He was truly laying himself bare. Perhaps her words about his incompetence had struck a chord. In addition to offering them some training, he was proving himself too. She worried for Mr. Miller. Mr. Pierce was going to give this everything he had.

"When running is not an option, when you perhaps are cornered and have no hope but to defend yourself against some ruffian, you must focus just as much on defending yourself and blocking blows as making strikes with your blade. Block with either your blade or forearms, like so."

He bent his arms at the elbows and thrust them up. "It'll hurt like hell, but once you finish your opponent, at least you be alive."

Mr. Miller came at Mr. Pierce with surprising speed. Amara

was sure he was going to make contact and draw a line of blood, but then he blocked him with the steel of his blade, the *ping* reverberating into the air.

"Keep your arms tight over your body—protect your chest and stomach most of all. Those are your most vulnerable spots."

Mr. Miller came at him again, this time aiming for his stomach. Mr. Pierce blocked the blow with his forearm; the blade got close, but Mr. Miller pulled back before making contact.

"Again, a cut to your forearm is better than your solar plexus," Mr. Pierce said. "One stab there and you'll bleed out. You're a goner."

Mr. Miller and Mr. Pierce backed away from each other again, circling. By then, a small crowd had gathered. They actually applauded. The women giggled.

"As tempting as it may be, don't try to grab your opponent to get in a strike. If you do come in for a strike, it needs to be a quick maneuver. You immediately want to back away. Don't expect all the blows to come from the front, either. Be prepared for them to run up behind you too."

Mr. Miller ran up behind him, but Mr. Pierce twisted around, his knife extended out and swiping left to right. Mr. Miller wisely jumped back.

Amara hoped she'd remember these moves. One day, it might be a matter of life and death. But when the moment really came, fear could very well empty her mind. She didn't know. All she could do was pretend to be brave.

They kept circling each other and Amara continued to hold her breath. Even if they were just sparring, one of them could still get hit. One of them could still end up bleeding out on the deck. After all, they were using real knives.

Mr. Miller slashed low, quick, and fast toward Mr. Pierce's stomach. But Mr. Pierce raised his arms up and hopped back.

"Stay on your toes," he said, turning on a heel. "Keep yourself a straight line and as small a target as possible."

Mr. Miller slashed high toward Mr. Pierce's face. Mr. Pierce responded by stepping deftly to the side. "High shots to the face or neck might unsettle you, but they also present the perfect opportunity to disarm your opponent."

Mr. Miller kept his hand in place as his sparring partner demonstrated slicing down across his wrist and forearm. "This should be enough to cause them to drop the blade."

Mr. Miller did just that.

"Losing your knife is one of the worst things that can happen. So do everything you can to keep it. Even if your opponent makes this move. Brace for it. And don't even think about throwing your knife, either, no matter how good a shot you think you have. It's not worth it."

The small crowd clapped again. So much for staying inconspicuous.

"Your parasol, miss." Mr. Pierce reached out for the white lace umbrella at Amara's side. He spoke to her as if she were just another spectator. Maybe that was the point. Maybe they were being inconspicuous, after all.

Mr. Miller asked to borrow a man's walking cane, offering him the ship's railing for support instead, then immediately came after Mr. Pierce. As if they were fencing, they crossed their improvised weapons.

"Grab your parasol with two hands, not one, and with the full weight of your body, thrust into your opponent's neck. Strike just below the Adam's apple if you can. A move that will land your enemy in the morgue, no matter how delicate your arms. The eyes are a good spot to strike as well. It may sound brutal, but a man who attacks a woman deserves little mercy."

Mr. Drake came up from behind Mr. Pierce, sandwiching him in front of Mr. Miller.

"If you come under attack by two, strike forward with your umbrella." Mr. Pierce made a stabbing motion to Mr. Miller's gut. "Then with the back of the parasol, jab it into the ribs of the person behind you."

Mr. Pierce examined the parasol, particularly its wooden tip.

"Next time, consider purchasing one with a handle made of steel, not wood."

For the third time, the small crowd clapped. If only just to blend in, Amara did too.

The three of them, Mr. Pierce, Mr. Drake and Mr. Miller, gave a little bow. With the spectacle over, the crowd dissipated, everyone but Amara and Granger.

Mr. Pierce came up beside her, bracing his hands on the railing and catching his breath. "Look," he said between breaths. "Not a scratch on me. Think I could hold up in a real fight?"

He was gloating now. Amara had been right. He was really just showing off.

"Was that at least helpful?" he prodded.

"I think so," Amara said seriously now. "But when it's time to defend myself, I hope I don't just…"

"Freeze?"

"Indeed."

"You're braver than you think you are. Especially after what happened with those men. You're still here, aren't you?"

"Oh, I didn't do much. That was all you."

"But you were able to stay calm. Calm enough to bring them to me."

He was right. She'd even been alert enough to grab the man's knife. She still had it, in fact, stashed away in her nightstand. One day, she thought it might be useful.

"An event like that would make anyone uneasy. Even me," he told her. "You may even feel that it's made you weaker when in fact, it makes you so much stronger. In strength and in mind."

"I hope you are right."

They were relatively alone now and Amara didn't know how she felt about it. Granger had lingered over to Mr. Drake, laughing as they chatted. Clearly, Amara hadn't been the only one noticing the physique of the fighters.

"Your demonstration gathered quite the crowd," Amara told Mr. Pierce. "I thought you said we should remain unseen."

"The woman they saw today was a lady. Tomorrow, they won't recognize you in your new choice of dress. Few in those garbs ever are."

He eyed her. "You're not worried, are you? You have me now."

It sounded so possessive, like they were man and wife. But, in a way, it was true.

"You're right," she forced herself to admit. She had asked him to prove himself beyond just words and he had done that. Going forward, she felt much more confident about their trip.

Mr. Pierce smiled and turned out to the sea, his eyes searching the horizon. "The ship will be arriving at Malta in a few days. What do you think, would you be comfortable getting off the ship and having ourselves a little excursion? Dinner together, perhaps?"

He turned his gaze on her fixedly. It was an invitation to something more. The sort of request she had heard from other men in a much more lascivious tone. Of course, she had never agreed. But for the first time, she actually considered saying *yes*. Not just for the sights.

"What do you say, Countess?"

"Of course," she answered. "Granger has been complaining about feeling rather cooped up, haven't you, Granger?"

Granger paused in her chatter, turning toward her red-faced. A sort of guilt Amara had never seen on her before.

"Wouldn't an excursion to Malta be nice?" Amara asked.

She nodded. "It would be lovely to try some of the local cuisine."

"I think we're all sick of the food on this ship," Amara said.

"Then it is set." Mr. Pierce folded his arms and shot her a smile that made her question everything. He had the type of charm that could make anyone do anything.

But she had other reasons for agreeing, she told herself. Even if she didn't want to admit it. She couldn't bear to say *no*.

CHAPTER TEN

The Blackbird

DARREN PREPARED A pen and inkwell for the telegraph to his father. Just one of the promises he'd made to the countess. He planned on keeping them all.

Gripping the pen, he struggled to steel himself. He hated to revisit the event. Dread was already filling his stomach. Those ruffians hadn't been just some random group. He had a feeling the man had been telling the truth. He was part of some larger organization, some larger conspiracy, just as Darren was.

Of course there was something larger at play. No organization with few men, few resources, and few connections could possibly learn the name *Silver Order*, let alone know its members. Was it a rival organization? The lesser scholars who called themselves 'the Ravens'? Or was it one of their own?

Guilt stabbed at him. Was the countess right? Was it possible that, in their travels, the Order had brought her and her mother to some villains' attention?

He didn't know how, but the secrets they guarded so tight were getting out. The Order couldn't be responsible for the attack. It was a trespass on a myriad of levels. To her people, her family, herself. The Order couldn't be the reason the dowager countess died, either. It was bad enough what had happened to Lady Webb's father. If she believed the Order had had a hand in killing both her parents, she'd never speak to him again.

They had been on the ship for near a week and he had barely made any leeway into her heart. The way she'd hesitated when he'd invited her to visit Malta, not just that, when he'd practically asked her to dine with him, it had been clear she still didn't trust him. He kicked the wall with his foot, cringing at how forward he must have sounded.

Ink dripped over the blank page before him. He needed to get to writing. He pulled out a new blank piece of paper and got straight to the point of the matter.

Father,

The countess has agreed to let me and my men join her party for the sake of protection. I'll be following her closely. Not only has she agreed to take us to the cave, she's promised me a few of the emeralds.

I imagine you will be pleased. Although we've seen our share of setbacks. A storm and also a group of three men demanding a map to the cave. They nearly killed the countess for it. Fact is, they know too much. Not just about the emerald cave, much worse about us. He said there're more like him. I don't know how, but they know what we are doing. They know what I'm doing. Perhaps more, perhaps what we do across the world.

Every night, I'm on guard just waiting for another one of them to show up. Miller, Drake, and I each take turns watching outside the countess's door.

I have her dressing less lavishly, in her servant's clothes, in fact, but I worry that won't make a difference. The villains, whoever could be after us, might already know what she looks like, no matter how much she tries to hide.

Our protection may not be enough. We'll need reinforcements.

D

Darren folded the note. Later, he would hand it off to Drake to be encrypted into their usual code and then burned.

As he placed it in an envelope, he still couldn't believe what he had just written. Someone else knew about the Silver Order. Outside their membership, he had never heard of a single whisper of the Silver Order. Something had to be done. Thankfully, his father would receive the wireless message far faster than a letter. Though there was no knowing how his father would respond.

For the time being, he tried to put it out of his mind. There was the excursion to Malta he had to look forward to. He had to ensure the countess had a diverting time. Maybe then she would trust him? What more could he do? He would all but serve his heart on a platter if it meant changing her mind.

What I really need is more danger, he thought sardonically. The only reason she had actually agreed to his protection had been those three ruffians. If more came after and he proved successful then too, she'd have no choice but to fully hand over her trust to him.

He shook his head. That woman wouldn't be satisfied until she drove him mad. To wish for danger, when it was already so rife...he couldn't possibly be this desperate. Was her trust really worth another bloody nose? Damn it all. His nose still ached. He picked up his lucky crystal, hoping that might offer him some relief, still wishing Lady Webb had it instead. He'd been lying to himself when he'd said it hadn't meant anything. It had meant everything.

He was still at his desk in quiet contemplation when Drake and Miller stumbled in, drunk off wine from dinner, no doubt. Darren rolled his eyes.

"Missed you at dinner," Drake said. "I think the countess was expecting you."

Darren sniffed.

"If she really cared about dining with me, she would have accepted my invitation to Malta without reservation. Rather than acting like it was some favor to her servant."

It sounded silly saying it out loud, but he couldn't help being offended.

"To be fair, Miss Granger *is* eager for the chance to get off this ship." Miller nudged Drake and gave him a look. "I believe she told you herself."

"If we want the countess to warm up to us," Drake said, ignoring him, "Cassie may be our only hope. I'll say good things about you."

"That means you'll have to remain close to her, will you?" Miller rolled his eyes.

Drake shrugged. "It's all part of the job, I'm afraid. If I have to spend time with Cassie, then—"

"'Cassie'?" Darren held back a laugh. "Sounds like you two are intimate."

"We are merely friends. That's more than I can say about you and the countess."

"What did she say at dinner tonight?" Darren asked. "Anything about me?"

It had been childish, perhaps, skipping dinner in an attempt to stop seeming so eager. He didn't care.

"For someone who hates the Order, she is rather superstitious," Miller said. "We saw a blackbird cross the sky and she said it may be a bad omen. Something about the direction it flew."

"I can't help feeling the same." Darren stared at the folded telegraph.

"Is trouble afoot?" Miller and his usual teasing self turned serious.

"I don't think those men were lying when they said there're more of them," Darren said. "As much as I would like to think otherwise…they know too much."

Miller nodded, full of thought.

"Then we'll continue to watch the ladies' rooms at night," Drake said with gusto. "Do you think the rogues are on board?"

"It's possible." Darren lifted a shoulder. "If they're not, Malta is likely where they'll try to board next. If we leave the ship for the island, I'd wager they'd try to follow. If we stay, they'll stay. It won't make a difference."

"You think they want the emeralds too?" Miller asked.

"Not exactly," Darren admitted. "I think they really are trying to protect them."

The Order was the true villain here. In most cases, probably. He should abandon this whole trip. Get off at Malta and take the next ferry to the Continent. It was becoming too dangerous, not just for him, but for the whole of the Order. He very well might run if not for the countess.

"We'll be ready for them," Drake said, all too confident.

This time, there would be no element of surprise. Because they'd released those men, their enemy may now know exactly how many guards traveled with him, the weapons they carried, and everything else they needed to know to plan a more successful attack. All those ruffians had to do was send off a letter or get a visit in jail. They could have been gathering additional reinforcements as they spoke.

"We'll need help soon," Darren said.

"Your father—" Drake began.

"Even if I send this on the wireless, we don't know how or when my father will respond. We're cut off, you understand?" Darren raised his voice with bitterness. "We're on our own...for now."

Just how his father wanted it.

"We could alert the captain of suspicious activity. We'll come up with something," Miller put in. "We'll get the crew to help us..."

"This is a passenger ship. They have butlers and chefs. They won't have the men we need."

Drake laced his hands behind his neck and stared up at the ceiling. He was distracted, just as Darren himself had been with the countess, except Drake had set his sights on Miss Granger. If he were in a better mood, Darren would have teased the man for it. Just as Drake had teased him. As it was, Darren was too troubled. They had too many problems on their hands.

Though he didn't want to admit it, this was all a first for him.

He had trained, yes—he had fed the countess no lies on that matter. All the same, he had never faced any real danger. Neither had his guards. They were bodyguards; they weren't accustomed to being stalked. He had a feeling that was exactly what was happening. Trapped on this ship, there was no losing their stalkers. Short of jumping into the ocean, that was.

From every angle, they were in dire straits. All they could do was restock their weapons.

CHAPTER ELEVEN
Malta

AMARA LAY AWAKE, tossing in bed, long before the horn signaled port. Just like the morning she'd had to board this ship, her stomach twisted in knots for what was to come. Except this time, she was more excited than nervous. And she was far more optimistic.

All night long, she had been thinking of Malta cuisine. At least that was what she told herself. More than that, she was picturing the person who would be sitting across from her. There was an implied intimacy to Mr. Pierce's invitation. She supposed she might have been mistaken. But since she had gone to bed for the night, there was no getting that part of it out of her mind.

She hated that her default reaction had been to turn his attention to Granger. As if she were only going for her servant's sake. Did she really have to be so horrible? Aside from his connection to the Order, he had never done anything to her personally. To the ladies of the ton, he was perfect. His looks were far from lacking and he had plenty of money; his only imperfection was his lack of noble blood.

A fact he'd been more than well aware of ever since he had returned from school. A change had occurred in him then. Though Amara had still liked to run in the woods, he'd been too grown up for it. He had pushed her away, forcing her to make friends with one of the servants' children instead.

When she'd next seen him again, years later in London, her first instinct had been no different than that of the other ladies of the ton. But by then, she'd begun to resent all the time her father had been away from home. Because of the Order. Everything was because of the Order.

She had tried so hard to turn a cold shoulder even when the London Season had kept bringing them together. Fat chance of that now. She needed him.

So for once, she resolved that she would be nice. She had to be.

That morning when she stepped out onto the deck, the weather was balmy and the breeze smelled sweet. Just as she had hoped, Granger's clothing was much more relaxed than her gowns, though they made Amara feel a bit less vibrant. She supposed that was the point.

The guards, who were in step behind her, seemed to approve, anyway. Amara turned to say as much to Granger, but she had already disappeared behind her, dragging her feet just long enough to speak with Mr. Drake.

A connection that was progressing faster than Amara had realized. Apparently, Granger didn't care who knew it. After all the terrible things that had happened, Amara couldn't blame or even scold her. She was just glad Granger was enjoying herself. She deserved to have a little fun and adventure. If that meant romance too, then so be it. At least one of them would find love.

"Just this way, miss." One of the crewmen directed her toward their guide, who was leading their tour group off the ship.

If it was any indication, Mr. Pierce was nowhere in sight. Had her rude reaction to his invitation been enough to put him off? He hadn't come to dinner last night, either. She was disappointed, she admitted to herself, but only because she wanted to change the course of their relationship toward friendship.

"Is Mr. Pierce otherwise engaged?" she finally endeavored to ask Mr. Miller. "I thought he promised to escort me across Malta. There is local cuisine he wanted to try, no?"

"He should be meeting us soon." Mr. Miller craned his neck above the crowd. "Ah, yes. There he is."

Mr. Pierce pushed his way through a group of young, well-dressed ladies. Amara couldn't help but notice how they glanced at him through their eyelashes. It was just his tall stature, imposing enough to catch anyone's attention.

"You've come, after all," Mr. Pierce began without hesitation. Apparently, he wasn't going to explain why he was late.

She didn't understand.

"I told you I was coming," Amara said tersely. So far, her plans to be amenable weren't going well. He didn't exactly make it easy.

"No," Mr. Pierce insisted. "You told me your maid Miss Granger was interested in going."

Mr. Miller stepped back then, likely preferring to assume the role of distant bodyguard now. Though no doubt he'd be listening.

She cleared her throat and calmed herself. "I'm glad you mention it. I've given our deal some thought and decided we would benefit from another agreement."

"Yes, what's that?" Together, they moved along with the tide of the crowd, crossing the bridge onto land. Mr. Pierce extended his arm and she graciously accepted until they reached steady ground, her feet finally feeling stable again.

Though part of her was tempted to stay attached—for protection, of course. She thanked him and released his arm, opting instead to remain close.

"Well..." she began somewhat nervously. After all the twisting and turning thoughts last night, she wished she had given more thought to what exactly she might say.

"If we are going to get through all this, we're going to have to be more than just civil, don't you think?" She swallowed. "We could, perhaps, be friends."

"I've never wanted to be anything less than friendly with you."

How was it that he could make anything, even something so innocent, also sound lascivious?

"Unfortunately, I can't quite say the same." Amara frowned. "But I want to change that. I want our trip today to be nice."

"Oh, not so fast. Don't hurt yourself now."

She ignored the sardonic comment, turning her attention to the tour guide instead, a young, lean man who stood on a crate so he could see over the entire party. Just then, he projected his voice loud enough to silence them all. He was giving an overview of all that they'd been seeing that day.

First, they would tour the city of Valletta, particularly some cathedral, then they'd take a carriage ride to the medieval fortified city of Mdina, enjoy lunch, and visit the ancient catacombs of St. Cataldus in Rabat, where they'd also get to enjoy the views from Dingli Cliffs. Lastly, they would gather souvenirs from the artisans of Ta-Qali.

Amara smiled at the sparkle in Granger's eyes. This was why she had ventured to come on this dangerous journey. Or maybe it had more to do with Mr. Drake. His eyes were just as bright.

Mr. Pierce noticed Mr. Drake and Granger too and exchanged a look with Mr. Miller. Both of them trying to hold back laughter. To Amara, what Granger and Mr. Drake had was sweet, really. What could be more romantic than the island of Malta on this perfectly temperate day?

On the island, the buildings took her breath away, particularly St. John's Co-Cathedral. As the tour guide explained that it had been dedicated to Saint John the Baptist, Amara could feel Mr. Pierce's gaze on her skin. Almost like he were touching her. Whatever he was doing, it made her face feel hot. He couldn't have just been watching her for her protection. It was something more.

Inside a church, what risk of attack could there have been? Here, where they were surrounded by centuries-old art and Baroque architecture, they were perfectly safe. The building was simply serene. No one dared speak much beyond a whisper. In the empty, cavernous space, a single word carried for days.

Amara tried to put his watchful glances out of her mind. The rich scent of frankincense oils and other incense was too intoxicating. Buildings this old just had a different smell and feel to them altogether. It was a collection of things, old woods or maybe the incomprehensible number of people who had passed through here over the years, somehow leaving their mark.

When they exited, the tour guide informed them that they would be having lunch by picnic. With just napkins and without plates, they ate fish sandwiches while overlooking the ocean.

There was little else to top it, except dinner by candlelight, perhaps. The sort of scene she had always pictured alone with a man but had never actually experienced.

Their next stop was Mdina. The carriages that would take them there came in multiple sizes. Some could fit four, even six occupants. Somehow, Amara, and Mr. Pierce ended up in one of the few that could only fit two. It was going to be a long drive. But she was going to be nice, she reminded herself.

Mr. Pierce helped her into the carriage. The hand he touched momentarily seemed to burn.

"Thank you," she said. "You've always been friendly to me. Even when I'm not."

With the exception of those few years after he'd returned from school. Those years had been awkward for everyone. So they didn't count.

Mr. Pierce was silent for some time, clearly taken aback. "Is that your way of apologizing?"

"Yes, why, yes it is. I also… Well, I've often wondered why."

She placed the hand within the folds of her skirt. It was much more coarse than she was used to, not even close to the comforting softness of satin.

Mr. Pierce paused again. "I suppose I always thought it might be enough. That, one day, you'd change your mind about me and we'd return to our previous friendship."

"That is the past, though," Amara remarked. And there was

no returning to that happy time. Too much had changed.

Mr. Pierce turned around to Mr. Miller, Mr. Drake, and Granger, who all shared the carriage behind them. There was room for one more with them, but she wasn't so cruel as to force Mr. Pierce to take the journey alone. Plus, Granger, if anyone, was the one who needed a chaperone. If she'd been born a noblewoman, she'd have been dragged to the altar or squirreled away at the nunnery already after her quick work forming an attachment with Mr. Drake.

"But I know you will," Mr. Pierce went on. "Change your mind about me, that is."

Like everything else, he sounded rather confident about that. *Too* confident. Not even she knew if she'd ever truly come around.

"I know because whether you like it or not," he said, "you're going to get to know me better these next few weeks. That alone makes this trip well worth it."

"Then you don't require the emeralds any longer?"

He snorted back some laughter. "Afraid my father still does."

At the mention of him, Amara looked away. His name was quick to conjure memories, both the good and the bad, and with them, a pain in her heart.

"You don't like when I speak of him, do you?"

"Or the Order at all, as a matter of fact."

"I understand, of course. But don't worry. Soon enough, you shall find out how different I truly am."

He kept saying that he and his father were different. Were they really or doth the gentleman protest too much?

"Everyone is a little like their parents," she argued.

"That is because most people spend a great deal of time with them." He shifted in his seat, swatting scornfully at a fly. "But I've been spending less and less time with my father, especially since he has become so tempestuous. It is only a recent development, you know. He was never that way while my mother was alive."

"Yes, I was sorry to hear of her death. Six years ago, was it?"

He nodded. "Unfortunately, my father has not gotten over it. Nor has his grief improved with time. Six years is more than long enough if you ask me, but I don't think he's so much as spoken to another even remotely suitable woman. And he's only gotten worse. He's angry about it. So angry. If only he would talk to me about his grief. But he remains distant. At times, it feels like I've lost both parents."

Amara didn't know what to say. "I'm… I'm sorry."

"You understand perfectly well how hard it is, don't you?"

"It's like losing the ability to breathe. It feels like you've lost something so vital."

"I'm sorry too. The Order expeditions are dangerous and the one your father took to South America was no different."

"So is this one."

"If it's any consolation at all, we made sure he was well aware of the trip's dangers before he left."

Amara knew where this was going. He was reminding her that it wasn't the Order's fault. Maybe he was right. Maybe in her anger over his death, she was just looking for someone to blame. Her father had known the dangers. And he still had gone away knowing she could end up fatherless. It wasn't fair.

Maybe it also wasn't fair how she'd treated Darren all this time. Just because he was directly associated with the thing that had been her father's obsession and had eventually led to his death didn't make him a bad person. The more time she spent with him, the more she realized he wasn't like that at all. He was actually kind of sweet.

"Look there!" Mr. Pierce shouted out, rather excitedly.

She took in the salty air, watching how the sea breeze brushed over the tall grasses. Up ahead, the fortress of Mdina came into view, even if it was just as small as her hand on the horizon.

The sandstone brick reminded her of the pale setting sun the day before. The colors here were a world apart from London, where everything seemed to be either black or gray. Here everything seemed polished in gold, even the sea, the way the sun glimmered off the waves. Even the air, for that matter, was different too. Warm and soft, it wasn't sharp and cold like England's. She was beginning to wonder why she lived someplace so bleak in the first place. Back home, her whole life was bleak.

Suddenly, enjoying the day felt impossible. How could she when she remembered the real reason they were there? It wasn't to sightsee. Even if she knew her mother would want her to enjoy herself. She felt like they ought to be doing something productive, not this.

"What happens if the crystals don't work?" she blurted out. It was a fear she had been holding on to more tightly than she'd realized.

"Forget your doubts. I know they do," Mr. Pierce said. "My father wouldn't have sent me here otherwise."

"You can't be so sure," she pointed out. Theodore Pierce acted that way about everything.

"But I am. As a member of the Silver Order—hate it though you may—I've seen things. Enough to know that crystals with impossible properties do indeed exist. Your father believed it too. Do you really think he would have wasted his time visiting the islands otherwise?"

"He always said his trip to the islands resulted in just one precious find: my mother." She smiled at the memory.

"Not the emeralds, eh?" He arched a brow, his eyes gleaming with mirth.

"He traveled for the adventure, not for loot. Unlike *some*."

"You mean me?" He laughed. "Of all the reasons I decided to travel across the ocean, loot isn't one of them. I thought I made it clear. My father wants the emeralds, not I."

She couldn't even begin to surmise all that his comment might imply. Not with him so near.

"Surely, you wouldn't allow him to force you." He was his own man and a confident one. Not the type to be pushed around or so Amara thought.

"He thinks this trip will bring me back into the fold of the Order. That it will reignite my passion for our little experimentations. He doesn't seem to realize what he's become. I don't want to get away from the Order. I want to get away from *him*."

But if he wanted to get away from his father, he could have gone anywhere. Instead, he had taken his directive and followed her. If he wasn't after the emeralds, what was he after? Something told her this trip had everything to do with her. It was a thought that set her face on fire.

They remained silent for some time. In the closeness of the carriage, she couldn't miss how he had turned away, swallowing a lump in his throat.

Amara tried to pretend she didn't notice.

"He was a good man once," Amara said, hoping to make him feel better. "He was kind to me as a child."

Mr. Pierce nodded in agreement. "That's the only reason I've stayed. That and duty, I suppose. It would be easier to never come back."

"Maybe you should. Maybe one day, you'll wake up and decide to abandon this journey and run off for good."

"You know I would never do that. Not to you. You must trust that."

"I'm trying." She didn't know why but she wanted him to trust her too. They were bound in this together now. Whether she liked it or not.

She had already given him so much. In exchange for her fears and insecurities, she had gladly taken his reassurances.

"Don't let the smooth waters of the Mediterranean deceive you. This journey will require more strength than either of us possesses. We will have to build on that strength as we go."

Amara tried not to show any fear. She simply nodded.

In Mdina, they walked up the sandstone steps up on top of the walls of the fortress. There, they could see almost the entirety of the island and far out across the sea.

Amara paused in her steps. She saw something out in the

distant sea. Then she saw it again. A spray of water, then the arch of a whale.

"Look!" She pointed. Everyone on the walkway took notice, even those not in their party.

Mr. Pierce stepped in close, his shoulder pushing into hers. "You're supposed to be incognito, remember?"

She lowered her hands. How stupid could she be? She had just brought attention to them in the most obvious way. If someone was looking for them amongst the passengers on the ship, they were sure to find them now. The whale mattered little now.

Mr. Miller and Mr. Drake closed in too.

"Let's keep moving," Mr. Miller said. "Fast now."

Maybe it was her ease with her companion, but she had completely forgotten the need for caution or the likelihood that someone was following them.

Mr. Pierce eased back an inch, relaxing slightly but still not completely off guard. Even here, they weren't safe. Danger could strike at any moment. She was aware of that now more than ever.

CHAPTER TWELVE

Candlelight

BACK ON THE ship, Amara's thoughts kept shifting to Darren. She thought she'd played rather nice. She'd even enjoyed herself during their outing. Maybe her perception of Darren really was changing, just like he'd hoped.

With all this time they were spending together, she would have thought she'd end up hating him more. Instead, it was quite the opposite. She liked him. How could she not?

The day had been filled with so much beauty. When they'd returned to their rooms, it was all Amara could think about. For once, she focused on all the good and none of the bad. She had had that slip at the end, but it was only because she had felt so safe.

It was unexpected how his eyes had filled with wonder at all the history. Even though he'd been keeping watch, he had paid close attention to the tour guides and every fascinating word they'd said. When she had asked a question, he'd nodded, eager for the response.

It was an image that remained with her until she drifted to sleep. When she woke, all the lamps were out except one.

Amara expected Granger to be up reading, but she was nowhere to be found. She could have gone out for some fresh air, but if that were the case, she would have taken the lamp with her. Amara counted again. All four were accounted for.

She waited several minutes, but Granger never returned. Amara started to grow not just worried, but fearful.

She had no choice. She threw on her dressing gown and stepped outside. She had barely made it to the stairs when someone stepped out of the shadows.

She almost screamed when she caught Mr. Pierce's face in the weak glow of light. He must have been keeping watch.

"What's wrong?" He pulled her into the shadows with him.

"Nothing… It's just…Granger is gone. I'm worried. Have you seen her?"

He shook his head. "You were right to find me. You shouldn't be alone. Come on. You can stay in my rooms."

"Are you sure?"

He nodded, leading her down the steps.

Inside, she clenched her arms over her chest.

"Where are Mr. Drake and Mr. Miller?" she asked, suddenly embarrassed that she was in nothing but her dressing gown. Worse than that, he was alone.

"They're at the bar. They needed the respite," he said. Amara wrung her fingers and shifted back and forth on her feet. She didn't know what to do. Stand or sit? She didn't know which one was more proper.

"What if something's happened?" She grasped at her throat, trying her best not to imagine the worst.

"I doubt it. Please, sit." Mr. Pierce motioned toward one of the chairs surrounding a small table. In everything he did, he was so casual and nonchalant. Amara, on the other hand, was anything but at ease. She was in a room with him. Alone.

"Then why did you bring me down here?" She blinked.

"I thought you could use the company."

He wasn't entirely wrong.

Mr. Pierce sat down across from her and poured her a glass of wine. She didn't even have a chance to refuse.

"Are you feeling all right?" he asked.

Amara shook her head. "When Granger finds out I spent the

evening alone with you, she'll never let me hear the end of it."

She was supposed to loathe him, after all. At least that was what Granger thought.

"I think once we discover Miss Granger's whereabouts, *she'll* be the one who needs to do the explaining." Mr. Pierce raised his eyebrows meaningfully.

"What do you mean?"

"I have a feeling her goings-on this evening will be far from godly."

"You mean with your man, Mr. Drake?" Her mouth fell open. She couldn't believe she'd been worried when all this time they'd been… She cleared her throat.

Mr. Pierce smirked and she felt herself growing warm, not just in her face but everywhere, across every pore and surface of skin. Her thoughts were abound with ideas. Maybe he was no longer the dangerous one. Maybe *she* was.

A silence descended over them until Amara found the courage to say something. "How long were you keeping watch?"

"Just a few hours."

"Do you need to sleep?"

"Not when I'm on watch."

"When do you sleep?"

"I find pockets here and there. In the meantime, I read." He pulled a book from the inside of his jacket. "About orchids, actually. Specifically, the vanilla orchid. When we get to the islands, I'm hoping to find a few specimens. I'd like to do some drawings."

"You draw?"

"For scientific purposes, yes." He blushed, or at least she thought he did in the weak candlelight. "I hope to bring home some chocolate too. Not for study, though, just for culinary purposes."

"Anything you don't plan to take?"

"Perhaps you."

Amara blinked, trying not to seem scandalized by the bold

remark. He was drinking, she told herself.

She snatched the book from his hands. The page he had bookmarked had a black-and-white illustration of the lady slipper orchid. It was so detailed, Amara could have stared at it for hours.

"Are these your drawings?" Amara asked.

He nodded. Amara flipped through, looking at other orchids. They had so much variety just in the shape of the petals alone. She had seen some in London, but not like this.

"The Order's botanists are always looking for new varieties. Perhaps we'll discover them."

"'We'?" She swallowed.

"We will be traversing through the jungle, won't we? Maybe into parts man has never stepped foot before."

Amara nodded. She knew this well enough and yet the thought still chilled her. The jungle itself brought out a very specific fear: fear of the unknown, not knowing if they'd ever return. Everything was a danger there: poisonous plants, carnivorous animals, even the ground that could look stable but was actually quicksand.

"You will have to be careful what you take. Especially in the parts protected by the diwata."

"Or what? A curse will befall me? You're growing into more of a believer with each day."

"Your men called me superstitious."

"They don't see the world as I do."

She swallowed.

"Is this a deep passion for you? Plant illustrations?" She tried to distract herself from his all-consuming glare.

He raised his eyebrows. "You could say that. Among other Order-sanctioned interests, yes. There are worse things one could do."

"I can only imagine. Dare I even ask?"

He laughed a little to himself. "I doubt they're suited for your nerves. They're quite awful."

"Tell me," she insisted.

He shrugged, probably only because he'd had a few drinks. "One time in order to keep some specimens in our hands and our hands alone, one of our members set an entire forest aflame. In Ecuador and a few other countries."

"That is awful." She shook her head. "Indeed."

"Mind you, I insisted we put a stop to it. The orchid business is a competitive one, I'm told. We don't fund orchid hunts for the sake of profit, I've had to remind our members. But for study."

"Your father approved of the arson?"

"One of our many disagreements. I've tried to talk to him, you know."

"Maybe you should try to do more of that. Maybe even—"

"Unseat him?" he whispered. "Just the words are treason."

"Not if you're successful." Amara shrugged.

"He's grieving." Mr. Pierce stiffened.

"I happen to know all about grieving. I still can't imagine turning to violence."

"Not you. You're far too much an angel."

Amara went still at the words. To anyone else, it might have sounded sarcastic, but something in his tone told her that it was really a compliment.

"You haven't touched your wine," Mr. Pierce said, changing the subject.

She dared not. The stuff always went straight to her head. It made her wild despite her lifelong efforts to be quiet and demure like society wanted. She needed to remember that Mr. Pierce was just a friend. Though lately, she didn't need wine to forget that.

"You seem distracted." He sipped his glass. "Do you wish to be alone? I could stand right outside your door."

"That is kind of you, but no," she said quickly. Lord help her, that was the opposite of what she wanted. She felt safe with him. She felt alive.

"I have all my life to be alone," she said, more to herself than him. She couldn't believe she had said it at all. Where had her thoughts taken her? She sounded desperate, like she wanted love, after all.

"Surely, you don't believe that to be your fate."

Amara stared down at her wineglass.

"I don't think you're destined to be alone at all," he went on.

"Tell that to London society. My third season has already come and gone. I've already abandoned the hopeless pursuit. Gladly, I'll have you know." And yet, she still felt guilty. She didn't want her father's name and legacy to die with her. It was her duty to produce an heir.

"Forget London society. I have other reasons to believe so. Mainly because I'd never allow you to die a spinster. My hand is as good as any, no?"

Amara laughed. He was being facetious. It was the wine in him talking. He couldn't have been serious.

"My mother requires my husband to be the son of nobility, you know."

"Oh, she'll come 'round. I have other things to recommend me. Namely, influence…connections…"

"I shall consider that." Maybe she would have, if it weren't for the Order.

"You need someone," he pressed. "Everyone does. What other meaning is there to life?" he asked with dramatic emphasis.

He was really into his cups now. As much as she wanted to, she couldn't take anything he said seriously.

"What will it take, Countess? My life? I only have one to offer you, I'm afraid."

"Maybe if you didn't drink so much." She snatched his nearly empty glass away.

"That's what our agreement entails, you know. Any half-decent guard should be more than willing to give his life. I know I am."

She didn't doubt it. He would go to any lengths to protect her. And that was no small thing, she reminded herself. Would it be so bad to have a man like that in her life? For however long? To at least have a night when someone kept her warm?

She shook her head. It was impossible, just like the emeralds. But he had a way of making the impossible possible.

With a fortune of her own, she could indeed be alone, she told herself. She was strong enough. She just didn't want to be. And Mr. Pierce was so much more than just some consolation prize. That was evident enough. The way he looked just then, aglow in the candlelight. It brought out the rich auburn color of his hair. No longer combed back, it hung loosely around his face.

When he smiled, casual and reassuring, the remaining barriers between them fell away. Here at this table, they could say anything they wanted, all decorum forgotten.

And yet, her mind went blank. Before she could find something, anything to say, the doorknob turned. Mr. Drake stumbled in then stopped in his tracks.

"My lady…" Mr. Drake straightened.

"Miss Granger is back to her room then, I presume?" Mr. Pierce stood.

"Yes, yes, yeah… She's there." He turned away, red in the face.

Served him right. He was gallivanting with her servant so unabashedly. Never mind that Mr. Pierce and herself had been forced to be alone together. They could have been doing anything. She'd had no idea this trip would allow her so many indiscretions. Someone less well-mannered and gentlemanly than Mr. Pierce would have taken full advantage. Maybe *she* would have, if she weren't so determined to keep playing the role of proper English lady.

The night had held so many possibilities she couldn't get out of her head. But it was all in the past now.

"Come," Mr. Pierce offered. "I'll take you back to your room."

Mr. Pierce stepped out first, checking the decks for anyone who might be inclined to start rumors. Once she got the all clear, she moved as fast as her coarse, cotton skirt would allow.

At the door, she could already hear Granger, rustling around inside. No doubt frantic that Amara was missing in the middle of the night. Just as she had been about her.

"Promise me you'll get sleep." She turned to him before opening the door.

"Once Miller returns. And don't worry, I shall have a word with my man about his behavior tonight."

"Don't be too harsh, I pray. After all the beauty and romance today, can you blame them?" Could she blame herself? She should have been glad Mr. Drake had interrupted them. Was Mr. Pierce?

Something flashed across his eyes. He nodded and looked down awkwardly at his feet before turning away. The words were caught on her tongue as Amara watched him walk all the way until the end of the deck.

CHAPTER THIRTEEN

Escape

AMARA FACED THE wall while Granger changed into her night habit.

"I know what you were doing," Amara said at once. "How could you leave me here by myself?"

"Lawrence, he… I'm sorry. I was only supposed to be gone for a few moments."

"*Lawrence*, is he now?" Amara arched a brow. There was no doubt they'd been intimate now.

Amara turned around. Granger had to be dressed by now. She needed to see the look on Granger's face so she could tell just how guilty she really was. Based on the deep crimson shade of her face, she was *very* guilty.

Where had they even gone for their private tryst? Mr. Drake didn't even have his own room. So it was anywhere but a bed. Amara's imagination went wild with ideas. The library? A storage room in the kitchens? A covered lifeboat? It couldn't have been very comfortable.

"This isn't just some fling, you know." Granger sat down on the settee.

Amara gave her the side eye. "What makes Mr. Drake any different than that footman or Lord Willowby's valet?" Still, even Amara had to admit she had never seen Granger so happy.

"This isn't a bit like Joshua or Benjamin." She shook her head fervently "I tell you!"

"But how can you be so sure?" Both of those men had broken her heart. The valet had gone so far as to make her believe he'd had true intentions. Granger had even been preparing to leave her post when suddenly, he'd disappeared. So it had been incumbent upon Amara to find out why. Granger, a mere servant, couldn't simply go over and ask the elderly neighbor where his valet had gone. He'd had no idea they were even together. So Amara had agreed to pay her old neighbor a visit.

She had to, the poor woman had been absolutely bereft. She simply wouldn't stop crying. At the time, it had made Amara glad she planned to marry to continue her estate and not for love. She didn't want to endure what Granger had. Not when love could so easily end in more than disappointment, but to Granger seemed closer to death. In just her first season, Amara had already lost hope. But Granger hadn't.

As it turned out, her old neighbor had died and the valet had been offered a position to which he couldn't say *no* on the other side of the country. But rather than bring Granger along, he had left her behind. Who knew why. It was one detail they'd never get.

"I just know." Granger lifted her chin stubbornly. "And it's not just the things he says."

Granger was nearly vibrating with excitement.

"Try to contain yourself." Amara sighed. She wanted to tell her that she shouldn't see him again, but that just felt bitter. Who was she to deny true love?

"It's the best feeling in the world. How I wish…" She grasped both of Amara's hands. "One day, you'll find someone. Soon, I bet."

"Don't concern yourself with me."

"After your third season, surely, you've given up trying to catch a member of nobility. You could still catch someone, though. You could marry like we peasants do, you know. For love."

"I have a few other things I'm trying to focus on at the moment, thank you."

"Your mother wants to see you happy," Granger pressed. "More than anything, she wants you to marry. She'll be a little disappointed if the man isn't nobility, but still… I just want you to know how it feels."

If Amara were being entirely honest, she wanted to know too. Not just about love, but about all the other things that had been on her mind when she was with Mr. Pierce. The things she wouldn't dare say out loud.

"There's this—this tension that builds up in your body and then it bursts, releasing all at once and—and—"

"You don't have to explain such things to me…" Amara covered her eyes. There were plenty of ladies in the ton who were bold enough to discuss such things during afternoon tea when their chaperones weren't looking. She already knew far more than she ought to.

Granger narrowed her eyes, like she didn't believe her. "If you really knew, you'd be out there trying to attain it. Mr. Pierce has eyes for you, you know. Is he really so detestable?"

Amara shrugged.

Granger knew of her reservations. "Because of what his father supposedly did to your father?"

"He really didn't do anything." Amara finally admitted.

"Even if he did, it wouldn't be his son's fault," Granger said. "Even if he is part of the Order."

"What do you know about the Order?"

Granger had likely known whispers of something for a time, but it was the first time she had ever spoken about it out loud, at least with her. Because of Mr. Drake, Amara realized. He'd probably spoken of the Order often enough that it was no longer a secret.

Granger just shrugged. "Would you just consider…perhaps he's a victim too? What if Mr. Pierce wants to escape the Order just as much as you wish your father had?"

"Who told you this? Mr. Drake?" Amara didn't know why, but her heart was thudding in her chest, tears were welling in her eyes. She sat down next to Granger to catch her breath.

"He cares about him. He says Mr. Pierce *must* leave the Order behind. Especially if things don't change. If his father doesn't change."

"Then what?"

"We could all go off somewhere. Once your mother is well. She could come with us. Anywhere that isn't London."

She made it sound so easy. But this was just some fantasy Mr. Drake had filled her head with.

"You have to talk to Mr. Pierce," Granger continued. "You have to convince him to leave the Order. Lawrence thinks you're the only one he might listen to."

Amara could have laughed. So that was where she was supposed to come in. "Of all people. Me?"

"Lawrence says Mr. Pierce is stubborn and obsessed with duty. His so-called birthright. But what good is that if one's dead?"

"I'm sure it's not so dire."

"But it is. You don't know the inner workings of the Order or the politics like Lawrence does. Lawrence is convinced that Mr. Pierce will soon have no choice but to turn against his father. That would mean an all-out coup."

"Mr. Pierce has never mentioned any of this. Nor his intentions to—"

"Of course he hasn't. Still. A wife is the one thing that could finally pull Mr. Pierce away. He wouldn't want you to be in any sort of danger, either. Lawrence told me he's a good man."

"So now you're talking about marriage?" Amara threw out her hands. "You spoke of this with Mr. Drake?"

Amara prayed he wouldn't repeat a word of it to Mr. Pierce. He was supposed to be her guard and nothing more. At least that was what she had demanded.

"Would Mr. Pierce be so terrible?" Granger asked. "Mind you

this is Mr. Pierce outside of the Order, far removed from it."

An hour ago, escape hadn't been Amara's advice to Mr. Pierce at all. Quite the opposite, in fact. She'd recommended he confront his father.

"He might not be happy with his father, but he still loves him." Amara could tell as much. "He wouldn't just abandon him."

Granger put her hands on her hips. "And how are you so sure of that?"

"He would have left already if he'd wanted to. His father's been like this for years." Plus, Mr. Pierce was hardly the one to take the easy way out.

"That doesn't mean you couldn't change his mind. Lawrence seems to think you can."

"As flattering as that may be, I—I can't."

"Lawrence's worried about us too," Granger said. "He says they still don't know whom those ruffians answer to. The Order has too many enemies. The worst kind that only power attracts."

"I can't believe—" Amara got up and started pacing. "He really told you all this?"

"He told me I ought to stay away from him. His life is full of too much danger. But I can't, you see…"

Amara resisted the urge to roll her eyes. There was no reasoning with Granger. She was just a young woman in love. Mr. Drake, at best, was a fool in love too.

"It is best to leave. Honest, it is. Lawrence doesn't like the direction the Order is going under Mr. Pierce's father. Not one bit. But what can he do? Just saying so could be dangerous."

Amara chewed her lips, feeling sorry for the guard. She owed him her life. The least she could give him was her pity.

"He must feel so trapped."

"Every servant knows the feeling."

"Even you?" Amara had never thought she might be so miserable, but maybe it made sense. Granger's life wasn't really her own. Everything in her life revolved around her job and Amara's plans.

"Not since I stepped aboard this ship." Her eyes brightened.

It was true. Slowly and subtly, Granger had changed since she'd boarded. She had become so bold. Someone who was willing to take risks and fight for what they wanted. And Mr. Drake was what she wanted.

But if they were going to marry and have a family, Mr. Drake needed to leave the Order. And Mr. Drake wouldn't leave Mr. Pierce to his father. So Mr. Pierce had to leave the Order too. Generations of his family's work. It would be madness to him.

But it wasn't just his sense of duty that would stop him—it was his love for his father. That night when they'd been alone, Amara could tell. Just one off word about his father and Mr. Pierce had gotten defensive.

How could Mr. Drake possibly think Amara could sway his boss to walk away from the Order?

Were Mr. Pierce's feelings for her truly that deep? Enough to convince him to betray his own father? She was consumed by the possibility.

As Granger went on about her paramour, Amara remained lost in her disbelief. All she had the strength to do was nod.

"Will you do it?" Granger finally asked in the end.

"Convince Mr. Pierce to leave the Order?" Amara's eyes went wide. "I'll try."

It was the only answer that could get Granger to drop the matter.

CHAPTER FOURTEEN
The Offer

DARREN DIDN'T SEE the countess the next day. Not even for a moment. He was avoiding her, and for good reason.

He had grown irritated by some of the things she'd said the night before. How he should have done more about his father. How he should have confronted him. She had no idea what he was dealing with. Or the type of brawl he'd be risking. The kind that only one of them was likely to survive. Obviously, the younger and stronger of the two: himself. Now did he really want to end up killing his father in the vain hope of changing him?

He looked out across the sea, leaning down on the railing as the sun descended. He was supposed to be planning and strategizing, but he was far too distracted.

A voice was nagging him, telling him the countess was right. If he had any brains, he'd do something. He just didn't know what. Force the old man to take folk medicine? Speak to one of those mentalists?

There was so much Lady Webb didn't understand about his family. And so much he didn't understand about her. God damn it, if only she would let him. He'd never met anyone more stubborn. He was already willing to risk his life for her. He'd even admitted that. What more did the lady want?

Footsteps echoed behind him, loud against the silence of the sea. Most guests were dining at this hour. Everyone save for Lady

Webb. She approached with trepidation.

"We missed you at dinner," she said with hands clutched at her waist. "What are you doing out here?"

"Just keeping watch is all." Darren tried to shove away his anger—he'd wasted so much energy on the countess. Thinking of her at all hours of the day without earning so much as a second glance when she passed him at a ball. He didn't know why he'd expected her behavior on this ship to be any different. Their routines and the amount of time they spent together had changed, but she despised him, as always. Frankly, he was tired of it.

"That's all you seem to do these days," she said. "Maybe you deserve a break."

"I can't let my guard down. Ever. Least of all now."

"What do you mean?"

He hesitated to tell her. He didn't want to worry her. Especially if it turned out to be nothing. But Lady Webb kept her gaze on him. She wasn't taking silence for an answer.

He reached into his pocket and handed her his small, collapsible eye scope. "Two o'clock."

When the sun went down, he wouldn't need the contraption at all. He could already see the twinkle of the ship's lights.

"It's so tiny on the horizon," Lady Webb said. "But it's coming closer, isn't it?"

"Straight for us."

The countess swallowed.

"I can barely make out the colors of their flags, but I don't have a good feeling. We'll have to wait until they get closer."

What then? He was still considering their options. They could abandon ship. Try their luck in lifeboats. He could alert the captain. But if the ship was what he feared it was, the warning would do little good.

"What do you think it is?" she asked. "Pirates?"

"Perhaps I should find you a knife."

"You're scaring me." Despite that fact, her voice was hard

and angry.

"Don't worry. We have time until they reach us. It's better to be prepared. Just in case. But it's probably nothing."

She breathed out. "I don't know how many more of these close calls I can take."

"Come now, you're more strong-willed than most. Like your father."

"You think so?" She smiled shakily.

"You have the same itch for travel too," he said, trying to distract her from her fear. "Once your mother is healed, there will always be other expeditions. I've been considering them myself."

"But not because you love to travel. As a means to avoid your father."

He huffed. More of this talk again.

"Perhaps it's the Order you should be avoiding," she went on, undeterred. "Perhaps you should be cutting ties completely. Mr. Drake said—"

Darren pushed away from the railing. "What has the fool revealed now?"

Lady Webb sucked in a breath but quickly composed herself. "He said the Order isn't safe for you any longer."

Darren knit his fingers behind his head in disbelief. This was all news to him. "What does he think, that my own father is going to come after me?"

"Maybe he just thinks it would be better if—"

"Forget what he thinks. He knows nothing of duty. All he cares for is a good time. With your servant, no less. It's despicable."

Lady Webb bit her lip. She was probably taken aback by the words, but Darren didn't care. Drake had no business talking about such things.

"But clearly, you're avoiding your father for a reason," she said. "If there weren't any truth to the matter, then you wouldn't be—"

"I've never said I'm avoiding my father."

My God, she was bold. He paced around. She didn't know when to stop.

"Is there any truth to Mr. Drake's concerns?" she pressed. "Tell me."

She wasn't going to stop until he answered honestly.

"My father…" he bit out. "He's unpredictable. Drake doesn't like it."

Miller didn't seem to like it, either, but he was smart enough to keep his mouth shut.

"If you can't address that, then perhaps the best way to handle your father is to just leave."

It was one way. Darren even found himself considering it from time to time. Damn all the generations that had come before him and all that would come after. He wanted to steer his own life for once.

A wish neither he nor Drake dared say aloud. It wasn't worth the risk of sedition. Deep down, Darren was too scared to leave, anyway. Too afraid of what it would be like to make it entirely on his own without the helping hand of his family's generational wealth and privilege. He wasn't used to living in potential poverty. But it was the price he might have to pay.

Not just him—Drake and Miller would be lost too. They weren't ready to return to the dirty, shit-filled streets of London. Darren had a duty to keep them as far from that kind of life as possible. He had told them once that working for the Order was secure employment. They'd never have to worry about starving again.

He couldn't be wrong.

"Leaving would mean the fall of the Order," Darren said with certainty. "If my father remains in place…alone…"

He didn't like thinking of it. He didn't think he could allow it. He couldn't watch generations of his family's hard work and sacrifice just crumble. Even from afar.

"All I must do is become a coward," he said sardonically. That was what it was. The cowardly way out. But one day, he feared, he might not have a choice.

"If it makes you feel any better, Mr. Drake would never leave. Not without you."

"What's standing in his way? He even has a sweetheart to drag with him," Darren said with a bitter tongue.

"You," Lady Webb said fiercely. "He pledges loyalty to you."

Darren stared back at her. He was a terrible person, after all. Just as bad as his father. The bastard who'd started this all.

"But if you leave…" Lady Webb stepped closer. "Mr. Drake for some reason believes I can convince you to do just that."

"Then Drake and Miss Granger can go off and have their happily ever after?"

"Only if we do."

"Excuse me?" He pulled back.

Was she taunting him now?

It was all he could do not to grab her and try to shake the truth out of her. No, he'd much rather lean in an inch, reach for her hand, maybe next her chin. Again, for the millionth time, he hesitated. Whatever existed between them was entirely a game of inches. Every night felt like his last chance.

He would have settled for a touch of her arm. It was just the feel of her skin he wanted. Soft and supple, he imagined. God damn it, he was tired of imagining. He was primed to take it. She was truly testing the limits of his control. In truth, that wasn't how he wanted her. More than anything, he wanted to have her yield to him. To have her beg *him* for once. It would be a nice little change of pace. If she just gave him a chance to do something, anything, he was certain he could have her begging for more.

"Would you?" she asked softly, huskily. "If you could have me?" In case that wasn't enough, she added, "All of me?"

"You are taunting me."

At the same time, he hoped she might come nearer. Was she really offering herself to him? Frankly, he didn't care what she wanted in exchange. Even the whole of the Order itself. It was too late for reasoning, let alone negotiating. He was too weak with want. His body was leading now, not his mind. He couldn't pull himself away, not even if he bit his own tongue.

It was simply a knee-jerk reaction to months, if not years, of wanting. Always so close yet so far away. He was too scared that she hated him to ask. But she didn't hate him, not with that look in her eye. Either way, he needed to know for sure. Better to have her reject him than continue to bleed out like he was, a slow and agonizing death.

This time, he refused to wait. He was done with hopes and dreams. He had finally snapped and there was nothing to be done about it.

He grabbed her by the waist, tugging her in as sudden as a jolt of lightning. Almost involuntarily, his hand reached around the back of her neck. A grasp that offered little escape. Her breath caught, and his Christian name spilled from her lips, but she didn't move.

Inches from her neck, his lips moved up to her ear. "I would," he admitted. "Just one night."

She swallowed loudly, almost achingly. Did he imagine it or did her knees buckle ever so slightly? It was all the permission he needed. Burying his fingertips deeper into her hair, just under her braids, he kissed her. Something he'd wanted to do for what felt like centuries.

He deepened the kiss, not quickly, as he'd expected to. Rather, he savored slowly and firmly, only parting his lips when she did. He felt rather than heard her moan into his mouth. When she leaned into him, he lifted her slightly. Gads, she felt as light as an angel. But the way she pressed into him, every inch of him, was anything but angelic.

The devil in him wondered where they could go. Where had Drake taken her maid? There had to be plenty of clandestine places aboard this ship.

He moved his hands lower down her torso to her hips, pressing her to tell him she wanted the same thing.

He grasped her hand, ready to lead her away somewhere, even if he didn't know where yet. "We could—"

"We could what?" she asked breathlessly.

"I want you," he said simply. Was it not obvious enough? "Just like all the other men in the ton."

She stiffened. "Those men who want nothing more than a mistress."

"No, I—" He was such an idiot. He hadn't been thinking. He didn't think he was capable at the moment.

"I wouldn't settle for that." She pulled away. "Not for them, not even for you."

He tugged her back. "I would marry you. *I will*," he said with emphasis. "The moment everything has been squared away with my father, once—"

Before he could finish, she snatched her hand away. It spoke volumes. They might have been inches away a second ago, but now they might as well have been miles.

"And when would that be?" she demanded.

"I can't know that. Things are just so unstable. I can't have you exposed to it, not until things are safe. And they will be. I'm going to make sure of that now. You're right. I need to act. I promise you I will."

She shook her head. She hardly seemed relieved that he was going to take her advice.

"I don't believe that for a second," she spat, suddenly furious. "You don't think I've heard these promises before?"

How could he convince her that his were different?

"Amara—"

"Lady Webb. *Sir*. Even if I could forget what the Order did to my father...it doesn't matter."

"It *does* matter," he hissed. What more did she want from him? He would have given her anything.

For Christ's sake, he had just agreed to forsake the Order and everything his family stood for. He just wanted a little bit of time to find his father's replacement. For her and her alone. Didn't that mean anything?

Before she could run off, he grabbed her arm. "If I leave my father, my only family, and never return. That still wouldn't be enough, would it? Not even for one night."

"Never." She broke away. Before he could pull her back a second time, she disappeared down the deck.

CHAPTER FIFTEEN
The Fight

AMARA HADN'T EXPECTED Mr. Drake to be right. She hadn't expected Mr. Pierce—Darren—to say *yes*. Neither had she expected the passion that would suddenly consume them both.

She had been so close to giving in. She had almost let him have her. She had been that drunk on lust.

In that moment, he wasn't Mr. Pierce anymore. He was Darren—the name that she invoked in a breathless whisper. Darren was what he'd always been. Since childhood. Even when she tried to deny it.

All that talk of marriage, however, had shattered everything. It had brought back all that she had tried to forget. She was back in the ton, amongst those philandering men, one dinner party away from true bitterness.

Now she felt as though she were already there. Securing a proper marriage had been her only task in life and yet she had failed.

She preferred to think she was too quiet, not entertaining or gregarious enough to enter into the right circles. She didn't want to face that it had anything to do with her "less than favorable" background. Or that her lips were too big, her nose not aquiline enough, her skin too dark.

Heavens, she was supposed to have given up on love. A life of solitude might not be so bad. So long as her mother was around, that was. When she was gone…

Her body froze instantly with pain. The same storm of emotions when her father had died. The kind that demanded screaming for any kind of relief. She'd never let herself do it, of course. She merely swallowed it down. The lump in her throat was growing thicker and thicker. She couldn't handle grieving both parents. Amara didn't even let herself think of it.

She needed to focus on her own failures.

As a child, she'd imagined things differently. She'd thought she'd be married by this age. Maybe with children of her own already. She didn't have high demands for her partner like her mother or some ladies of the ton, who wanted any number of handsome features, a title, *and* money. She merely wanted a man who was loyal, gentle, and kind. Someone who could actually hold a conversation about something other than the weather.

So far, Darren had indeed proved himself to be all those things. She'd been alone with him on multiple occasions and not once had he even tried anything. Not so much as a kiss. Until now.

But he wasn't supposed to be transactional like all the other men of the ton, who always wanted something for merely playing nice. His deal would have been nothing more.

When he offered marriage, it hadn't seemed real. Would he have really gone through with it? She wanted to believe so. She wanted more than one night. What she couldn't endure was waiting. How could she ever be certain he'd make good on his promise?

How could he expect her to wait for such a thing as crucial as marriage? There was so much that could happen if they waited. She couldn't bear it if he cast her aside. After all they had been through, could he really do that?

Could he?

There was so much more to him, and she could no longer ignore it. He was not just a perfect gentleman and more handsome than she ever dared to admit, but honor-bound, fearless and determined.

If he was just one of those things, he wasn't like the other men of the ton at all.

He was different from his father too. Of course he was. She had never seen him hurt someone unnecessarily, nor had she ever heard a single nefarious rumor, just those about his eccentricities. So how could she blame him for her father's death?

Her anger had justified it. Anger that had seeded from unbearable grief.

It was unfair, really, when all this time, he had done everything in his power to protect her. He hadn't just gotten a broken nose, he had put his life on the line. His father's demands had had nothing to do with it.

More than anything, he had come on this trip to protect *her*. From the moment he'd heard his father wanted those emeralds. He didn't need to tell her. She already knew it in her heart. She had always known.

Now that her anger had cleared, she could actually feel it. For longer than she herself knew.

She squeezed her fists.

Why didn't she just give in to her feelings? The lust he had built up in her earlier was still simmering. Possibly for good. No matter how base, she didn't want the feeling to dissipate, never to be felt again. More than anything, she wanted it back, that moment back.

She hated herself for being so difficult. Since her father's death and her mother's sickness, that was all her life had been. She hadn't expected anything, least of all love, to come half so easy like it had with Darren.

She would accept a promise of marriage. He wasn't like the other men of the ton who wouldn't keep their word. She just needed a moment to realize that.

Was it too late to reverse all that she had said? Maybe if she went to his room, offered him an explanation, admitted that her father's death had been no one's fault but his own.

No more wasting time. She flung open the door and started to run.

Forget their so-called protocol. She didn't want to have to wake Granger and explain what she was doing. She just wanted to do it.

Outside, it was pouring. How had she not noticed? As if the world was tilted, the rain fell in diagonal streaks that jumped with every gust of wind. Not even the covered deck could keep her dry.

She slowed. Something was off. It was still early in the evening and the deck was oddly quiet. Usually, she could hear footsteps from below or distant chatter from the covered decks, but somehow, the boat felt empty.

This was probably a terrible idea. But she was already soaked and turning around back to her empty room felt unbearable. She couldn't leave things between her and Darren like they were. So against her better judgment, she proceeded down the deck.

The silence continued. It was late, but not that late. Where was everyone?

A distant scream jolted her. What in the world? It had come from the other side of the ship. She backtracked toward the noise. There was something else in the air. The rain was blocking it out. It was a gentle roar, the kind that could only come from a crowd.

What was going on?

She considered returning to her rooms, but her curiosity was too great. She ran toward the noise. The rain was falling harder now, obscuring her senses even more. It was getting harder not just to hear, but to see too.

Again, she considered turning back, but surely, a crowd would be safe. Who knew? Maybe something had happened on the ship. There was any number of things that could have gone wrong.

She had never been to this part of the ship. Most of the passengers had their rooms on the third floor and that was where she had taken her walks. Here, the deck was tighter, busy with lifeboats and equipment. A small, gathering crowd made her feel borderline claustrophobic.

She wanted to ask what was going on, but everyone, mostly crew members, had their eyes fixed toward the center. Even if she wasn't in Granger's servant's garb, she doubted anyone would notice her. Amara got on her tippy-toes, struggling to see over everyone. She caught a flash of movement, but nothing more.

"What's happened?" she steeled herself enough to ask the stranger next to her.

"Fight," a uniformed crew member said.

"Then why is no one stopping it?"

"Too dangerous. They have knives."

The crowd opened up just enough to see two figures circling each other.

Amara stiffened. Was it Darren? This was an all-too-familiar scene from the other day, only they weren't just play fighting. Not in this intense downpour. The flash of movements were too fast and panicked, whereas Darren's movements the night before had been measured and steady. There was always the chance it wasn't him. But there was also a chance it was him. That was what kept her there.

"There will be a victor soon," the crew member said. "They're getting tired."

Amara sucked in a breath. She knew what that meant. Someone was about to get stabbed. Maybe even killed. She couldn't go anywhere now. She had to see this through.

She hopped on her feet, just high enough to catch a glimpse at a dark-haired man with pale skin. He was dressed finely. He had to be an English gentleman, of that she was sure. Although she was well-acquainted with most of London's prominent society, she didn't recognize him. She hopped again. This time, she caught a flash of brown hair. The exact shade of she knew to be Darren's. There was no doubting that.

Her heart started pounding in her ears. She pushed through the crowd. Something was pulling her, fast and sudden like a full moon tide. She didn't know why. It wasn't like she could help him much in a fight. Foolishly, she thought that maybe if he saw her, maybe if they were to make eye contact even for a second, it might help him survive. Maybe all he needed was to hear her voice. She tried to shout his name, but in the rain that continued to pound, that would have been futile.

Everything felt futile. Darren could be stabbed by this man, this stranger, at any moment and there was nothing she could do to stop it, save for taking the hit herself.

"Darren!" she screamed wildly as she continued to push through the crowd. It was all that she could do. There were some annoyed grunts, but the people let her through until she was standing at the very front. Except for the raindrop that occasionally caught on her eyelashes, she could finally see the fight crystal clear.

It was so much worse than she feared. Darren was already injured, bleeding down his right arm and left cheek. So was his opponent. Whoever he was. She had never seen him before. But they were equally matched in terms of stature, build, and probably age. The winner would depend on skill alone. A fact that renewed her faith in Darren. He had trained. More than just his strength, he was smart too.

"Please," she found herself saying through chattering teeth. He had to get through this. Her clothes were soaked through and so was every inch of her skin.

Darren must have seen her, then. He paused. For a second, he was captivated. Maybe it was just an illusion, but the rain seemed to slow. Long enough to fully take him in. His hair clung to his forehead like straw. He had never looked so utterly exhausted. She wanted more than ever to pull him away. But it was too late. His opponent lunged for him, taking advantage of Darren's brief moment of reverie.

Amara screamed out. She couldn't be sure exactly what had happened, just that Darren had collapsed backward. The whole crowd seemed to panic with her then. They pushed against her, forcing her to the left then to the right. Moving in all directions, the crowd was thinning. The rain had picked up again.

Something was going on. Something more than Darren getting injured. Men were shouting. Someone pushed past her again, knocking her to her knees. The second she got up, she slipped down the deck. She didn't know what had happened. The entire boat seemed to shift on a wave. With the deck so slippery, she had no traction. She flailed her arms out, desperate to grab something. If she didn't do something fast, she'd be hurled right into the sea.

Her hand smacked the railing with an explosion of pain. Wincing, she grasped it, but finger by finger, she slipped again. Midair, her lower body flung out toward the sea. By mere chance, her arm caught the railing at her elbow.

But her feet weren't touching the deck. She was still hanging and not on the right side of the ship. She was dangling out toward the sea. A wave of mist smacked into her cold and sharp like needles.

She might have yelled for help, but she was momentarily distracted by the bright lights of another ship, bouncing on the waves. It was about one-fourth the size of their ship, attached crudely around the railing by a rusty chain.

Was this the ship Darren had seen coming toward them?

Up ahead, men were still huddled on the deck. Were they the pirates? They were hovering over something. Was that Darren? It had to have been. They were dragging him, bringing him over toward their ship.

As bad as she wanted to scream, she held her tongue. She'd find a way to pull herself over the railing and back onto the safety of the ship so she could run and alert Mr. Miller and Mr. Drake. But she had no idea where they were. Why weren't they here now? Where were they?

Again, she wanted to shout their names, but she couldn't draw attention and alert these potentially dangerous men to her already precarious location. Another wave was coming—the railing was already aching with the movement. She couldn't help herself. She screamed.

Every man on deck turned in her direction.

CHAPTER SIXTEEN
The New Dawn

AMARA WOKE TO white. Her world was supposed to have been dark, rainy, and foreboding. She shouldn't be squinting against bright white. When had it become morning?

When she tried to go over the night's events, a rush of emotion washed over her. She'd been terrified. She still was. She was running in the rain. All the while, the ship had continued to tilt. The sea was raging. Just as much as the ship leaped and pulled, so had her heart.

Then everything went black. Every possible worst-case scenario ran through her mind. She must have hit her head. Someone had taken her. Those pirates. If they had harmed Darren... Her stomach clenched. She couldn't bear it. Would they hurt her too? Who were they?

One face in particular stuck out in her mind: the man whom Darren had been fighting. He'd been dressed as a gentleman, but just because he'd looked the part didn't mean he actually was one.

The chair creaked next to her. As if she'd materialized him with her thoughts alone, she snapped up to see the man she'd just seen in her mind. He was so much closer than he had been the night before. So close, she could make out the gray gleam of his eyes.

Somehow, he appeared much friendlier and more handsome

than the night before. His hair was dry now, the color of a raven. She shifted backwards.

"You're safe." The man held up two hands.

But inching backwards, Amara didn't believe him. She looked about the room. The bed she was in was pushed up against the wall. The only way to get to the door was to run through him. His frame was so imposing, he could probably stop her in an instant.

"Here." He twisted to the nightstand to grab a glass. "Drink this."

She didn't move. She didn't trust it.

"Where is Mr. Pierce?" She immediately demanded. "Where is Granger?"

"'Granger'?"

"She's my lady's maid."

"Still on the ship, I suppose."

"And the other guards?" For all she knew, they were… She couldn't even think it.

"I can't speak to the others, but Pierce… He was injured in our little scuffle last night. We're treating him below deck."

So he was alive. Thank God. Amara sat up a little more. "I want to see him."

"Now's hardly the time. Here." He pushed the glass toward her again. "Drink this. Please."

Amara gathered up the sheets around her waist, realizing she was in naught but her underthings. She checked for her amulet. Thankfully, it was still there, hanging at her neck.

"I'm no thief, miss."

"Then where is my knife?" She raised an eyebrow.

He smirked. "You won't be needing that here."

That should have told her everything she needed to know.

"Now, please," he said. "You must drink."

"What is it?" She eyed the glass. "Poison?"

"Of course not. Although I understand the distrust. We haven't been introduced, have we? I'm Victor Julius. And you are Miss Webb…"

"*Lady*," she corrected.

"Oh, yes. I might have forgotten, given your plain clothing yesterday. Forgive me." He bowed his head slightly.

"Who are you?" She leaned forward, hesitantly. "How do you know my name?"

"No one of consequence to you. But to the Silver Order, I am of great consequence, indeed. We have a long and complicated history, I'm afraid."

"Considering that you tried to kill Mr. Pierce last night, I'd say so."

His lip quirked to a smile. He didn't deny it.

"Now that we have been introduced, are you sure you wouldn't like a drink?"

Quite parched, she snatched the glass from him and took a gulp. She swallowed deeply.

"I may be Pierce's enemy, my lady, but I'm not yours. Not in the least. That storm nearly threw you overboard. I saved you. Singlehandedly."

Amara considered this. Last night, the ship had rocked so ceaselessly, she should have ended up in the sea. If Darren had been incapacitated at the time, then someone had to have saved her.

"And I saved you from more than the sea," he added. "I saved you from him. From Pierce."

She stared at him unblinking. "Mr. Pierce is a member of my guard. I've known him for years. He's my…my friend."

"It's a little more complicated than that, isn't it? I, for one, know that he and his family are far from perfect. Just as I'm sure you do."

Again, Amara stared at him blankly, trying hard not to reveal herself. His father had his issues, yes, but who was he to question Pierce's whole family? Who was he to know any of this?

"Am I wrong?"

"I want to return to my room."

"Your room? You mean—" He shook his head, as if to say,

"Poor woman." "I'm sorry, but you cannot, my lady. You're on the SS *New Dawn* now."

She almost spit out her water.

"The w-what?" she sputtered. "I'm no longer on the *Evangeline*? I demand you let me off this ship at once, then."

"'At once'?" Mr. Julius questioned. "Where, exactly? There isn't land for miles."

That was when it hit her. Aside from Darren, who was being treated for wounds below deck, Granger, Mr. Drake, and Mr. Miller had all been left behind. Amara couldn't be sure if any of them were still alive. She took a deep breath. Somehow, she wasn't panicking. In fact, she was quite subdued. How? Her vision was fuzzy around the edges and so was every other sensation.

She took another sip of water. At least what she thought was water. The more she swallowed, the more she noticed the slightest hint of lemon and lavender.

Was it really just for taste? It was something only the most eager of hosts would provide and for grander occasions. And this was hardly that. Or was it meant to cover up something?

"You did drug me, you bastard." She was not often one to swear, but the moment called for it.

"Just a little bit. It's meant to calm you is all. We could all use a bit of that, don't you think?"

Mr. Julius—or simply "Julius" since he hardly deserved a proper form of address—took the glass from her hand and drank some himself. He let out a sigh of refreshment. "Delicious. It's my own special cocktail. Like liquor, but without the taste. I drink it every day."

Was he mad? Lord knew what other concoctions he imbibed.

"What have you done with Mr. Pierce?" Amara asked calmly, though she would have preferred to scream it. All Julius had admitted so far was that he was below deck. Even though he was injured, she was relieved. Almost. If this fiend was even speaking the truth.

"My dear, you need not worry. As I have said, he is your enemy."

"I told you he's a member of my guard," Amara said firmly, even though he was so much more.

"Seeing that he's failed at that, it's best you forget about him."

As if that were even possible.

"I'm going to protect you now, my lady. And I shall explain everything in due time. Don't fear."

Amara's head was spinning. She didn't know what to believe, only that Darren wasn't her enemy. Far from it. What could Julius possibly say to change her mind?

"I know you are headed to Manila. You have an important task, do you not? We'll be there in just a couple of weeks' time. You won't even have to change ships. Not again, anyway."

Her stomach sank, part of her relieved the ship was still taking them to the islands. She wondered what he knew about the emeralds, though. It was probably only a matter of time until he asked her for a map.

"I assure you, you'll get there faster this way. Your mother's life depends on it, does it not? Now, please, you must be hungry. I'll have some servant sent up—"

"I won't eat, not until I see Mr. Pierce. I insist."

"We can discuss it over dinner. It seems crude to discuss such things when you're in this state."

"I will not take a single bite," Amara said firmly. She was filled with so much worry, she didn't think she could eat anything.

Julius grit his teeth. "Fine. Eating or not, you should at least be properly dressed. In something better than that hideous servant's garb anyway."

Before Amara could argue, he stormed out, leaving her in a state of shock yet calm all the same thanks to his drink. The bastard.

Before she could even attempt to get out of bed, a succession of servants came in. Everyone but Granger. Even if Amara wished more than anything she were here, it was a good thing she'd been left behind. It was better than being taken prisoner. Perhaps her hunch was right. Those men *were* pirates. Amara didn't want Granger anywhere near them.

While they did her hair, the servants—all young women—didn't speak much, even when she asked questions about Julius. Amara decided not to press the issue. She didn't want them to get in trouble for her sake. But it did nothing to calm her fears. Maybe she should have accepted a second serving of Julius's drink. After an hour, it was already starting to wear off.

As they filled a copper tub and fussed with her hair, she was too alone with her thoughts. Who was this new Victor Julius person who had swept into her life as sudden as that storm? And what kind of history did he have with the Order?

If she had met him in any other circumstance, she would have recognized him as someone of consequence. He had the right manners and upper-crust accent. She might have even thought him kind. Aside from the whole drugged drink, that was.

But Darren couldn't be her enemy. Not unless Julius knew something she didn't.

How could she even think it? She couldn't, not without proof. Tears swelled over her lashes. She prayed Julius didn't have any. Her feelings for Darren were too strong. In fact, they were set in stone. It was too late to change her mind without completely crumbling.

One thing was certain: Darren and Julius were enemies. But she was being treated like the closest of friends.

In the next hour, Amara's hair was braided and she was dressed far more finely than she had been the day before. Multiple layers of light-blue, ruffled lace covered her bodice and skirts. Lined in rose satin ribbon, the design was intricate, handmade, no doubt, not that cheap machine lace she sometimes saw on dresses. There were even pearls and rhinestones sewn in for sparkle.

Yes, it was beautiful, but she never would have worn something so ostentatious. And she wasn't even going to some grand ball; she was simply dining on a ship, however nice it was. Then she realized. She wasn't dressing so fine for some occasion. She was dressing for *him*. It angered her. As if she were some prize. As if she could be expected to have a good night knowing Darren was somewhere injured and suffering.

There were no bars, not even the door was locked, but she might as well have been in prison. In the middle of the sea, there was no escaping this man. She was already starting to shake just at the thought of another meeting with no chaperone of her own. Who knew if there'd be any servants in attendance…

She could grab one of the lifejackets and jump if she truly got desperate. She could do that now. But at the same time, she wanted to know why. Why were Darren and Julius such great enemies?

CHAPTER SEVENTEEN
The Prisoner

A N UNNAMED SERVANT took her down the inner halls of the ship. As she passed the crisp, white, metal walls, she was growing more certain that this wasn't just any passenger ship. It was too small, too pristine. No, this had to be a private ship.

She tried to picture its layout in her mind. From what she could tell, she was somewhere above the hull of the ship, where the windows looked out over the sea. And yet, instead of walking to the outside decks so she might see the sunset, they remained within the confines of the white, bolted walls. Instead of moving through doors and more open space, they walked down another flight of stairs.

She was so confused. This couldn't have been where Julius wanted to dine with her. The floor had changed from fine carpets to bare metal. Without windows, there was no more natural light, just cold, hard steel.

"My lady?" Julius called out from one of the doorways.

The moment she'd passed the threshold, the servant scampered away. Just as she had feared. There would be no chaperone. She wanted to shout at the young woman to come back. What good would that do? Julius would just order her away.

"Hello…" Her voice shook. The slightest tremble she wasn't sure she could stop once it started. Being alone with him was most untoward, but it was just one of her many concerns.

She pressed a gloved finger to her nose. The lower bowels of the ship had already proved dank and musky, but here, the smell had worsened.

"Surely, you don't expect me to dine here." Could this be where Julius meant to dispatch her? Down here beneath the sea, where no one would hear her scream? But if he wanted to kill her, why save her from that storm?

"I refuse to—" Amara's voice cut off when she searched the rest of the room. She didn't know what clued her in first. Sight or smell.

Behind a long row of metal bars, Darren was on the floor covered in so much soot, she could barely make out his porcelain skin.

"Darren." She reached through the bars to rub his shoulder, cold as ice. If only she'd had a shawl. But since these last few days at sea had been growing warmer and warmer, she hadn't been provided one.

"Why have you done this? Release him at once."

"He's more dangerous than you know." Julius just stood there with his arms folded, unmoved by her plea. "Better to keep him caged like the animal he is."

"He at least needs a blanket," Amara demanded, suddenly furious. She wanted to tear the bars apart.

"This is cruel!" she shouted, her voice echoing in the small chamber. "To keep a man like this, innocent or guilty, makes you a monster too, you know."

"So you'll entertain the possibility that he is guilty after all."

"There's blood," Amara noticed with a wince. "He could be bleeding out."

"That's from earlier," Julius said casually. "We've already treated his wounds. Enough to ensure he survives."

Julius kicked the bars of his cell.

"Come on, wake up," Julius said. "You have a visitor."

Darren didn't move. He merely groaned. She rubbed his shoulder.

"I'm right here," she tried to reassure him. It was mad, but she wanted to believe she could heal him just by making her presence known, just by touching him.

She needed to tell him how grateful she was that he had tried to save her. Even if he had failed and taken a knife through his flesh nonetheless. He deserved to hear that she loved him. In that moment, she had not a single doubt in her heart or head.

Julius sighed. "I had hoped he'd be awake for this, but alas…"

"Why are you doing this?" Amara snapped at Julius, aghast.

He turned away from her, moving to a table complete with a white cloth, two space settings, and a candelabra. She hadn't even noticed it when she'd stepped in. He really did mean to dine with her down here. The truth was he wanted to scare her, but she vowed not to bow to his manipulations.

"You told me you wouldn't eat without seeing Pierce first."

Amara stared daggers at him. "Now you mean to rub it in my face, yes?"

"Please," Julius implored her with the graceful sweep of the hand. "Join me and we can discuss."

Amara got back up off her knees. By then, her lace dress had been stained with grime. She didn't care. She hoped she'd ruined it.

"You told me you'd explain," she said, still fuming.

What was he waiting for? He was taking his time, like this was just any other leisurely dinner. And Amara was losing her patience fast.

She heaved a breath. She needed to stay calm and keep her wits about her. It was time to negotiate and be clever, not crumble apart. That would only give Julius the upper hand. She had to have something he wanted. She was certain of that. Otherwise, he wouldn't have saved her.

She didn't care what it was. She just needed to find out. She would have done anything to free Darren from his chains, to at least give him the smallest scrap of blanket. How long could she just sit there watching him suffer? It was unbearable.

Completely unaffected, Julius spread butter over half a roll. "Please...indulge yourself. I've chosen an excellent red to pair with our mutton."

He reminded her of society. Keeping up manners even in the most undignified of situations. Dining rooms of Mayfair and the other fashionable parts of London were always filled with secrets everyone knew. The mistress who sat beside the wife. The best friend who stole the silverware. Julius was another one of those individuals who turned manners and hospitality into a most annoying art. To Amara, it was all just showing off and pretending you were more than the next person.

"You must have an appetite after your injuries, hmm?" He took a small bite of his roll.

She had a few bruises, but nothing compared to what Darren endured just a couple of yards away.

"Mr. Pierce is the one who needs medical attention, not I." She tried to speak calmly, though her voice quavered. "Has he been to the infirmary?"

"We've treated his wounds. I've told you already." He blinked hard, as if *she* were irritating one.

Amara couldn't believe the man's flippancy. He just kept on sipping his wine.

"He doesn't deserve this." Amara crossed her arms. No matter how delectable the food looked, she still couldn't eat, not with Darren suffering so up close.

"Then you must be ignorant." He sighed, shaking his head. "Better than being complicit, I suppose."

"And you know so much? How?"

"I was a member once." He lifted his chin.

"You're a member?"

"I said *once*. They excommunicated me."

"Is that why you've done this?" she asked through her teeth.

"You may not be aware, but Pierce's father and his father and so on have committed many crimes, not just in England, but across the world. Manila is next on their list."

"Mr. Pierce is helping me."

"Is he? The Silver Order is nothing more than a group of smugglers. They steal even the smallest things that interest them. It doesn't matter to whom it belongs. And sometimes it's no small thing."

"I take it they've stolen from you?"

"Not me, but my family. Years and years ago. Back when we still lived in Rome. It was a gem, something like the ones you're after."

Amara huffed. "I doubt they could be *anything* like the ones we're after."

"The world is full of the unusual." He reached out, his finger grazing her wrist. "If you are aware of the Silver Order, then you must be aware of that."

"Perhaps."

"T'was a sapphire. We had but one."

"All this for one little sapphire?" How big could it even have been?

"Not with what this one could do. Like your emeralds, this sapphire has very special properties. Ever since it was stolen, my family has been doing everything we can to get it back...for generations." He straightened, the next words full of pride. "Even infiltrating their membership at one point in time."

"And after all that work, you were found out." Amara frowned mockingly. "It was a good try. But perhaps you should move on." If he could be flippant, then so could she.

"I'm afraid I can't. More than just a gemstone was stolen from us. Life itself was taken. Years of it. You see, the stone gives life to whomever wears it. For however long they wish."

Amara's eyes narrowed at him. It couldn't have been true. But it must have been, only because the emeralds needed to be. For her mother's sake.

"The Pierces might as well be murderers," he said. "I'm sure they are in more ways than one."

"But if that happened years ago, none of that changes anything," Amara said. "Mr. Darren Pierce, the man you're imprisoning, is innocent."

"I've not finished!" Julius roared, his voice building with each word.

Amara fell silent.

Julius cleared his throat. "Darren Pierce is not innocent. And neither is Theodore Pierce. His father is a loose cannon and yet Darren allows him to carry on. More than that, he took his father's directive to follow you."

"To protect me."

"How can you believe that?" He leaned back, seemingly aghast. "Has he manipulated you so well?"

Amara couldn't help but consider it. Could it really be a lie? If so, Darren had played the infatuated gentleman so well. When all the while, he'd simply wanted to take the emeralds? The moment they got to the islands, it would be so easy.

"They are master manipulators, dear. They are trained from birth to be. A skill they hone for years."

Darren had told her that he had received training in fighting. But that was different from being taught how to masterfully lie.

"Nonetheless, the sapphire is not the true reason why I have him. It's more what he plans to do." Julius looked over at the prison cell then went back to cutting his meat. Amara took a healthy sip of her wine. She was going to need it.

"What are these plans?" she asked.

"The same that every Pierce has had. To continue their pillaging of ancient artifacts, all for the sake of their own study."

"My father was once one of their members." Amara rolled her eyes. "I'm more than aware of the Order's mission."

"You find it acceptable?"

"I never have. But for the sake of my father, I have come to tolerate it." Though it wasn't easy.

"There are some of us who refuse to, who would prefer to see the Order's downfall."

"They are more powerful than you may be aware, Mr. Julius."

"I'm more than aware, my lady. Like I said, my family has been following them for generations. But nonetheless. It shall happen. I've dedicated my life to it. Strategized for years. Waiting for the perfect time to strike."

"Are you going to kill him?" Amara struggled to force down her building panic. If he wanted to do that, what could she possibly do to stop him? She gripped her dinner knife. If she tried to stab him now, how quickly would he overcome her? Would he hesitate to return the favor?

"Not I." He waved away the idea with a pinched face. "I won't be the one who kills him. That would make me a murderer…but he will face justice. And he will die."

"If you conspire to his death, that still makes you a murderer," Amara said matter-of-factly. "Whether it's done by your own hand or not."

"I've not had to *conspire* to anything. I'm just going to put him in the right place at the right time."

"What are you going to do?"

"There are men who want him in the islands. We're getting closer to them every day. I'm simply going to deliver him."

"You think they're going to kill him for you?"

Julius nodded.

"You were the one who hired those ruffians, aren't you?" she asked.

Julius smirked in a way that told her everything she needed to know. What Mr. Drake had told Granger was right. The Order had many dangerous enemies and Julius was merely one of them.

"If you want the map, I—"

"I've never wanted the map, my lady. I only want to stop the Order. One day, you'll be glad for what I've done.

Amara didn't know what she believed. Only that it didn't seem fair. She still wanted to pull Darren out of that cell and into her arms.

When she didn't respond his eyes widened.

"This is justice, my lady."

"It doesn't feel like that at all. Not to me."

In a way, it was true, she supposed. Their families, hers from the Philippines, his from Britain, had been opponents for centuries. He came from her oppressors and she from the oppressed. Just another reason why they didn't make sense together. There were thousands, but somehow, she didn't want him any less.

Even if the Order had done horrible things, those were Darren's ancestors' crimes. Not his own. Though there were some parallels. Darren was still after the emeralds, but through what means?

Julius blinked hard. "It's not just what I want, it's what the islanders want, my lady. You wouldn't deprive them of that, would you? Those *ruffians*, as you call them, were only too easy to hire because they believe in my cause."

"Mr. Pierce is different than his father," Amara said, brightly, realizing then it was true. "I'm sure his plans are different too."

"I wouldn't be so sure about that. He nearly killed one of my men, you know. That was before our little scuffle."

"I'm sure he was only trying to defend himself," Amara said. She wouldn't be swayed by what could only be lies. Not with the feelings Darren had begun to stir up in her. They'd been so strong, she didn't think anything could weaken them.

"Please trust that he's in that cell for *our* protection. The whole fight you saw, it started when he pulled out a knife."

"How can I trust anything you say?"

"He *is* like his father. No different. Is that really so hard to believe? Who raised him? Who provided him training in all things devious?"

Amara kept shaking her head. She didn't want him to see the tears welling in her eyes. She didn't want him to know that maybe she believed him. She had thought it for some time now. Even if his father hadn't always been that way, even if Darren hadn't been around it, what if he was still destined to become so?

Sometimes, that kind of madness ran in families.

A servant came out and switched her untouched plate to some other dish. She didn't notice what.

"Someone will find out what you did." She went still. "You can't keep this a secret."

"Aren't you listening to me? Theodore Pierce is a tyrant. A violent tyrant. And Darren Pierce will be no different: sweeping through country after country and stripping them bare of anything ancient and magical. It has been this way for centuries and will continue if I don't stop them. Generation after generation."

If the same power, connections, and funds were put into his hands, Amara wondered if he'd handle it any better. He too was from the West. Did he really think he was so different? Amara saw right through him.

"Do you have any idea what he meant to do with you? He wasn't going to carry on with you on a pleasure cruise. He was going to force you to show them the way to the emeralds. Then he would have taken them. All of them."

She couldn't help but think of what one of their members had done after finding a special type of orchid: burned down an entire forest. Were they all like that? Not Darren. He had tried to stop it.

"Care for dessert?" Julius asked.

The plates before them were slices of chocolate sponge cake. As Julius cut into one, strawberry syrup oozed out like blood.

Amara was disgusted. "I'd rather die."

These words, summoned with as much venom as she could muster, seemed to send Julius over the edge.

"Then you should return to your rooms." He threw his napkin down on the table. "You have much to think about. I pray you come to your senses."

Amara bit down before more angry words could bubble up. He was talking to her like he would a child. But becoming combative would do her little good if she was truly trapped with him. She had to get out of here before she erupted any further.

Being so close to Darren yet unable to help him was too unbearable.

She happily gathered her skirts and sat up.

"One of my servants will show you the way."

"No need." She had memorized every piece of the ship from the moment she'd stepped out of her room. At some point, when she tried to escape into the sea, it would come in handy.

She stopped at the doorway and turned back to Julius, who was standing up and watching her every move. No doubt he'd confirm with one of the servants that she had indeed returned to her room.

"I won't change my mind about Mr. Pierce," she spit. "Not in a thousand years."

"Maybe not tonight, but eventually, you shall see reason."

Amara grit her teeth. Worse than a child, he was treating her like she were mad. Love, she heard, could do that to people.

CHAPTER EIGHTEEN
Ache

WHEN HIS CELL went black again, Darren let out a breath. He had forced himself to stay still as long as he could. Thank God their dinner had ended early and they were finally gone. He threw his weight to one side and flipped over onto his back. He groaned, but he would have preferred to yell out.

Every inch of his body ached. Julius hadn't lied. They had indeed stitched up the wound and slapped a bandage over him. As for the pain, they hadn't bothered about that. What he wouldn't do for some brandy.

He gripped the lump of cloth at his ribs, fully prepared to feel hot blood. But pressing all his weight down onto the wound seemed to have worked. At some point that day, he had finally stopped bleeding.

There was so much he wanted to say to Amara. He knew he shouldn't call her that, but she was more than a countess to him. She was everything. It was the only form of address that made sense.

First he wanted to say that he'd made a serious misstep. He never should have told her to wait for him. Whether it kept her safe or not. Of course, she'd see the delay as a false promise. Even if it hadn't been. Even if truer words had never been spoken. Words he wished he could remain loyal to.

Instead, he wished he could tell her to stay away. Not from

Julius, but from him. He had gotten her into enough trouble.

He didn't want Amara to see him like this, with pain radiating down to his bones. That would only be playing into Julius's manipulations. He wouldn't give the man the satisfaction.

Bringing her down here had been a threat, pure and simple. If she didn't agree to conspire with Julius, she'd end up in a cell too. A thought that sent his stomach roiling with the words and assurances he had been forced to keep in. If nothing else, at least he'd learned Julius's plans for him.

It was bitter and grim, but at least he knew. At least Amara would still get the crystals she needed. He still had hope for that. If she followed Julius's rules and helped him end the Order, she might very well live.

And Darren would get death. Once they arrived on the islands, he'd never leave.

Julius's plan tied everything together. He was why those men had known about the Order. They'd been his errand boys. They hadn't been difficult to convince. Grudges, hatred and bitterness—it had all been bubbling inside those men, not just for years, but for generations. Now it was coming to the surface. It was coming for Darren.

Julius had informed those men of everything. What the Order was planning, who they were. Things no one could know. Secrets people had died for.

There was only one way he could have gotten those secrets. Darren had recognized him right away. He'd been a member once. That had ended years ago, after his father had found him sneaking about in their storage rooms, looking for something.

When he'd admitted his true intentions—rather stupidly— he'd been excommunicated. Now he was after revenge. What better revenge than killing the next in line?

He should have never had the chance. His father must have made a misstep as all excommunicated members never lived to tell the tale. Julius was supposed to be dead. Somehow he'd escaped. If he could do that, maybe he could succeed in killing him. Maybe he could take down the Order too.

But just because he was already dead didn't mean Amara had to be. So long as she no longer associated with him. Better he start the disassociation sooner rather than later. Better for her to believe he was already dead. He prayed she still despised him. He never thought he'd hope for that, but he did. He truly did.

He'd been mad for thinking her feelings had turned for him. The night before had proven it. Rather than disappointed, he should have been glad. Otherwise, she'd never give him up.

The worst part was a man like Julius probably wanted Amara too. The way he'd tried to dine with her... Rich men always wanted what they couldn't have. That would be the cherry on top of his already ultimate revenge.

I won't play into it, Darren kept telling himself. He couldn't let his thoughts of Julius forcing Amara—or even worse, convincing her—to marry him tear him apart. But no matter what he told himself, the sharp pain in his heart never seemed to go away. It was the worst of all. The pain in his bones didn't hold a candle to it.

He couldn't be entirely sure Julius wouldn't just toss her away, ruined or worse. She deserved someone better, better than himself. She deserved a man who came from nobility. Someone who could keep her safe. Someone who could bear abstaining from her until marriage.

He was neither of those things. He was supposed to be her guard, her protector, but he had only brought her danger. If she had carried on without him, she might not have faced any of this.

For him, the danger was nothing new. His birthright had always been a curse. He'd inherited money and power, yes, but also the many, many sins of his forefathers. His father had been no exception. Maybe Julius was right. Maybe one day, Darren would be committing the same crimes.

Even Amara had confronted him about it. She had asked all the hardest questions of all. Why hadn't he done more about his father? If the man was so bad, why hadn't he altogether left? He'd had every opportunity and yet he hadn't.

The Order was vulnerable because of it. Their enemies were just waiting in the wings to take advantage. His father's neglect of the Order, all of it due to his grief, had been the fracture that had allowed a villain like Julius to seep in after years and years of waiting. Now that Julius had started this war, he wouldn't stop until he got what he wanted: the destruction of the Order.

But if there was anyone who could save the Order, it was Darren himself. Even if that meant sacrificing his father. How could his father argue? The success of the Order always came first to his father. At least that was what he had claimed.

Darren wouldn't give up just yet. He would find a way to escape the islands. But first, he'd have to give up Amara.

CHAPTER NINETEEN
Story of the Order

THE NEXT MORNING, Amara ate breakfast on deck, open to the sea. The gentle sea breeze slipped through her hair as if she hadn't been through hell and back the past two days. As much as it pained her, she couldn't allow herself to forget the image of Darren lying half-dead. No matter how far removed from it she was now. He was still down there, below deck, suffering.

Aside from a few bites of buttered toast, she couldn't eat much. Especially when everything around her looked so indulgent. How could she when Julius was unlikely to afford Darren even a crumb?

The *New Dawn* proved to have much finer accommodations than the *Evangeline*. That morning, another one of the servants took her from the infirmary to her new quarters abovedeck. Her room was almost double the size of her previous stateroom, covered in more gold trim and inlaid wood. An arrangement of at least five different varieties of orchids greeted her atop the dresser, nightstand, and tea table.

To own a boat like this, the wealth required would be immense. The same kind of wealth needed to take down the Order. Her thoughts continued to spiral.

What hope did she have against resources like this? He had too many servants and a guard at every turn. She had no chance of escaping unseen, even if she could find a way to make it to shore.

Amara tried not to think about it as she looked out into the waves. One day, she would see the islands. If Julius kept his promise, she'd get the emeralds and soon, all of this would be over.

But what would happen to Darren? She was determined to set him free. As helpless as it seemed, she just needed to think, to figure out a plan.

Julius joined her at the table then. She'd expected him sooner. What had he been so busy doing? Torturing Darren? Her heart twisted at the thought.

"How long have you been tracking us?" Amara stared out into the sea.

Julius flung out his napkin before placing it on his lap.

"Forgive me." He pulled the silver dome off from his plate. "But I'm ravenous."

He started with his ham, cutting it into small, bite-sized pieces. Amara could only stare in disdain.

"Well?" Amara pressed for an answer. "How long?"

"Longer than you think. Everything that's happened, it's been in the works for generations."

He'd already told her that. But Amara still didn't understand exactly what that meant.

"Some could even say it was fated," he said smoothly.

Amara sniffed.

"Even if it takes time," he continued, "criminals always get their due in the end."

"Mr. Pierce's forefathers may have been thieves, and they may even have had violent tendencies, but Mr. Darren Pierce does not. I assure you." Amara kept defending him, but she was starting to lose steam. What was the point when Julius seemed so set in his beliefs?

"How can you be so sure? Forget everything he's ever said to you. Put aside the sweet words you wish so badly to believe, and look at what he's doing. Before I intervened, he was on a ship to Manila, ready to do more pillaging."

"He's really only helping me."

"But he *does* plan to take at least some of the emeralds."

"I've—yes," she admitted. "The emeralds are for his father."

"Regardless. He is still the one retrieving them. No?"

Amara crossed her arms. She had to admit, it was possible. "What do you think he really means to do?"

"The same thing they've been doing for a thousand years. It's a pattern, you see."

"You think he's really going to take them all?

He nodded slowly. "Heavens, they'd likely turn the place into a mine."

Amara cringed at the image of workers teeming over the land, pulling up plants, cutting down the trees. Who knew, maybe they'd set the whole jungle on fire. It didn't matter to them that it was ancient and sacred.

Darren had even scoffed at taking some orchid specimens. At the very least, he didn't understand how closely the diwata protected the mountain.

Was Darren really all that different? Was Julius?

"And you, what will you have me believe that you would do?"

Julius raised his hands in the air. Feigning innocence? She wasn't certain.

"I wouldn't touch it," he said. "I am hardly in want of funds."

"Of all the places in the world. How did they find out about us?" Maybe it was morbid curiosity, but Amara wanted to know.

Julius placed down his fork. "That's an awful long story, and I'm getting rather restless. Care for a turn about the ship? I'll tell you all, everything that my family has learned through the years."

"Fine." Amara grumbled at his sweet tones.

She threw down her napkin and quickly walked ahead, hoping to keep at least some distance between them. Julius, however, was quick to keep pace with one hand in his coat pocket and the other up across his torso. As if she'd dare place her hand in the crook of his elbow. Rather, she kept her arms clutched to her sides.

"It all started centuries ago," he began. "When Britain tried to take the islands from Spain. They invaded Manila for months. Not very long, compared to the Spanish, just long enough to take home a few of its secrets. Albeit at the cost of many lives. I happen to think that was the reason they were there in the first place."

"But how did they discover them?" If her people could keep the secret from the Spanish, then why not the British?

"Because the invasion involved more than military men. It included the Silver Order. Adventurers. Namely: Pierce's own great-great-great grandfather. My family would argue that the Order funded the entire invasion. If it wasn't for the generous Pierce VI, it never would have happened in the first place."

Amara sucked in a breath. It was bad enough when she'd believed the Silver Order had funded an expedition that profited from her people's land, but entire invasions? Darren had never mentioned it. Of course he hadn't.

And what for? What could be worth the death and suffering that undoubtedly came with the invasions? The Silver Order studied everything strange and mystical, as far as Amara knew. But it wasn't worth all that.

"I don't know what initially turned the Order's attention to the islands. It must have been some enchanting tale or another. Enough to make them want to investigate. An open mind can make quite the difference, you know. Most will simply keep walking when something is not what they expect. Even when something's right in front of them."

He smiled, his eyes sparkling with interest. The very same she might see from an interested suitor at a London ball.

"Have you ever experienced something supernatural, something you couldn't quite explain?" he asked.

Amara shrugged. Little things seemed to happen all the time.

Like the way Lola's special tea had relaxed her almost instantly. The one time she'd found a dead bird, or rather what she'd *thought* had been a dead bird. But when she'd reached out to touch its black wings, the moment she'd made contact, it had fluttered away. Perhaps it had just been stunned from flying into something, but perhaps…

"You have. I know you have…but growing up in tight-laced London, you never thought to investigate it, did you? Let alone give it a second thought?"

She shook her head. She might have been raised in London, but her blood, her mind, part of it at least belonged to the islands. A way of life that she was completely ignorant of. It made her sad, almost, that she might never fully know it.

"I don't know all that the Order discovered during the invasion, but it was enough to make the Order eager to return." He was speaking of her father's expedition. Also, her own. She was leading them there herself. It seemed a betrayal, almost.

"The islanders haven't forgotten what happened during the invasion. It wasn't just the items that were undoubtedly stolen. It was the people who were massacred. And for what? It was no different than highway robbery, but because the Crown approved it, that made it acceptable? Not to me."

Julius was trying to tell her that she was a victim, same as he.

She didn't know why, but all the pain and suffering seemed to hit her at once. Everything she could imagine. It brought tears to her eyes and shivers all over her skin. It was too much pain for any one person to bear.

"And Darren Pierce means to do the same. It's a pattern, I tell you. One that repeats over and over and over throughout history."

Amara nodded. She didn't want to believe him and yet with every word and his stony face of conviction, she was starting to.

"You and Pierce are enemies, not just in this lifetime, but in many. Since the British invasion at least. When you're with him, can't you feel it?"

Amara eyed him. Julius might have been an enemy of the Order, but he still believed in their practices. He believed in the same mystical world that Darren did, and its threadbare hold on the physical world.

"Do you believe trauma can be passed down?" Julius paused to stare out over the sea with a faraway and distant gaze. He looked back at her expectantly. Really, he was trying too hard.

It was a strange concept, indeed. "What do you mean?"

"Like a mother to a child. Down across the generations. Whatever traumatic things happened to your ancestors, no matter how long ago, a part of you still clings to them."

"But how?"

"Through your blood, your flesh, or perhaps through some inherited, long-established connection to another realm, a sort of collective consciousness. I believe that the deeper and more intense the trauma, the deeper and more intense the effect. So you must feel it. You must."

Amara furrowed her brow, not sure if she believed. "What is it supposed to feel like? What sort of effect would it have on me?"

"Everyone reacts differently. But perhaps you become less trusting of certain people. More cautious, whether that's for good reason or not."

Amara knew where Julius was leading her. But his words couldn't all have been lies. Some of it, she had to admit, made sense.

"People like Mr. Pierce," she said.

"I can only imagine what his forefathers did to your fore-mothers. Who knows, maybe there were more of you." He waved a hand through the air. "People with your…your talents."

She eyed him. How did he know this? How did he know everything else? Perhaps these sorts of interests and curiosities were passed down in his family, too, like trauma was in hers.

"We shall never know for certain," he said. "But you do. Somewhere deep inside you, you already know."

"You think they wiped them out?" By *they*, she meant Ba-

baylans, but she couldn't be sure he'd know the word.

"Nearly. My guess is that during the invasion, at least one of your ancestors were wise enough to escape. Perhaps into the mountains the moment they saw the white sails on the horizon."

Amara tried to imagine what living in the mountains would have been like. How had they gotten food? Where had they slept? It all must have been so challenging. On top of having to leave everything behind, vulnerable to pillaging.

"I don't know what, exactly, the Order found," he continued, "but during those few months, they heard tale of the cave. They just didn't have the time to find it."

"But my father did. And now they mean to find it again," Amara said aloud. She'd known this all along, but perhaps she'd never really known what that might mean. She couldn't limit Darren to just a few of the emeralds like she'd hoped. She didn't know why she'd ever thought she could.

She had been too preoccupied with escaping danger. Beside Julius, she still was. Maybe she was being silly. During their walk, Julius continued to keep a healthy distance from her. He didn't force her to place her hand in the crook of his arm. Even his eyes were well-behaved. They didn't travel down her neck like the eyes of most men of the ton.

He wasn't interested in her or even the emeralds. For those reasons alone, she should have felt more than safe. But she didn't. At least not completely.

"For what it's worth," he said, "I'm sorry your family had to go through that. It's a mark on not just the Pierce family, but the entire British people. Well, I suppose a lot of things are."

"It's more than a mark. It's a stain the size of the ocean."

He laughed deep and heartily. His eyes seemed to have changed since yesterday. They were so friendly now. Had she really considered this man her kidnapper once? She couldn't believe she was already warming to him.

It was too easy. Suppose he put something in her food to make her more amenable like he had with that drink? But what could she do to avoid that, starve?

For all she knew, Darren already was. The thought of him in that cell again stole her breath. It was almost like she had forgotten entirely. Her mind wanted to. Thinking of him there was too difficult to endure. But even worse was warming to his enemy and doing nothing to help him.

"I'd like to bring some food down to Mr. Pierce," Amara said softly. She turned away when Julius stepped in closer. "If that would be possible…"

"He has had plenty of food and it's far too dangerous, I'm afraid."

That was a lie. Darren was the only gentleman with whom she'd ever felt truly safe.

"He could manipulate you," Julius said. "He already has."

"I doubt he could do much worse."

She looked up at him through her eyelashes. It was only too easy to play the demure English rose. She knew how to play the role all too well.

"Really, I must insist," she said in a diminutive tone. "I know if the roles were reversed, he wouldn't grant you even the smallest mercy. But that is what makes you two so different. Your morals."

"I suppose in that way, I am superior…*far* superior."

She nodded, deciding to play along. At least for now.

He threw out his arms in a sign of surrender. "Very well. I will have food of your choice brought down to him by one of the servants. What do you think? Will that suit?"

Amara sighed. Maybe this really was pointless.

Even if he had allowed her to see him, there was nowhere to run. Just miles and miles of ocean. If she had counted the days right, they should be in the Pacific. The largest of all the oceans, not to mention teeming with sharks.

She ought to just bide her time until they got to the islands. While Julius dealt with Darren, she could easily run off and find the cave. She wouldn't have to share its location with Darren and the rest of the Order. She should be embracing this. But she couldn't.

It was too late. In spite of what Julius had said, Amara had already fallen for him.

Even if his family had done all the horrible things they'd discussed earlier. Darren was different. He represented hope that maybe the future could be different. There wouldn't have to be so much pain. Not forever, anyway.

All this time, he had protected her. Julius, on the other hand, had *kidnapped* her. She couldn't forget that, no matter how nice her accommodations. Or the fact that he had taken her knife and drugged her.

"I know the circumstances that brought you here might not have been the best," he began, as if reading her mind. "But I feel the need to remind you that you are not my enemy, my lady. Only Pierce. Once we get to the islands, you'll be free to do as you please. I promise, the emeralds are no concern to me."

Amara nodded, but it didn't seem to satisfy.

"Think on it. If I hadn't stepped in, you would have had no choice but to lead Pierce straight to the emeralds your family so fervently protected for generations."

On that score, he was right. Perhaps that was the true reason Darren had protected her. It was very much in his interest to do so. She was the map. To him, perhaps that was all the value she held.

"You don't want the emeralds for yourself?" Amara asked. "Truly?"

"Gads, no." He shrunk back, clearly disgusted with the idea.

"But those ruffians. They were your men, weren't they? They demanded the map from me. They—"

"They wanted to take the map from the Order. They knew you were working with them. They were going to destroy it. Nothing more."

"How did you even know we were on that ship?" she questioned further. "The trip was so last minute."

"We have spies everywhere. Even within the Order."

"Does that mean…" Amara's heart clenched. "You had spies following me?" For how long?

"The Silver Order had spies following you too."

Amara shook her head, feeling the sudden urge to look over her shoulder.

"But if you don't want the emeralds, then why am I here? Why take me at all?"

"I'm just trying to do a good thing. You nearly fell off the edge of the ship, Countess. And you were injured. I couldn't just leave you there."

"Yes, you could," Amara said stubbornly.

"And do what?" He stepped closer into the small inch of space that separated them. "Toss you back on deck? Tie you to the railing and let the sea have its way with you?"

So he'd actually meant to rescue her. Not kidnap her? She still wasn't completely convinced. As logical as it was, the moment she thought of Darren, all of Julius's persuasive words seemed to dissolve. She went cold.

"It is the Order that is our enemy," he said. "They cannot continue to throw aside morality and ethics all in the name of research and discovery."

Amara agreed, but was more blood really the answer? She didn't dare to speak up, though, not when she could sense an impassioned rant coming. What hopes did she have of undoing a longstanding vendetta that had festered in Julius's family for generations? One she wanted nothing to do with.

"It's also what they do with their knowledge," he continued. "They don't share it willingly, you know. Only with those who can afford their price. That's the only reason why they're able to do so much."

Amara didn't nod or argue. She only wanted one thing: to see Darren.

CHAPTER TWENTY

Carnival

OVER THE NEXT few days, Amara couldn't stop thinking about inherited trauma. Trauma that was so awful, so horrific, and so deep that it lived on for generations. The more she thought about it, the more she believed what Julius said. Perhaps it was why she had been all too willing to give up on love, especially with Englishmen.

Even at the start of her first season, finding a suitable match had been a chore, not the exciting quest for love that most debutantes considered it to be. Marriage was something she'd wanted so badly to get over with. To her, it was just a business transaction, like so many mothers preferred to think of it.

But as the season had worn on, she hadn't even tried. She'd remained a wallflower, shrinking away from dances and conversation. She had never really thought about why. It was just a gut feeling she'd had every time she'd entered a ballroom stuffed with gentlemen. She'd had an inkling that it was because she was different. But now she wondered if it went deeper than that.

"My lady?" Julius called her attention away from the sea. "I've come to beg for the honor of your company."

For the last few nights, she had been feigning seasickness and taking dinner in her room. It was just easier than Julius staring her down because she couldn't eat. She much preferred to be leaning over the deck just outside her door.

Whenever she thought about Darren, the sea breeze was the only thing that could calm her. The farther out to sea they got, the stronger the winds became. They were still warm and balmy, but at the same time so sharp and cutting, they made her eyes water.

She felt sorry for Julius, almost. To come to her like this, the last few nights had evidently not been easy for him.

Didn't he have anyone else to entertain him? Then again, someone like him could hardly be satisfied with staff.

"We're near Alexandria and I'm told we'll arrive just in time for the carnival tonight."

"We're going to dock?"

"In just a few hours, I'm told. I thought it would be just the thing," he said with slight unease, as if bracing for rejection.

She wasn't sure how she felt about that. She wasn't sure how she felt about anything anymore. Here on this ship, it was like someone else was in control of her life. She was not just at Julius's mercy, but the sea's.

"There will be a number of festivities," he went on cheerfully, almost overly so. "Not to mention private and public balls. Some months ago, I was able to secure an invitation to the ball of a very kind British officer with whom my family is well-acquainted."

"In Alexandria?" She couldn't help but feel a slight lift at the words. She had studied the city—its ancient history, anyway. What intrigued her about it was that it was a true melting pot of cultures and all their biggest accomplishments. At one time, the city had held the best of what the human race had come to achieve, all in one place. To this day, no other city in the world had ever come close. Unless one considered all the discoveries collected by the Silver Order. There was no knowing how many countries and cultures they spanned.

How Darren would have loved to see it too. Just the thought made her heart sink.

"Have you ever been? Just off the banks of the Mahmoudieh

Canal. The crème de la crème of Alexandrian society will be in attendance."

Amara bit her lip, her heart lifting again. She couldn't help it. She had never been to a ball outside England, let alone to a place where there might be several cultures, not just a pool of white faces. For once, she wouldn't stand out. She would be one of them. As much as she wanted to say *no* to an all-too-confident man like Julius, she found herself nodding.

"But…" Amara looked down at her lace dress. As nice as it was, it still had the stain from when she'd knelt beside Darren. The memory made her lose her breath before she could say the words.

"Fear not. I have something just for the occasion."

He led her back to her room. Inside, her armoire was left open. "I see one of the servants has already delivered it."

Julius went to the armoire and pulled out a gown that shone like pure rubies. The red silk of the bodice was trimmed in black with plenty of ruffles.

"You'll absolutely shine."

"Yes," Amara said seriously as she studied it. All the dress needed was a petticoat or two. She rubbed the silky material between her fingers. The thick, high-quality silk she knew and loved. Against her skin, it would be like butter. She had to admit this, too, lifted her. Julius knew just how to appeal to someone of her background. She might have been different in some ways from the English roses of London society, but in many ways, she was just the same.

After the last few difficult weeks at sea, she longed for her gowns back in London. Even if she didn't much care for all the balls and dinner parties, she did love dressing up. She always felt better when she looked her best. To all those who thought she didn't belong, it almost felt like revenge.

She couldn't wait to get the gown on. Still, the details of the evening gave her pause. Not to mention how prepared Julius seemed to be for the occasion. How long had he been planning this? He seemed to have every minute figured out.

"I assume you'll find me a chaperone." She continued to study the gown. The black lace along the plunging neckline was even more delicate than her previous dress. The sleeves, made up almost entirely of black beading, hung off-shoulder.

"Don't even think of it. Alexandria isn't London, my dear countess. The customs are quite different."

"Well, then..." Amara hesitated. A chaperone was the only thing that would have offered her some protection. But here on this ship, she was starting to realize she had none. It was just another reminder that she was at his mercy, that whatever he wanted to do, wherever he wanted to take her, she needed to oblige.

She swallowed. "Speaking of customs, is there any of which I should be aware?"

"Fear not." He smiled. "You'll do splendidly, I'm sure."

"Have you been to the city before, then?"

"Indeed. It is among my favorite in the world. Society can be quite varied. You'll see."

Amara had no idea he was so well-traveled. Was that how he came to understand the Silver Order's dealings so thoroughly? She had to admit, a part of her wanted to get to know Julius a little more. Only to make out the person he was, of course. His ideals were so refreshing and progressive, but he certainly wasn't the hero. As much as he tried to make himself sound so. Even if he claimed to have rescued her. What about what he'd done to Darren?

"Many customs are the same, you'll see. You do know how to dance the quadrille, don't you?"

"I'll do fine," she drawled. With three Seasons under her belt, she'd had plenty of practice.

"Wonderful. I shall be proud to have you on my arm," he said. "I daresay you'll find the ball quite diverting. There will no doubt be plenty of interesting music. Compositions you've likely never heard before."

He waved his hands up excitedly. "But I don't want to give away all the surprises of the evening."

Amara wondered if there would be fireworks. "You'll send someone to help me dress?" she asked.

"Of course, of course." Julius backed out of the room. "I shall send for someone right away. There is no time to waste."

Good, she told herself. She didn't need any more time to hesitate. She could hardly believe that she was even entertaining the thought, let alone agreeing to go. Julius had no doubt put that special drink in the wine that had come with her dinner tonight and quite possibly with all her meals.

It was the only thing that explained why she so badly wanted to go.

Plus, she needed to be amendable.

For all she knew, he'd force her somehow or imprison her for declining. While she was there, she couldn't just run, though. As much as she wanted to. She had to stay. For Darren's sake. She could never leave him. At least if she was on Julius's good side, someday, they'd have a better chance of escaping.

"Wait," she called out just as Julius entered the hall.

He turned back, his eyes darkening, perhaps fearful she'd change her mind.

"Do you have more of that drink? The one…"

"Oh, yes." He dug into his jacket and pulled out a flask, his face brightening. "Now it's very concentrated, remember. Like whiskey."

She snatched it, taking a sip before what was given to her at dinner could fade.

It was the only way she would be able to endure him.

CHAPTER TWENTY-ONE
The Dance

IT WAS DEEP into the night by the time the ship had arrived on land. On the deck, Amara stretched over the railing toward the faint din of the carnival. At midnight, the whole city seemed to fill the streets. The party was already in full swing. Beside her, Julius had donned a mask and a cape. A moment ago, he'd handed her a velvet mask too. It was so light and smooth, she barely noticed it on her face.

Ahead, amidst the warm glow of lights and sounds of laughter, she didn't know what to expect. She had never actually attended any carnivals. She had only heard of them, particularly those held in Venice. She expected others to be in costume. Since this was a night people liked to throw caution to the wind, there was no knowing what depravities she might see. Would she see animals being butchered in the street for feasting? People running naked? The latter might have been a little much, but instead of feeling trepidation, she was eager to take part in the melee. Why not loosen her corset strings and do as she pleased? Behind a mask, who was going to know? Wasn't that the point?

Carnivals, she'd heard, were all about indulgence not just for meat—hence the root of the name—but also for drink, merriment, and sometimes even violence.

"Shall we?" Julius asked. His mask, unlike hers, covered his whole face, disguising not just his face, but his voice too.

"Yes." She took a sip from the flask and handed it off to Julius. The liquid had no harshness, but its effects, she was starting to realize, were stronger than whiskey.

They walked the streets briefly. The attendees, varied in all aspects—age, race, social status—had one thing in common: they were all deep in their cups.

"It's too bad we're only just arriving. During the day is when they host all the games and races. And of course the parade."

Amara was a tad crestfallen that she wouldn't get to experience any of that, but only temporarily. At least until they walked up to a great estate lined with carriages.

Right on the water, the white, stone manor seemed to glisten. Was it possible that it was made entirely of marble? It had to have been just a trick of the light. Every window was lit with candles. A hundred tiny flames cast a glow all the way onto the water.

"I have so many people to whom I must introduce you," Julius said. "I hope you don't find it too tiring. In London, it must have been exhausting for you."

"At times..." Amara said, slightly ashamed by the lie. He might as well have been asking how many offers of marriage she'd gotten, which, quite sadly, was none, or rather one, if she included Darren's. But she still wasn't sure she counted that or if he truly meant it. At parties, men had made her many false promises.

She searched her mind for another subject, anything to take her focus off her failed Seasons in London.

Luckily when they walked into the crush, there was plenty to distract them. Everyone wore masks like they did. The costumes were far more elaborate than her own. She saw a Marie Antoinette, a lion, a medieval knight, and even what had to have been a crow with a sparkling black beak.

Julius immediately grabbed her a glass of champagne. "You must try this dessert."

Though it was sticky with glazed nuts that dripped over Amara's gown, Julius insisted. In consolation, it tasted wonderful, not just sweet, but full of cinnamon and other spices she couldn't quite identify.

"Shouldn't we find the host?" Amara remarked.

"This late into the night? I doubt we'll find him."

Amara pressed into him as someone pushed past her. Perhaps he was right. This was a crush to challenge London's wildest of gatherings. But what of the other introductions? Amara was starting to wonder if he knew anyone here at all. Even if he did, they'd be impossible to find.

"Ah, the waltz." Julius hummed as they ventured into the dancing room.

With the room packed to the edges and ballgowns twirling, the scene was mesmerizing. For a moment, she just stared. She was back in London, at home. As much as she thought she hated these balls, the familiarity was welcome. She breathed out, relaxing for the first time in the busy crowd. A laugh bubbled up in her throat.

"They are far better dancers than us English," Julius said.

Amara agreed. They moved with such grace and ease. Like the difficult steps and spins were nothing to them at all.

"You know the waltz, too, don't you, my lady?"

She nodded. It was practically a prerequisite for any high society London gathering. If the occasion called for it, one had to be able to show off.

"Your dance card was always full, I bet. Lending you much practice."

Amara said nothing, but that only seemed to encourage him.

"I should remember there's more to the London Season than just dancing," he said. "There're all those endless callers. How exhausted your mother must have been."

It was the last bit about her mother that sparked something inside Amara. It was something she had been storing inside her for quite some time. Something dark that came out like fire.

"My mother was exhausted, indeed, but for many other rea-sons." She sighed. "If you must know, I had none. I was quite rejected by the circles of high society."

She just couldn't take the false words and expectations anymore. At least Darren seemed to understand this about her.

"Oh…I see," he fumbled not just his words, but he stumbled in his steps too. "Fools, the lot of them. I can't imagine why—"

"I think you know perfectly well why, Mr. Julius. Not everyone is as free of prejudice as you."

"Indeed. Of course. My sincerest apologies." He bowed his head. "I've distressed you, haven't I? When all I wanted was to ask for a simple dance."

Amara shrugged, but deep down, she was starting to hate how practiced his words had become. Their conversation wasn't easy like it was with Darren. It was always so forced. She took out the flask and drank deeply this time.

"You?" She coughed, raising it up toward his lips.

He took a sip with an eager smile. When he held out his hand, she had no choice but to take it.

Assuming an assertive lead, Julius began moving them more swiftly across the ballroom. Her layered skirts flitted around her, opening like rose petals. She caught sight of herself with Julius in the mirror. It was quite picturesque how well they moved together.

"You dance well," Amara commented with a giddy laugh she knew could only come from the drink in that flask.

"For good reason." Julius smiled. "The way to a man's heart may be through his stomach, the fastest way to a woman's is through dancing."

He really was trying to win her. But why? If he had no interest in the emeralds and he truly thought taking them was wrong, there could be no ulterior motive, could there?

Just because *she* had one didn't mean he did.

She could do it, she told herself. Something she had been considering for days. If she got close enough to him, she could manage it. All she needed to do was discover where he kept them. Were they in his coat jacket? His pants pocket? The key to

Darren's cell had to be somewhere on his person. It was too important to ever be left behind.

As much as she wanted to start feeling for them all along his body—as difficult as that may have been—if she was really going to find them, she needed to be careful and convincing…

"I've been foolish," she whispered to him. "I don't know how I could have been so foolish. Naïve too."

His arms went rigid for a moment, then he nodded in understanding. "That's behind you now."

"I just hope…I haven't messed things up too royally. Otherwise—"

"Don't fret, my lady. Not tonight. You have me now. Not to mention every one of my resources. So long as you'll allow it."

His *resources*. Amara had a feeling the word implied more than just money, but other things like ruffians who were willing to kill at the snap of his fingers. He was beginning to sound more like someone who was part of the criminal class than high society.

He was truly despicable.

She took another drink of her flask.

"More?" She offered to him again. If he was looser, that would help greatly.

"Why not?" He took another sip.

"You're going to need to drink more than that if you're going to keep up with me."

He nodded, smiling, and took another sip, this time more deeply.

Then he pressed up against her so now nothing, not even a sheet of paper, could pass between them. They were so close, she could feel the in and out of his breath. She held her breath wanting to shove him away. Instead, she went perfectly still.

She could feel something else too. But it wasn't what she feared. The *thing* that uneasy debutantes chattered about. Thank *god*.

Right at his hip was something much less lewd.

Keys. Maybe it was just her imagination, but as he swept her across the ballroom, she heard them clatter slightly. Among them could be the very one that could release Darren from his cell.

Suddenly, the memory of him in his cell, the way it pulled at her heart, snapped her awake. Hot anger began to bubble in the pit of her stomach, sobering her. The daze Julius's strange drink had had her under completely gone now.

She didn't care if Julius was right about all the Pierces had done. She might even be suffering deep trust issues from the leftover trauma, but that didn't matter. That didn't make it right for Julius to do whatever he wanted to Darren. That didn't mean Darren should be executed for crimes that weren't his. Even if it was by the people his family had wronged. No matter how hard Julius had tried to convince her, that wouldn't be justice. And she wouldn't stand for it. With the carnival and this grand ball, he had only meant to distract her. But he hadn't. Not in the least.

Instead, her thoughts had honed in on finding a way to lift the keys from his pocket. She was already winning his trust. As hard as it was, she had pretended all evening. She just had to take it a little further.

"What's on your mind?" Julius widened his smile. He was clearly relishing in the fact that she hadn't yet resisted.

It wouldn't be easy to take the keys now. His focus was too much on her.

"I think I'd like to see the stars tonight," she found herself saying. "Tonight the sky is especially clear."

"I hadn't noticed."

Amara had hoped he might glance upwards and give her a moment to reach out and at least confirm the location of the keys. Instead, Julius's gaze bore into hers. She swallowed. Perhaps if she gave him enough of the drink, he might pass out early. He had to.

To avoid suspicion, that meant she needed to at least drink some herself.

"There's an excellent spot back on the ship," he said. "It would be far more quiet, wouldn't it?"

"And secluded," Amara remarked. She made a point of taking out the drink. This time, she offered it to him first.

So thrilled at the idea of being alone, he grasped it at once.

Julius was only too eager to lead her out of the ballroom and into the open sky. He knew exactly what her earlier request meant. It was only something she had been asked by the so-called gentlemen of the ton a thousand times before. *"Let us sneak away so we can gaze upon the stars. I want to show you the little dipper..."*

What it really meant was that they wanted to get under her skirts. She knew the look of a man who wanted her like that. Julius had that expression on his face and then some. He couldn't seem to believe his luck. At any moment, he was ready to pounce.

CHAPTER TWENTY-TWO
Open Sea

A MARA GRIPPED THE silk sheets, struggling to free herself from the weight of Julius's body. She had had to drink almost to the point of vomiting to finally get him to pass out.

She'd begun to panic when he'd led her down into his sleeping quarters. But the way he'd stumbled, she'd known he hadn't had long. At least she'd prayed that would be the case.

Her heart had been pounding fast when he asked her to have a seat on the bed.

"One more drink," she said. "I heard it helps increase the… You know…"

Raising his brows, he obliged, taking one final sip before finally passing out. The only problem was that he'd landed on top of her.

She used all her strength to roll him over. It was better that he was face up, anyway. Especially since the keys were in his front pockets.

She winced as she dug into her right pocket, freezing when he began to stir. When he went still again, she watched for the slow rise and fall of his chest, making sure he was really asleep.

Amara started breathing again. Thank God. She reached her hand in deeper. It was quite the compromising position, indeed.

Enough to ruin her, if anyone knew or saw. She didn't care. When she found the keys, she would hide them within the fold of her skirts. She'd save Darren. That was all that mattered. Even if she still hadn't considered where she and Darren would go.

It didn't help that she had only a rough idea of where they were. Last night, the ship had pulled from port to continue on through the Suez Canal. But how far could they have traveled in the night? If she was remembering her geography correctly, they were somewhere on the Red Sea.

There should have been land on either side of a narrow strip of sea now. But what didn't look like much on a map could be far larger in person. To them, it would be a vast, open sea. How long it would take them to reach land, she had no idea. All she knew was that they needed to travel west.

Somehow, they'd find a way. They could steal one of the lifeboats, she considered. If they didn't make it to land, another ship might very well discover them.

But she didn't need to worry about all that yet. In the light of a single candle, she had to retrieve those keys first. Her plan was to take the whole batch and work through each one. By the time Julius woke up, they'd be gone. If she was lucky, they'd have at least until late morning.

She smiled. Along her fingertips, she felt the cold metal of the keys.

Everything was falling into place.

She grasped them tightly to keep them from clanging and ran to the door. At the threshold, she paused for a moment, checking one more time to ensure Julius was still asleep. She hoped, truly she did, that this was the last time she'd set eyes upon him. It couldn't have come sooner.

On his next breath, she was gone.

AMARA RAN THROUGH the halls, pushing past two bewildered servants. She hadn't forgotten the way to Darren's cell. In fact, she remembered it quite well. Getting to Darren had long been on her mind, during every moment with Julius. It had been agonizing to hide her true feelings. Knowing Darren was so close yet so far away. Like him, she had been trapped too. Not with the bars of a cell, but with Julius.

Even before she'd asked to see Darren, she'd known Julius wouldn't allow her to go down to his cell again. He wanted to do terrible things to him. She could see it in his devilish eyes, could hear it in his voice every time he spoke of him. Things that he didn't want her to see. At night when she could barely sleep, it was all she could think about.

Julius wanted her to believe he was a better gentleman than Darren could ever be. With a cleaner past and future. Basically perfect in every way, particularly when it came to his morals. But it was a mask. A lie. Especially his words. His actions, on the other hand—hiring those ruffians, kidnapping her, taking her knife—they all revealed what was hiding within.

Darren was the only man she had ever known who was totally unafraid to be himself. His topics of study were not commonly accepted, but that did not change how often he spoke about them amongst polite society. While some had turned away from him, there were always those who did not.

She shivered. The man she found in the bowels of the ship would be far from the fine-dressed gentleman she had bumped into from time to time during the Season.

There was no knowing what kind of condition Darren would be in. The only thing she could be sure of was that he wasn't dead. That was a job for the islanders. She believed Julius on that score. That was why when people asked, Julius could call his death justice. Not what it really was: murder. And she didn't doubt there were Filipinos who would remember the Pierces' crimes, who might be more than happy to dispatch him. But that wouldn't happen.

For once, she'd be the one to rescue him. Between heaving breaths, she smiled at the thought of it. She couldn't wait to see his relief.

She stopped at an opening. The one she believed would lead to the final stairway. What if there was a guard? It was one factor she hadn't thought of until now. Still, there was no going back.

She pulled open the door slowly, setting off a loud whine.

If there was someone keeping watch, they were onto her now.

"Sir?" A voice echoed up the stairs.

She cursed. There were guards. At least one. Her mind searched for a proper lie. She wasn't about to wait for them to go on break. She didn't have that kind of time. Who knew when Julius might wake up.

So she proceeded down the steps, anyway, taking the shawl from over her shoulders and folding it. She was grateful the night had grown chilly, causing Julius to find her one ever-so-sweetly. She needed it now more than ever.

A guard blocked the bottom of the stairs as good as a gate. She lifted her chin and tried her best not to show any fear.

"I'm to deliver a blanket to the prisoner."

"A blanket? Of all things—" The squat and stocky man sneered.

"I demanded it," Amara said, keeping her voice haughty. "I won't sleep until I can be sure Mr. Pierce can."

The guard seemed to believe her. The only trouble now was how to get rid of him entirely. She turned to Darren's cell, surprised to see him sitting up. So surprised, she shifted back. He was like a caged animal, watching her with dark, bruised eyes. Full of suffering.

"Drop off the blanket and go," he barked suddenly.

Amara jumped. Words she thought had come from the guard. Then she registered it. The words had come from Darren.

"I'm sorry?" she asked stupidly.

"You heard me."

She was in a daze of disbelief. She didn't understand why he was being so dismissive. Shouldn't he at least have been grateful?

Even if he didn't know she had the key needed to break him out of here, wouldn't a *thank you, it's so nice to see you* have been a better response? After being apart all this time, didn't he want to at least speak with her? If just for a moment? He didn't realize she could offer so much more.

She stared into his eyes another moment. Maybe he preferred death.

It didn't matter. Even if he told her to go to hell, she was still going to save him. Because despite it all, despite his mean words, she still wanted to kiss and embrace him. All this time, that was what she had wanted. A feeling that had yet to fade since that night on the ship. In fact, with his absence, it had only gotten stronger. She knew it had been the same for him, not just these last few weeks, but perhaps for years.

Amara rushed up to the bars and leaned against the cold metal, getting as close as her body would allow.

"Be careful..." the guard's shout echoed in the small chamber. "He bites."

His voice was fierce enough that she shifted back. But she had also recognized something. The guard was slurring. Clearly, he'd been imbibing on the job.

"A moment alone," she shouted back. "There's a bottle of whiskey in it for you."

The guard was silent for a moment, but Amara could tell she was considering it.

"Do you really believe I'll be able to break through these bars?" she demanded.

"A whole bottle, you say? How?"

"I know where Mr. Julius keeps the finest. In his room, he has an entire cabinet."

"You swear it?" The man crossed his arms and widened his stance.

She nodded.

"Watch yourself, then. If he does something, I'll have to clean up the mess."

The guard pounded up the stairs. The moment the door swung shut, Amara got to work. As focused as she tried to be, her hands still fumbled with the keys.

"What are you doing?" Darren demanded gruffly. "You're going to get yourself killed."

She shushed him. "I need to concentrate."

She had a whole set of keys to get through. She worked in each one. The first one didn't work. Neither did the second, nor the third…

"You're risking too much in this," Darren went on. "For what? I'm not who you think I am, Countess. I'm no different than those men of the ton. The men you hate."

She stilled. It wasn't true. "Why are you saying this?"

"Because if you stay with Julius, you'll live."

Amara shook her head. There was no way she was doing that. She stabbed in another key. But it wouldn't turn.

What if none of them worked? Judging by the look on his face, Darren wondered the same thing. What if she had grabbed the wrong set of keys? She couldn't stop her thoughts from spiraling.

"Amara," Darren whispered. "Don't. I know you think you must owe me something, but you don't. Just go. Please."

Was he mad? The right key was here. There was no way Julius wouldn't keep the lock anywhere else but on his person, where it was safest.

"Just a moment," she promised. There was only a handful of keys left to go. What they could all be for, she had no idea. Maybe they were simply meant to distract.

"What about Julius? I'm in no condition to fight him off."

"He's asleep."

She was on the last key. It had to work. It had to. Darren watched her work it into the lock. But she knew the look in his eyes. It was fear, not that it wouldn't work, but that it would.

Then the lock clicked. She never should have doubted.

"Well?" She swung open the door, expecting Darren to embrace her at once. That wasn't the case. He just stood there—in fact, he shrunk back. Perhaps she had been mistaken. All her previous imaginings had been a lie. He didn't truly love her. His promise of marriage had indeed been a weak one. Maybe even a lie. He had simply been caught up in all the charm of that day in Malta and the lust of that night. But Darren as a mere friend was still better than a fiend like Julius.

"Come," she begged. While she did her best not to sound hurt, her voice strained. "We have to get out of here."

"You don't know the dangers of involving yourself with me, Countess. Julius will follow after me no matter where I go."

Amara shook her head. "Julius can't have broken you so soon."

"You should go without me," he said without feeling. "I'm in no condition. I can't."

"What?" It was a ridiculous suggestion. She couldn't just—

"It's the most practical and logical thing to do," he told her.

"For me or for you?"

"For you. You still need those emeralds."

"Yes, but…"

"To do that you'll need to survive, no?"

"Yes."

"If you want the best chance of survival, you'll abandon this plan. You'll return those keys to Julius."

"No," Amara said flatly.

"You owe me nothing."

Again with those words. Didn't he get it? Didn't he understand? She was doing this because she loved him.

"We can make it out of here," she persisted.

He lobbed his head from side to side.

He was delirious. He wasn't really himself. Even if she decided to force him, he was twice her size. She couldn't just drag him.

"Give yourself a chance," she nearly shouted at him. "This is the only one you're going to get."

Julius would show him no mercy; neither would anyone in

the Philippines.

Amara pushed herself away from the bars. "You don't know what it's like with him. You haven't been up there. You haven't had to endure—"

"Stop," Darren said, clearly not wanting her to expound further.

"I'll not suffer another day with him."

"What has he done to you?" He ground out.

"What does it matter? If I want the emeralds, I need to endure it day after day."

Darren's jaw worked. She was finally getting to him. His sense of duty and self-sacrifice was nothing to him now, not if Julius was proving less than a gentleman.

"I only need you to row the boat," she lied. "I can't do it myself."

Darren eyed her, likely not believing. She didn't believe it herself. Earlier, she had imagined herself telling him just how much she loved him, gripping his face, and kissing him. She hadn't expected him to be like this. So emotionless. Like he'd never loved her at all.

"Then I'll leave you. All right? As soon as we reach shore."

"Why?" The crack in her voice was likely revealing all her feelings for him. "Can't we figure something out?"

"If we go our separate ways, he'll follow me, not you. You see?" Darren looked down, considering. "I want a promise."

"Very well," she lied again. "I promise."

Darren seemed to come to his senses then. He stood up with more alacrity than she'd expected.

"You're not..." she said. "I thought you were badly wounded."

"It was an act. You don't know our enemy. Julius will never forgive you for this."

"I don't care."

"Well, you should."

Amara picked up her skirts to run. They faced the long corridor that went deeper into the bowels of the ship, where cargo was stored. Neither of them could be sure where it might lead. But she also didn't want to go back up the stairs, where the guard was.

"I can handle the guard," Darren said.

He took off. The moment he got to the top of the stairs, the sounds of scuffle kept Amara back. Hoping to stay as far from the fray as possible, she pressed her back against the wall of the stairway, squeezing her eyes shut. She hadn't expected people might have to die during their escape.

If he had to break his vow now, she wouldn't blame him. He had simply no choice.

Darren returned to the doorway, waving her forward with a newfound knife in his hand. It glistened in the weak light, completely clear of blood. On the deck, the guard was tied up with rope from one of the life preservers and gagged too.

Thank God. No matter how badly he had been treated, he'd still held to his promise.

They ran down the deck under the cover of nightfall. She didn't know what she'd been expecting once she set him free, but it hadn't been this. Part of her feared that he'd be so broken, she'd have to carry half his weight. Frankly, she wasn't sure if she could handle it. Especially with how hurt and helpless he'd seemed the first time she'd seen him in his cell. But it all must have been an act. Though he had some bruises and lines of dried blood across his arms, he carried on like he'd never been hurt at all. He ran so fast, she could barely keep up—straight for the lifeboats.

She need only stand back and watch as he whipped off the cover and checked the support ropes. Then, when he was finally ready for her to board, he stretched out a hand as any gentleman might. For a moment, she even forgot they were running away. When she grasped his hand, time itself seemed to pause. She was ready to go wherever he wanted to take her, so long as they would be going together.

She lifted her skirts and stepped in gingerly, bracing herself and gasping when the boat swayed. She felt silly for the small outburst. The ocean ahead, she was sure, would be far worse.

Amara looked out over the edge and immediately regretted it. The sloshing ink of the sea seemed so far away.

Darren hopped in and started pumping the lever, sinking the boat closer and closer to sea. She couldn't believe they were going to make it. They were finally going to get away from this horrible ship. Though they had no idea how far they were from shore. At the moment, it didn't matter. All that mattered was that they got as far away from the ship as possible.

A shout erupted. She jumped. The voice was close and gaining. Darren didn't react much; he simply started pumping the lever faster.

Up above them, Julius leaned over the edge of the deck, just a figure against the ship lights. He was moving back and forth on the deck then turned to one of the lifeboats.

Amara panicked. "He's coming after us."

She had to do something, anything. If only Julius hadn't taken her knife.

"Hold on!" Darren shouted, forcing Amara to open her eyes. He turned over his blade and began sawing the rope holding up the boat, his arms straining as he worked it back and forth with great speed.

Though she promised herself she wouldn't look over the edge again, she had to see how far they were from the water.

She cursed and tightened every muscle.

"Relax," Darren managed to say between sawing. "Your body will take the impact better if you relax."

His knife was almost through the rest of the rope. When there was just a sliver left, he stopped. Amara was confused. He needed to drop them into the water *now*. Julius, who was still pumping the lever, was getting closer.

Instead of sawing, he pinched the blade between his fingers. She realized now that he was aiming. Julius was too focused on lowering his boat to notice. Darren launched the knife into the air. If Amara had blinked, she might have missed it. The blade didn't seem to travel at all. It cut through the air so fast, the next thing Amara saw was the handle wobbling in Julius's left arm. It wasn't a kill shot, but it was certainly enough to slow him down.

Julius screamed out, his body crumpling to the side.

She had no doubt that was exactly where Darren meant to strike him. He hadn't missed his heart; he was simply trying to keep his promise. No kills. She was impressed. She was about to say as much when Darren once more yelled, "Hold on!"

Amara grabbed both sides of the boat, trying to stay relaxed while Darren yanked down on the rope hard. The rope whined for a moment before snapping. Amara shut her eyes as she felt her body lift, suspended in the air.

Before her next intake of breath, the boat hit the water with a deep *thud* and, at the same time, a sharp smack of water. An entire wave of it splashed over her, chilling her in an instant. For a moment, she couldn't breathe. She had forgotten where she was and what they were doing. The water was so cold, it nearly wiped her mind clean.

As Amara gathered herself, Darren was already rowing. He didn't look back. She had been right, she had needed him to row. Against these waves, she simply didn't have the strength.

She turned her attention back up to the glaring lights of the ship. Everything else was black. Julius, she wasn't surprised, had given up. He was pumping the lever back up to the dock to get help for what was most likely just a flesh wound. If he had been really determined, he would have yanked the knife out, tied a cloth around the wound, and kept going. That was what Darren would have done. That was what made him the better man.

But it wasn't as though he were indestructible. Across from her, he was shivering too with hair matted to his face. The exertion of the rowing should warm him quickly, she hoped. With every pump of his arms, they were moving farther and farther away from the pull of the ship. That alone was something they could truly celebrate.

"We'll have to wait until dawn before we can find land." He pulled the oars in and heaved a breath. "Julius was an unfortunate detour, but we'll make it to the islands, I promise you. I have friends as close as India who will help us book passage at once. Your mother is still going to get what she needs."

She pressed a hand on his thigh.

"Don't worry about that now," Amara said, though she still felt worry building in the pit of her stomach.

If they could just reach land. She wanted nothing more than to be on land. After all they'd endured at sea, she could understand now why some sailors would kiss the ground the moment they arrived. The sea really was a tempest. Unpredictable and without mercy.

As the boat swayed back and forth in the darkness, there was no knowing where the raging sea was taking them. Even if Darren was rowing, there was a current in the sea that no one, no matter how strong, could fight against.

Under this intense darkness, Julius would never be able to track them. By morning, they'd be too far away. It was over. Even Darren seemed to relax.

"Come here." Darren crossed the small distance between them and pulled her against him. "You're shivering."

She hadn't even noticed. All she felt now was the warmth of his taut skin.

"Lift your skirts onto the seat," he told her. "Otherwise, they'll take up all the water."

On the bottom of the boat, there was still at least a half foot of what felt like ice.

Amara did as he instructed, feeling warmer already.

"I still don't get why you did it," he whispered. "I don't know how you got those keys, but—"

"What was I supposed to do?"

"Julius was going to take you to the island."

"You think I could have trusted him?"

"He never would have followed you to the cave. At least that much is true. He doesn't want the emeralds. He simply wants the Order's destruction."

Amara was dumbfounded. After all she had done, he still didn't understand why? But of course he didn't. Last they'd seen each other on the *Evangeline*, she had rejected him. She just didn't know how to explain. She didn't know how to tell him she had changed her mind.

"I'm on your side, Darren. I always have been."

Amara couldn't see his expression, but she felt him go still.

"You are?"

"You're next in line to lead the Order for a reason. You have to fix it. I'm going to make sure you do."

"It would be different under me," he whispered. "Much different. Amara. Blast what Julius thinks."

She didn't correct the use of her Christian name this time.

She smiled, even if what she'd said hadn't been the complete truth. More than how he would change the Order, it was love that had driven her to him. Her ancestors and the trauma they had endured was no longer holding her back.

If only she'd had the courage to say it. She still feared he only wanted her the way all the other gentlemen of the ton did. Just for one night or two or several. His plans to leave her at shore only seemed to cement that.

When she'd rescued him, he hadn't kissed her like she had dreamed all those nights on the *New Dawn*. He'd shrunk back. If he loved her, wouldn't he have at least embraced her? Wouldn't he have gone with her without a moment's doubt? He wouldn't have promised to leave her behind.

CHAPTER TWENTY-THREE
The Whale

THE NEXT MORNING Darren woke with Amara in his arms, the sun shining hot on his skin. As gently as he could, he draped his moistened cravat over her face to protect her from the morning sun. She needed her sleep. Darren had no idea what would lie ahead once they reached land. If they ever got there, that was.

Darren closed his eyes, wishing he could fall back to sleep. The last thing he wanted was more time to think. Sitting alone in that cell, that was all he had done. Not just about how he'd ruined things, but about Julius and Amara together. It had unleashed a rage in him that had only gotten worse.

He should have been grateful for her rescue, but there were still things that bothered him. How had she gotten the keys that Julius had undoubtedly kept on his person? How had she known that he kept liquor in his room?

It shouldn't have mattered because it was his fault. He was the one who had failed to protect her. He was the reason she'd been on the *New Dawn* at all.

Now, she was the only reason he was free. He couldn't fail her. He needed to honor his commitment to their mission. After what happened, he had almost given up, but that wouldn't happen again. Not for the Order, but for Amara. Even if he couldn't have her.

It didn't matter where they ended up, so long as they could find an English embassy. Once they did, she'd get on another ship and back on her way to the islands fast. And Julius would come for him. Not her.

He had yet to spot land, however. Surrounded by nothing but glistening sea, he felt so small and so lost.

When he left her that was what he would be. But could he actually do it?

Part of him still held out hope. Perhaps she did want him. When he'd first kissed her, she had pulled back, yes, but for that brief moment, she'd also kissed him back. A memory his mind continued to savor and, at the same time, struggled to make sense of. She wasn't supposed to have returned the kiss. Not even for a second. Not if she hated him.

It wasn't just that. She'd called him by his Christian name too. It had sounded so strange yet wonderful on her lips, surprisingly new. That had to mean something.

Most importantly, she'd rescued him. Why? Maybe she'd just needed him to escape Julius. Maybe she was simply using him to row the boat, like she'd said. God, he hoped not. Nonetheless, he wouldn't let it be in vain. He would honor the rescue by taking her advice. Rather than running away like Drake wanted Darren to do, he needed to take his father's place. Dangers be damned.

Failing that, Julius would succeed in destroying the Order. He was sure to start his own faction. One that all their current members would be persuaded to join. It was the only way Julius would ever get the sapphire back. Not to mention all the power that had been lost with it.

He rubbed his eyes, irritated by drips of sweat. With every minute, the day was growing hotter. He didn't know how long he'd last in this sun. He wrapped his waistcoat over his head and dipped it back into the water three times now.

Under the summer sun, it wouldn't be long before Amara stirred. Her eyes just began to twitch when an impossibly large shadow crossed over them.

A spray of mist sprinkled over him. His insides clenched. He feared a storm. No matter how minor, they couldn't survive in this tiny boat. He began to fear the absolute worst. But when he looked up, he didn't see sky, gray or blue. He saw a wall of shiny and bumpy black.

Mist showered down over him again. He pulled back as far as he could inside the tiny rowboat. It was a whale. A massive one, at that. A humpback. Right across him was a blinking eye roughly the size of his hands.

Amara sprang up next to him.

"Is it raining?" She squinted.

Darren grasped her hand, watching the large eye before him blink. His mouth worked for the words, but he couldn't find any.

When another spray of mist rained over them, Amara laughed and even stretched out her arms. Darren followed suit, catching more of the droplets and mist over his skin. It was remarkably refreshing. Frankly, it was just what they needed.

"What do you think it's trying to say to us?" Amara asked.

The whale shifted downward, swaying the entire sea and their tiny boat with it. Amara clung to Darren, gasping.

"What's it doing?" she whispered.

"Don't worry." Darren tried to reassure her. "It won't eat us. At least I don't *think* it can."

"Of course not." Amara smiled. "It's just curious."

More mist sprayed over them. But this time, it wasn't just sea water. Mingled in were drops of blood.

Darren cursed. When Amara's mouth opened to scream, he clenched a hand over it. "Don't scream. You'll just frighten it."

The poor thing had been injured somehow. By what? As large as it was, it didn't have many predators. Except for a giant squid perhaps or a kraken, but those fights tended to happen under the sea. Was it sickly? And the sharks were taking advantage? No, he'd likely have seen them swarming by now. What was more likely was humans.

The whale sank deeper into the sea, suddenly exposing harpoons protruding from its left side. It was being hunted. The harpoons had been there all along. For hours, most likely. Farther back, Darren spotted a small boat. Not too far behind that was an even larger ship.

Darren didn't think—he immediately started waving. So did Amara. They didn't know who these men were, but they had to take the chance. They were the best chance at survival that they were going to get.

"Ho there!" someone shouted.

As if in response, the whale let out a massive moan that vibrated their boat's frame. The whale was expiring, but it likely still had a few hours yet. Its massive body swayed, the small movement likely all the poor creature could manage. Yet it was enough to bring their boat ever closer toward the whale's ribs. Close enough that Amara reached out a hand over its rough and bumpy skin.

He couldn't hear what she was saying, but it sounded like an apology.

The whale shifted again, its long fins flopping in the water right at the front of the boat. Darren got an idea.

"Grab that fin." Darren pointed at the one floating beside Amara. "Now."

With both arms, she clenched on to the base of it, right where it met the whale's body. The fin wiggled a little, but not much.

"Why?" she questioned, swaying with the movement.

"I'm sure the sailors will take us in, but just in case, tying ourselves to the whale will ensure we get to the ship."

"Because they're going to pull the whale in?"

"To the larger ship, yes. Either that or sail toward it."

He heard Amara say, "Thank you." But she wasn't thanking him. She was thanking the whale.

While she held on, Darren started unbuckling and removing his trousers.

Amara stared for a stunned moment, but getting hold of her senses, quickly turned away.

"I'm going to use them to help us hold on to the fin."

Otherwise, it was too slippery. As soon as the ship started pulling, they could easily lose their grip. He tied his trousers together with his waistcoat and shirt so it was long enough to wrap around the entire fin. If it held, they wouldn't lose their grip. It was the best solution he could think of. The alternative was climbing onto the whale itself. But if they slipped, they'd end up helpless in the sea.

"We could row," Amara said, evidently unsure of it all.

"They'll have every deckhand trying to bring in this whale," he said. "We'll be the least of their concerns. And if we're forced to wait, the sea might force us farther away. Farther than we can row. I'm afraid we'll have to tether ourselves to the thing."

Unfortunately, this meant he had to be half-naked. Amara, the lady that she was, continued to avert her gaze.

Despite his ungentlemanly state of dress, the fact that Amara didn't have to be naked herself hopefully made up for it.

Just as he'd predicted, the ropes attached to the harpoons went taut and they began slicing across the sea at surprising speed. Soon, Darren could hear the shouts of the men and their grunts as they tugged on the rope.

As they pulled closer, Darren could make out their flag as well. They were Americans. He sighed with great relief. That meant they could speak their language. He prayed they had plenty of food too.

Every tug was bringing them closer, but with every one also came a shriek from the whale. Sometimes they were low grumbles and other times they were so high-pitched, Darren winced.

Amara rubbed a hand over the whale's skin. They were going to let it bleed out, which would take hours.

Wasn't there a more humane way? Couldn't they take a pistol to its brain? Though where exactly that was on such a strange creature, Darren had no idea. It didn't have a distinct skull. It was buried too deep within all its blubber.

Amara shot a pitying look at Darren. They were going to have to watch the whale suffer all the way to the ship.

Poor creature. When he looked into its one eye, he saw intelligence, sentience. It wasn't right that this should happen just to light lamps. He didn't think he could light another one ever again.

Amara closed her eyes as the whale released another low, drawn-out roar. The whale's agony was clear. And yet they could do nothing. This was the price they would have to pay if they wanted to escape the sea.

The whale blew up more water. This time, it was completely saturated with blood. Amara's dress, thankfully, was already red. Otherwise, it would have been forever stained with it.

The sailors gave celebratory cheers as the whale crashed into the small boat. Lord knew how long these men had been tracking the whale, cornering it up into the Red Sea. Days? Weeks? No wonder they were in raptures.

One of the men, who appeared to be their leader, waved Darren and Amara over to the skiff. To board, they'd have to walk over the whale's body.

Rather than go one by one, Darren decided it would be best if they crossed together into the fray of unknown men. Amara held on tightly as they weaved between shuddering harpoons, many of them still attached to the corresponding cannon. Then they jumped onto the wooden skiff with a *thump*.

"I suppose we could always use another hand," the captain said, gruffly handing Darren a harpoon. "You have the strength?"

Darren nodded. He had no choice but to oblige. The least he could do was kill this poor creature as swiftly as possible.

He made sure Amara was comfortably seated before he walked with the other men atop the whale. Darren didn't like leaving her alone with the sailors, not even for a moment. Luckily, the men were too preoccupied with the kill to pay Amara much heed.

A whale this size was their payday. At least a half-dozen men, all in cheerful spirits, were on top of the whale now, using all their might to send iron down into its quivering skin.

Amara had little choice but to watch as Darren drove down his harpoon, blood thrown back onto his bare body in murderous streaks. Amara hadn't included whales in their initial agreement against violence, but it was a vow he considered broken nonetheless.

CHAPTER TWENTY-FOUR

The Marsala

THE SAILORS WERE a bit rough around the edges and far from the society that Amara was used to, but they at least spoke English.

Better yet, the food tasted fresh. It was only fitting on a ship named the *Marsala*—named after what they were told was the captain's favorite meal. Down in the mess hall, she shoved an entire chunk of salted beef into her mouth. She swore it was the best beef she had ever had in her life. Or maybe she was just that hungry.

Either way, she couldn't fully enjoy it. Guilt continued to pool in her stomach. She shouldn't be hungry after what she'd seen. The whalers had spilled all that blood and they still hadn't killed the whale. Even after they'd winched it to the ship and Amara had climbed on board the much larger factory ship. For two hours, the creature had continued to suffer, releasing low moans that had grown weaker and weaker until it had finally expired. By then, it had been a great mercy.

But that didn't mean the violence was over. Soon, sharks had moved in and the whalers had had to protect their prize. So they shot their harpoons at them too. Then another team of men had begun cutting its blubber. Amara had been grateful to be taken below ship, though she couldn't completely escape it. She could still hear the slicing and the *thump* of blubber landing on deck.

"They're headed straight to Bombay for a supply pickup." Darren returned to the table in a long, leather jacket that made him look like just another member of the crew. Seated with the whalers, who stared and ate with their mouths open, she was grateful he hadn't gone far. He'd pulled on his clothes right on deck and she knew why. Amongst these men, who hadn't seen a woman in God-knew-how-long, he wasn't going to let her out of his sight.

"It will be a few days," he said. "A week at most."

"There's an embassy in Bombay, isn't there?"

"Better yet, I have friends in Bombay. You should have no issue booking passage to Manila."

Amara nodded slowly, reminded that he really did mean to cut his journey short. If it weren't for the other sailors, she would have argued and begged for him to reconsider. She might have even confessed her feelings for him. But how could she muster the courage when his proposed departure meant he wouldn't return them?

"Good news," she said instead.

"Of course, on this ship, we won't have the accommodations you're used to—"

The man next to Darren sniffed. Darren ignored him. "But we have been afforded a room."

"*A* room?" Her eyes widened.

"We *are* man and wife."

"We are?" Her mouth went slack.

He raised his eyebrows, tilting his head to the other men.

"Right." Amara cleared her throat.

A bachelor traveling with a young lady would have been horribly lacking in propriety. Like these men would care.

More importantly, it might make them think twice about assaulting her if they believed she was under his protection. She was the only woman on the ship full of whale killers—she couldn't forget that.

"Are you sure, there isn't—"

"Is there another man on board with whom you'd prefer to share a room?"

"Fine," Amara muttered. They'd likely be sleeping amongst the cargo.

"*I'll* share with you." One of the men smiled.

Darren shot him a look before turning back to her.

"How's the food?" He stabbed a fork into one of the potatoes.

"Surprisingly delicious."

"Once we're finished, we shall retire."

"You think so? I thought I could watch the sunset and personally thank our host."

"I've already thanked him for the both of us."

"But—"

"Not a chance." He leaned into her and whispered harshly. "The last place you want to be is on deck when these men turn to their drink."

In the tightly packed mess hall, some men had already started.

"In this room..." Amara kept her voice low. "I imagine there's but one bed?"

"Naturally...though I did manage to convince the captain to allow you use of his privy."

"Thank God." Amara sank with relief.

She didn't even want to think about the privies the crew were using. They were likely buckets. She winced just at the thought. She would have given anything to be back on the *Evangeline*, but this ship was still preferable to the *New Dawn*.

"You must be careful aboard this ship," Darren said with his head down.

"I know," she whispered back. "It's still better than...than—"

"Being with Julius?" Darren placed his fork down and raised a brow at her. "What's worse, sharing a room with him or me?"

Amara guffawed. "It doesn't compare... It's... It's much different..." Just a little fast was all, if she was being honest.

She shook her head. She wanted him and no one else. Wasn't

that clear enough after what she'd done? She had risked so much to *rescue* him. It was his turn now to come to her like he'd done on the *Evangeline*. If he felt anything like she did, he would.

"You're right, I shouldn't do this." Darren turned back to his plate. "It's irrelevant."

Irrelevant? Was he angry at her? Why? She wanted to scream, just not in front of these men. But no matter how low they were whispering, the whalers were still trying to listen in on their conversation. Every single one of them. The newcomers were the crew's best form of entertainment probably in months.

After Amara had finished eating, Darren found the captain, who led them down deep into the ship. Amara was right. They would indeed be sleeping amongst the cargo. The room wasn't really a room at all. It was just the deepest part of the ship with a folding cot. Amara wasn't sure if it could be called a bed, let alone if they could both fit on it.

The captain handed them both two small oil lamps. Darren winced slightly. They were both thinking the same thing: this was why the whale had been killed. For something as insignificant as this.

Even if their quarters weren't much, they thanked the captain before he left.

Amara swallowed, bracing herself when the ship swayed with a wave. The bed slid toward her, but Darren caught it with one hand, just before it slammed into her.

Darren tried to reassure her. "I can fix this."

He placed their oil lamps into a pair of hanging baskets then pushed the bed between two large crates and slapped the sheets.

"Nothing should fall on us this way."

Amara walked toward the bed in a daze, fully considering jumping back into the ocean.

"It's only for a few days."

Amara gasped. Something scurried along the wall. What could only have been a rat.

"They shan't bother you." Darren shrugged. "The cot is raised up."

Amara nodded. She was stronger than this. She could do this. If she could traverse the mystical jungles of Manila in the coming days, then she could deal with a few rats.

Darren sat down on the cot. "Want to see if we fit?"

Amara bit her lip. He was always doing this, always acting so familiar, always pushing her too far, rather than just taking things slow, as she preferred.

At the same time, she wasn't so cruel as to force him to sleep on the floor with the rats. They would have to make do. Amara sat down on the bed. Even though the mattress was thin, she was surprised how nice it felt.

"It's much cooler down here," Darren commented awkwardly. "We should be able to get some half-decent sleep. Better than under the blazing sun, anyway."

Next to him, Amara wasn't sure she was going to get any sleep.

"You should take off your gown, Countess."

Amara crossed her arms.

"It's damp." He laughed.

Amara clenched her jaw and turned around. This was all turning out to be quite humiliating. She pulled her dress down over her hips, leaving her in just her stays and a thin petticoat.

"That's still damp," Darren said as she tried to return back to the bed.

Amara sighed, exasperated.

"Come now," Darren pressed. "We'll be freezing. The blanket is thin enough. Barely a sheet. I promise I won't look. Even if you've already seen much more of me."

"I didn't look," Amara retorted.

"Not even a second?"

But of course she might have looked for a second. Enough to know to look away. That didn't stop her from holding the image in her mind. She saw it again and tried not to blush.

"Fine, I'll remove them. The moment they're dry, they'll go right back on again."

Amara untied her skirt, leaving her just in her lace drawers. Darren immediately spread the blanket over her, keeping to his promise not to look.

He truly was the gentleman. She just hoped that throughout the night, he'd remain so. For a long moment, they didn't speak. In the silence, her mind couldn't help returning to the morbid scene earlier.

"The whale is right there, you know." Amara nodded her head to the starboard side of the ship.

"Yes, but it's at peace now."

"Do you think I helped it? I mean if I really do have healing powers like my lola says, maybe a touch from me only prolonged its suffering."

"Not in the least. I don't think your gift is like that at all." Darren's hands laced behind his neck. The movement caused her to fall into him ever so slightly, the heat of his ribs radiating into her. She should have moved, but she didn't. She found herself curving into him, their bodies aligning like puzzle pieces.

She deserved to be comfortable, she told herself. God, did he feel comfortable. Maybe something more than that if she could name it.

"How can you know that?" She craned her neck so she could watch his eyes as they bore into the ceiling, dreamily almost.

"I could see it. In one eye at least. I've felt it too."

"You did?"

"When you first saw me in that cell. When you touched me."

"What did it feel like?" She sat up on one elbow, suddenly intrigued.

"Like the warmth of a fire and the cool dew of water all at once."

"Truly?" she asked, their faces so close. Again, she should have backed away.

He nodded.

"Then I'm glad I touched the poor whale while I could. I never imagined it could have such intelligence." She could sense it, though she didn't quite know how.

"It's a mammal just as we are. We have a kinship with them…'"

"Some *kinship*," Amara drawled.

"If one harpoon blow would have done it in, I would have—"

"I know, Darren." Amara sank down from her elbow into the bed and somehow closer to him than before. "You tried your best to dispatch it quickly. So did those men."

"But it can't be done," Darren said. "That's the tragedy of it. Because of its thick blubber, whales can't be taken out quickly like a lame horse. Perhaps it shouldn't be done at all."

"You think so?"

"They're smarter than we may ever know. Maybe it came to us for a reason. Maybe it could sense your gift. Maybe it found something about you soothing."

"Be serious." Amara simpered. She rested her forehead atop his shoulder and she didn't even care. Neither did he seem to.

"It's just a theory, albeit from a reputable source. When it comes to the supernatural, I'm well-versed."

The sweet thought helped carry her to sleep. In the end, she didn't have much trouble lulling off at all. Despite her plan to keep one eye open, she was asleep in a matter of moments.

CHAPTER TWENTY-FIVE

Hero

FOR THE SECOND night in a row, Amara woke in Darren's arms. Rocking to and fro with the waves, she was back in the tiny rowboat, miles from land. The whale flashed before her, smeared in blood. Its eye blinked at her in a quiet yet desperate plea for help.

The boat swayed harder. At some point in the night, the waves had picked up speed. Perhaps they were nearing the Arabian Sea.

Someone was squeezing her. Darren. He was shaking her. But she wasn't in the rowboat at all. She was in bed. With Darren.

Amara sat up in horror, clutching her neck.

"I'm sorry." Darren shifted back. "I didn't want to wake you, but you were whimpering in your sleep."

"I was?" Amara dug a hand into her hair. "I had a nightmare."

"About the whale?" Darren asked.

She nodded.

"Me too. But it's gone now. Remember?"

Gone? In truth, it was no more than a few feet away chained to the ship. But she couldn't continue to dwell on that. Somehow, she needed to forget.

Darren rolled onto his back and stretched an arm over her side of the pillow. The distance between them could have been measured in inches.

"Do you mind?" she asked.

"What? Am I too close? Last night, you didn't seem to mind."

"I must have been cold. I was confused," she tried to explain. "I must have thought we were still in the lifeboat again."

"Or perhaps you just don't want to admit that you feel safe with me. Don't deny it. On a boat like this amongst those men, do you really want me in another room?"

Amara crossed her arms. "I'm not denying anything."

If she was really being honest, she still wanted him. She was just waiting for him to renew his own sentiments. When he did, she swore to herself that she would give in, no matter how temporary his embrace.

She regretted pulling back that one night. A mistake she didn't have the strength to repeat. All her life, she had been commanded to be chaste, as if it were easy. As if she didn't experience yearning. But indeed she did. She just didn't know how to show it. The only thing she knew how to do was surrender.

As much as she didn't like it, she was coming to terms. She was willing to take whatever she could get. For however long.

"The captain left those on the stairs this morning." Darren pointed to a folded yet still crumpled pile of clothing atop one of the smaller crates.

She picked it up with caution. As she guessed, it was men's clothing. A simple white tunic and the coarsest trousers she'd ever felt. Not that she'd felt many.

"It'll have to do, I'm afraid," Darren said.

She shrugged, pretending she didn't care. They were dry and they wouldn't weigh her down. She moved behind one of the taller crates. Worse than the clothing, something else bothered her. The comment Darren had made in the mess hall. Did he really think she felt the same disgust for him that she did for Julius? It had been on her mind all morning. Especially now as she got dressed.

Darren had no idea just how much more comfortable she was with him in the bowels of this ship and in men's clothing than she had been amongst the gold-gilded rooms of the *New Dawn* and in the finest of gowns.

As much as Julius had tried to provide her every comfort, she could never truly relax with him. Julius thought the past made them a perfect match. But it was the future that told her otherwise. A future with him would only be rife with violence and revenge.

He was stubborn and determined enough that he would likely spend his whole life trying to get even with the Silver Order. A life he didn't realize would never heal her wounds. Rather, it would only make them run deeper. One could not get even with the past. All one could do with the past was learn from it and, more importantly, move forward. A task Darren was already taking on.

She never had to hide who she was in his company. She could be everything she was all at once: British, Filipino, demure, domineering, sweet, and short-tempered. No matter how those traits seemed to contradict each other.

She trusted Darren. Not for his past, but for his future, one she could so clearly see from time to time, not because he had made any promises, but because of the kind of man she knew him to be. For the simple fact that he was willing to leave it all behind.

But she didn't want that for him. He loved his father too deeply to leave him behind. He simply needed to take his place as chair. No matter how challenging that would prove. She vowed to help him. If he allowed for it, that was. If he wanted her more than physically. If only she had the strength to ask. Right now, she ought to.

She didn't care for Julius; she never had. She swallowed a breath. "Darren, I—"

"I wanted to remind you," he interrupted, the cot creaking under his weight. "When we arrive in Bombay, that's where I shall leave you."

She swept around, only to face the crate. Was he serious?

"I'll make sure to book you safe passage, of course. I'll even see you board and wave you off, but I can't board with you."

"What?" She barely mustered, her voice weak and raw. "I don't understand. Why?"

"You know why. Julius will follow me wherever I go. He'll be expecting me to be at your side. Once he sees that I'm not, perhaps he'll leave you be and continue on after me. I'm the one he wants dead. Not you."

Amara cringed at the mention of death. Did he really think she could do that? Just leave him when someone was on the hunt to kill him?

"There's a whole history between us you know nothing about."

"I know more than you think," Amara countered. "He told me all. He said he wants to destroy the Order in its entirety. More than anything, he wants to keep you as far from the emerald cave as possible."

"As you once did as well."

She stepped out from behind the crate, facing him head on. She could only imagine how she looked. But he said nothing. He merely stared, too focused no doubt on the conversation at hand.

"Why didn't you just stay with him?" he asked her again. "Why did you bother yourself to rescue me?"

He wanted a real explanation this time. In his desperate eyes, he wanted all the words she didn't yet know how to say. Was he really going to make her beg? Couldn't he just kiss her again like he had before? If he did, she wouldn't stop and neither would he.

A moment passed then another and still, he did nothing. She wished for once that she weren't such a timid wallflower. Somehow, since she had learned her feelings for him, it had only made her shyness worse.

It didn't matter that they had already shared a bed and a kiss. Moments that replayed in her mind for the thousandth time, forcing her to look down.

She wanted a repeat, a do-over—she could admit that now—but she also wanted more. She wanted something that could last. Just the slightest possibility that he didn't want that was like acid burning in her gut.

"I couldn't stand the thought of you locked up like that." Those meek words were all she could manage.

"I would have been happy to die. It would have been better than knowing you were with him," Darren said harshly. "Knowing what you must have had to do."

Amara wanted so much to lie to say nothing had happened. But the truth was she had gone out with him late one evening, danced around in a ballroom, even. She had ended up in his room and he'd almost…

"Nothing happened."

Did he believe her? The conviction of his statement was all but cemented on his face. Was going out with Julius for the night, being alone with him in his bedroom, even if nothing had happened truly unforgiveable? For some men, it might be. Especially if others had seen. The rumors would be too hard to bear. Her heart seized. She hadn't considered any of this.

"As much as Julius has tried to convince you otherwise, he only thinks of you as a tool," Darren said.

"I know. I'm not stupid."

"I'm sure he tried to make you believe his efforts are righteous. Just because he doesn't believe in our secrecy. Because he thinks our knowledge should be shared with all. He cares not of the consequences."

"He also thinks that much of your knowledge has been stolen."

"Without a doubt."

"Then it isn't yours *or* his to share, is it?"

Darren set his jaw and nodded.

"I don't think Julius is some hero," Amara said forcefully. "Even if I could see some merit in his plans, he doesn't even come close. Not with the way he does things. The way he *hurt* you."

Amara wanted so badly to reach out. She should have paused just a moment to ask how he was feeling. To at least check him for injuries. So far as she could tell, the sea had washed him clean. Blood was no longer crusted in his hair. His stitches were holding his wound together nicely. Aside from that, he only had a few lingering bruises. She was sure there were other places he ached. Instead of coming to her and seeking comfort, something she wanted more than she'd expected, he turned away from her gaze.

"But leaving me in that cell, it would have been better for you. Think on it—you wouldn't even have felt guilty. What guilt does anyone feel for the villain?"

"You're not the villain." Amara shook her head.

"Nonetheless. You would have been better off leaving me."

"The only reason I'm alive is because you've stayed at my side. You can't leave. *Please.*"

"I told you my plans to part ways on the *New Dawn*. You agreed…" His face twisted with confusion.

"I know, but—"

"I find you a real and proper guard."

She bit her lip. That wasn't what she was concerned about at all. What mattered to her now was being together. But now that he was saying they couldn't be, something burst inside her like a flame.

"You truly are no different than all the other men of the ton," she said harshly. Why else did he kiss her when he only ever planned to leave? "You only want the basest and shallowest of things."

"Is that really what you think I am?" He stiffened. "Just another nob?"

She moved to the door. Darren followed after her, even though he was still half-dressed.

"Amara, tell me. Speak to me," he begged. Tell him? Bleed her heart out to him when all he was going to do was leave her behind? That would only make things worse. She couldn't endure such pain. She wouldn't do it to herself. Not a chance.

She gathered up her tousled, salt-laden hair and placed it over one shoulder.

"I'm famished," she said. "I'd much rather have some breakfast." She tried her best to appear angry and quite finished with the topic. Anything but heartbroken.

CHAPTER TWENTY-SIX

A Day in Bombay

AMARA KEPT HER distance from Darren. Even if she was sure he'd never try anything with her again, not after what she'd accused him of.

Amara hated herself for saying it—that he only wanted the basest and shallowest of things—and even more for getting so upset. Of course they hadn't lasted. It wasn't entirely her fault. It was simply fate.

And yet they still had to share a bed. They still had to spend day and night together on this ship, where there was nowhere else to run. How it must have been torture for him. It was torture for her too.

The only saving grace was that there was plenty to distract them. As a way to pay for their keep, Darren took it upon himself to help with the cutting of whale blubber. Amara, thankfully, was given tasks alongside the cook that included chopping vegetables and mopping. As difficult as the tasks proved to be, at least she was alive. She repeated this to herself as the day wore on. By nightfall, she was too exhausted to think.

There was one saving grace from it all. Once it was clear that the new passengers were willing to work for their keep, the whalers began to see them as peers. They no longer cared that Amara, being the only woman on board, was supposedly bad luck. Dressed like a man, perhaps it was easier to pretend she was one.

Amara and Darren began staying out on deck with the crew later and later, first in the mess hall in the early evening then out on deck beneath the stars. At nighttime, when the sailors were free from their work, they loved to tell tales.

A different man told a different story every night. Each one more fantastical than the last, but all proclaimed with the utmost vehemence to be true. Stories of impossible survival against sharks and giant squids and the women they'd had to leave behind. Women so beautiful, they made you believe in God, one of them said. Because who else could make something so divine? Even if the sailor lost her to another man by the time he'd returned from sea, he still believed. The most poetic words she'd ever heard—from a sailor, of all people.

She couldn't be sure, but for the briefest of moments, she thought she saw Darren's eyes glaze over with tears before he rubbed them away. The story of star-crossed lovers had perhaps made him think of their own. For that, she wanted to cry too.

The other more adventurous tales featured a sailor who'd slipped into the mouth of a whale. They had given him up for dead and gone ahead and winched the whale to the ship. But one night, they saw something moving violently in its belly. Curious, the whalers cut it open and discovered their shipmate still alive, his hair and skin bleached from the whale's stomach acids.

Out there surrounded by nothing but gentle waves and skies, it was only too easy to get carried away by the tale. Amara liked to close her eyes and listen, the words soothing her to sleep. The next thing she knew, she was at the bottom of the ship on the worn-out cot she shared with Darren. She slept so deeply on that ship and she didn't know why. Maybe it was the gentle warmth of the Arabian Sea or perhaps she had finally gotten her sea legs.

A few more days came and went. Each day, the bed seemed to grow smaller. And every morning when they woke, their bodies were closer. The last morning she was in his arms. She dismissed it as nothing, blaming it once more on the cold. While her conscious mind wanted distance, it seemed her subconscious wanted something entirely different.

Amara was surprised when tears welled in her eyes during her goodbyes with the crewmen. She owed them her life; it didn't seem right that she'd never see them again.

Back on shore, she might have to shed her servants garb and don her faded ballgown as a lady once more, but she still felt as if she were one of them, one of the working class. None of what they did was easy, but it was necessary. All it had taken was some hard, honest work for her to realize that.

Something else had returned to her mind too. Darren would be leaving her to continue on alone. Her mother still needed saving. Somehow, the *Marsala* had offered her a respite from it all.

In the hired hack that was to take the pair to Darren's family friend, the mood had completely changed.

Amara sat arms crossed. Even though Darren was just across from her with their knees nearly touching, they didn't speak. Was this his way of easing their soon-to-come goodbye? In her eyes, the silence was only making things worse. She hadn't said a word since she had said her goodbyes to the whalers. It was beginning to drive her mad.

Old memories from aboard the *New Dawn* had returned threefold. The pain he must have suffered while she'd been galivanting across that ballroom in Alexandria. The jealousy he must have endured then. Perhaps he did feel something for her that went beyond the physical. She might have been convinced entirely if he weren't about to leave. She might have even expressed her own feelings. As pointless as it was, she still wanted to.

Blast it, she should at least demand to know why he had kissed her. What was holding her back? His small stake in the emerald cave that some deep-rooted ancestral ties refused to let go? She didn't know, but with Darren giving her the cold shoulder, she found herself staying silent too.

The moment they'd arrived in the heart of the city, however, Amara was glued to the window. With its limestone bricks and column-lined buildings, the whole city shimmered in the sun. Some parts reminded her of London. The women wore the latest London fashions. The kinds of dresses she had only seen in shops.

"You need not worry about a language barrier here." Darren spoke for the first time. His voice sounded deeper than usual and rough, maybe even pained. "Most everyone here speaks impeccable English."

"We turned the city into London basically," she returned.

It felt odd to say, 'we,' but it applied. She was a countess, after all. She couldn't exactly deny her British heritage. However, to her other half, this place meant something else entirely. It was a cautionary tale. If the British saw value in Manila like they did with the cotton in India, this was what the city would become. All aspects of their culture would be washed away, lost and replaced.

The Romans who had come to Britain in ancient times had been no different. Like her father had once said, history really did have a way of repeating itself.

The sun was high in the sky by the time they'd arrived on the doorstep of Darren's family friends. Even if he hadn't known the address, it would have been easy to find. All they needed to search for was one of the biggest, most extravagant homes in the entire city. Iron balconies lined each of its four stories. One of the doors was open with a sheer curtain blowing in the wind, leading directly to a deep-cushioned chaise.

The place was so vastly different than the whaling ship, it almost stole her breath away. And she was a countess. A lady who was supposed to be used to these kinds of manors.

In her tattered and sun-faded silk gown, she certainly wasn't arriving like she was one of them. After all she'd been through, maybe she wasn't any longer.

What mattered to her now more than parquet floors and cushioned furniture was whether or not these friends were actually friendly.

Her first impression of Mr. Sylvester Darby was rather cold. Typical of an officer with high rank in the British Army, he was rather quiet and stern-looking. Fortunately, his wife had a much more outgoing composition. Before Darren could even explain all that they had been through, Mrs. Darby eyed Amara's state of dress and immediately whisked her away to a bath.

Amara had never experienced one so indulgent. The steamy air held scents of frankincense, lemon, and lavender.

Mrs. Darby even sent a servant out to purchase Amara more practical traveling clothes. Amara made sure to request something sturdy, offering to reimburse them once she returned to London, but Mrs. Darby waved her away, claiming it had already been covered by Darren. Amara wanted to argue and refuse, but it was not a fight that seemed fair to Mrs. Darby. Amara promised herself that she would discuss it with Darren the next time they were alone.

But when will that be? she wondered. She couldn't forget his plans to remain here when she booked passage onward to the islands. She had tried to prepare for his departure, but a part of her refused to believe it. Another part of her feared what was sure to be a quick and abrupt departure.

Her stomach continued to twist at the thought as Mrs. Darby's lady's maid helped prepare her for dinner.

"I noticed you were without a chaperone or even a companion," Mrs. Darby said from the settee in her boudoir. She had claimed the light was better here for braiding. "Perhaps you ought to think about acquiring one before you depart."

Amara didn't know why, but she suddenly burst into tears. She finally had to admit it: she was fearful for what lay ahead, especially without Darren at her side, and she missed Granger. The poor servant was probably on her way back to London. For all Granger knew, Amara was dead.

Damn it. She squeezed her fists.

She didn't care if Darren said his presence would only lead

Julius back to her. She needed him.

The servant muttered some excuse and left. Amara expected Mrs. Darby to do the same. But she didn't. She remained. She even rubbed a hand over Amara's back. Her own mother might have done the same.

"You're in want of more than a chaperone, aren't you? You would like Mr. Pierce to remain on the journey with you."

She nodded, slightly humiliated at the thought. It was untoward to travel with a bachelor. It was the sort of thing that elicited rumors and ruined reputations amongst London society. But aside from her mother, he was the only one who had ever made her feel safe.

"I could tell you two had formed an attachment."

"You can?"

"It's the way he looks at you." She shrugged, like it was nothing. Like this didn't flip Amara's whole world upside down. "And the way you meet his gaze merely for a second at a time. But who wouldn't be in love after what you have both been through?"

Months ago, Amara wouldn't have believed it. She wasn't supposed to fall in love. Only a marriage well-matched in terms of rank and income would do. In London high society, that was all marriage was: a business transaction. One in which she had come up surprisingly short.

That was what she'd once believed, anyway. What seemed like ages ago.

"He might say he doesn't want to continue on with you, but I can tell deep down, he fears for you. But it wouldn't be proper, would it? Not with what has happened between you two."

Amara looked up at Mrs. Darby, broken-hearted. Darren was much more than a guard to her. He always had been.

"But it's not all lost." Mrs. Darby squeezed her arm. "What of marriage? We could hold the ceremony right here in Bombay. Oh, it would be splendid!" She clapped her hands together.

Was she mad? "I don't think marriage is something he'd really follow through with." Yes, he wanted her, maybe even as a long-term mistress. Every piece of her minus her hand.

"Oh, please." Mrs. Darby rolled her eyes. "All you need do is say *yes*."

Could it be that easy? Would he actually agree? She almost didn't dare allow her heart to think it. But she did. Every fiber of her being held out hope that Mrs. Darby was right.

"We'll discuss it more over dinner," she said.

Before Amara could protest, Mrs. Darby left the room to call the lady's maid back in.

"She'll need to do it in a completely different style," Mrs. Darby said when they returned. "Something more suited to the occasion."

CHAPTER TWENTY-SEVEN
The Offer

B Y THE TIME Amara had stepped down to the expansive dinner room, Darren was alone, hovering over his place setting. The room was done in an especially detailed baroque style, but she saw none of it. Even in a sea full of people, all she would have seen is him. He bowed his head.

"The Darbys make their apologies. Some kind of business or another…though I hardly think it an accident."

Amara squeezed her fingers together. She was relieved, really. She didn't know how she was going to make it through dinner with all that she wanted to say to him. It would have been so hard getting through all the pleasantries. Apparently, their hosts knew it too. They were quite possibly the most courteous couple she had ever met. A friendliness that matched their lavish house, which was just as warm and comforting.

Darren stepped forward, his gaze pained. "Have you—have you been crying?"

Amara ignored the question. "You can't do it, can you?" she said in a tone that surprised herself. "Remain here, in India, while I go."

"I—"

"It doesn't matter." Amara interrupted, quickly realizing she wasn't brave enough to hear the answer. "You can't. You just can't. Especially if you believe Julius will come after you like you say. You haven't thought about what that might do to me. I'll always be wondering. Worrying about what happened to you."

"Why?" he pressed her.

She blushed, forcing herself to come closer to him as she laid herself bare. "The truth is, I do care about you. I care about you so very much." She exhaled. Was now when she should burst into tears, crying, begging him to stay? She could have done it any moment since they had arrived here.

He gave no indication he'd even heard her. He only stared back. In a state of shock, perhaps? Or maybe he didn't believe her. Maybe he needed her to discuss the elephant in the room first.

"Nothing happened with Julius…" Amara began. She knew he was suspicious. "You have to believe me."

Spending an evening with Julius had been horrible enough. If it hadn't led to Darren's freedom, she might have regretted it. How else could she have ended up with the keys? She hadn't the sleight of hand to do it while he was awake. She'd needed to be with him to get him to drink more and more of that concoction. He'd needed to pass out, off his guard.

Still, Darren said nothing. Why was he tormenting her like this? He turned away, staring at the large landscape painting. Rather than pay homage to the Indian jungles, it depicted the English countryside, just like a thousand others before it.

"Did you enjoy being with him?" he asked.

"Of course not."

She worried her teeth into her bottom lip. Despite what Mrs. Darby believed, she couldn't be sure if he'd forgive her. What she *was* sure of was the growing ache in her heart. Just for him.

"I can't take it back," she admitted. She couldn't undo the past.

"I know. That's not what I want from you."

"An affair is out of the question." Countless men had wanted that. She had to make doubly sure he didn't want that too, no matter what he promised.

Darren's eyebrows shot up. "Is that what you think I want?

All this time?" Darren grasped her arms before she could devolve into tears. "My proposal was an honest one, Amara. I meant it more than anything I've ever—I wouldn't leave with you for anything less."

He closed in—so close, she could feel the brush of his eyelashes.

"I just… I needed to be sure you returned my feelings," he continued. "After all these years, when I was so sure you didn't… I needed something more."

"You needed convincing," she whispered, understanding now. "Does that mean…You mean you'll go with me?"

"If you truly feel as you do, I don't think I'd have the strength for anything otherwise."

"You're certain?" Amara asked slowly, disbelievingly.

"Letting you go would be the noblest thing. The safest. But I'm no saint, you know."

"I see…" She swallowed.

"But I want the second-noblest thing. Marriage. I want your heart—your whole heart if you'll give it to me. For that and no other reason, I will go with you."

Even though the words were plain for her to hear, she still wasn't comprehending them. They were too good to be true.

"You'll marry me?" she questioned again. She was supposed to have given up on marriage. Darren made her reconsider. He made her believe she could have an entirely different life. A beautiful life. Because of the man she knew he could be.

"All that matters are your feelings for me." He straightened. "I'll not compromise. I'll have you all to myself. That's all I ever wanted, want now, and will ever want. Forever."

She knew now that he had been all she'd ever wanted too.

"In exchange, I promise you that what happened those last few days with Julius will never happen again. It was my actions that forced you on his ship and mine alone. I blame no one but me."

"You do?" Amara gaped at this. This was a turn in events. "I thought you would never forgive me."

"There is nothing to forgive. It's just… It forced me to doubt. To fear that maybe you preferred him or some titled gentleman…that I was too beneath you…"

Amara could have laughed. "None of them have ever impressed me. Not even their well-tied cravats."

"But I do?" he asked, self-consciously, almost.

"Thoroughly. Your fearlessness in particular." There was also how he made her feel: safe and warm in a world that was all too cold and unfamiliar.

The prison he had been subjected to would have broken a lesser man. Not him. It had only hardened his resolve. Even if that meant leaving her.

"In each and every London ballroom, I only ever noticed you," he said, his piercing eyes going right through her until he could see everything she was trying to hide. With him, she didn't need to be like everyone else. She could be herself in all of her dualities. His eyes were begging her to admit it.

"I feared you hated me," he said. "You're supposed to. You and your mother."

Amara wasn't sure if she'd ever really hated him.

"I was grieving," she tried to explain. It had been because of anger more than anything else, an anger that she never should have placed on him.

No matter how angry she was over her father's death, hating Darren wasn't possible anymore. Not after all he'd done for her.

"My mother might take some convincing," she said coyly.

Naturally, her mother had never considered Darren as a possible suitor. Heavens, they'd both been so naive. He might not have been from noble blood, but he was well-known in society and considerably rich. Was that enough to sway her mother? Although Amara didn't want to admit it, after her daughter's third season, Amara's mother was likely to accept anyone.

"I do hold some position," he said. "I have—what do the women of the ton like to call it?—social connections?"

Amara had no doubt of that. Within the highest circles in society, she spotted the insignia from time to time—the one Darren wore on a ring. She saw it on a cufflink, coat pocket, a timepiece, usually amongst the highest circles. It was a small sort of engraving that one might only notice if one was looking for it.

"I would contend that I offer more influence and power than most, title or not," he said. "More power than a countess could ever dream of. Not to mention a life of excitement."

The Order studied any number of strange and extraordinary things. The sort of things no one else dared explore, that were already in her blood.

He was truly making a case for himself. A proposal that was far more long-winded than it needed to be, but it was still a proposal, which was already more than she had ever expected. And she wanted to hear every word. She smiled and held back a laugh—because none of it was necessary. He'd already won her. She didn't quite know when. Long ago, perhaps.

"Would our lives really be so exciting?" she asked. She couldn't help it. She was enjoying this.

"Secrets are always so. Especially when only a select few have access to them."

"I would be one of them?"

"As my wife," he said, speaking the word boldly, "you'd have power and position too, of course. It is not something to take lightly."

"I see."

"There are plenty of women who hold power and position in the Order. It's been that way since before Britain was, well, Britain."

"What do you mean? During Pagan times?"

"We have a different name for that time. But yes."

"What if it upsets people? Our marriage, I mean."

Thankfully, she didn't need to lay out all her misgivings. He knew well enough the challenges she had faced in society.

"No one would dare. Don't even think of it. Think of the

influence you'd have, the interests you could pursue."

"What about your home? It's been in your family for generations. I couldn't leave mine…" She'd been to the Pierces' estate enough times as a child to know that it rivaled the greatest castles of all England.

"I don't care about the details. I just want *you*."

"You're certain?"

He laughed. "Bricks will keep. I don't have to live there." He cleared his throat. "Unless you think someone else in the ton might suit you better?"

"Those bores?" She chewed her lip. "For a long time, I thought they were the best I could hope for."

"Rather, I think you're destined for happiness." He leaned in and gripped her hands. "With me."

Finally, she let him know the truth. "It is quite possibly the only way I could ever truly be happy."

Through her hands, she could feel him shaking with excitement. So was she. Was this really happening? How hadn't it happened so much sooner?

"Why didn't you tell me how you felt on the ship?"

Amara swallowed. "What I couldn't tell you with my lips, I told you with every other part of my body. Every night. You just didn't realize."

"You blamed it on the cold."

"I'm a terrible liar. I wanted you every night… I wanted you to… Maybe I shouldn't have…"

"I will now." He pulled her in closer by her waist, the sudden motion making her warm all over. "Tonight I will."

"I came so close." She pounded him lightly on the chest, letting her hand rest there. "So close to leaving. I almost did. Almost."

More than going alone, she'd feared losing him. She already nearly had.

"Not a chance," Darren said, running his lips along her cheek and chin. "I don't think I could have endured it."

She smiled. The words were more than she could have ever dreamed. Even as a child, when she'd dreamed up proposals that would sweep her off her feet. It was so much more exciting, romantic—everything.

"I don't want to wait this time," he whispered. "The Darbys say we can marry here. Think of it. The Darbys are great friends of the bishop. We could get a special license."

As much as Amara's heart leaped at the thought, she had to be practical. "How long, do you think?"

"Days. The next ship to Manila doesn't leave until Friday. We could be married by then. The Darbys will facilitate everything."

Was this actually happening? She was about to be married. Even if her mother couldn't attend the wedding, wasn't that what she ultimately wanted? She'd come around to anyone at this point. More than that, they'd be able to travel as man and wife. At last, she'd be his. No matter what happened, they would have each other.

"Yes," Amara said, louder than she'd expected, almost with a shriek.

"Are we really doing this?" Darren pulled her in so tightly, he lifted her slightly.

When he dropped her back on the ground, she pulled back. "What about your father?"

The problems with his father and the danger that surrounded him were what had initially given him pause.

"I won't allow him to interfere with my life again or even delay it."

He had been truthful that night of their first kiss. He really had meant to marry her. It wasn't a weak promise like she had feared, but a real one.

"I've realized something." He smiled. "No matter what happens, it will be far better to have you at my side."

She thought about what life might be like when they returned home. There was so much to think of. Everything was moving ahead so fast. She understood why people called some romances a whirlwind. She already felt as though she were floating, being whisked away by it all.

He distracted her by inching ever so closely.

"You need not worry about any of that," Darren told her. "Not now."

He cupped her chin and took her mouth with his. There was no preamble to it, no need to ask for permission now. She had already agreed to the kiss, that and so much more.

CHAPTER TWENTY-EIGHT
New Passage

D ARREN STARED OUT into an unending expanse of purples and pinks.

After a whirlwind of a day, Darren needed a breath. He waited just outside their rooms as Amara changed out of her wedding clothes. At Mrs. Darby's insistence, her gown had been quite lavish: white silk with loops of pearls that hung over her bodice and like sleeves over her arms. Though not quite fitting for sea travel, he wished she could have worn it longer.

The special license had taken longer than they'd expected and by the time they had received it, they'd had to rush the ceremony in order to have time enough to board. Like he was still drunk on champagne, his head was buzzing from all the nervous energy. He feared they wouldn't make it. He didn't want to miss their ship, but he wouldn't miss marrying her for a kingdom. They hadn't even had the customary wedding breakfast. There hadn't been time. But they'd made it. They had exchanged rings and the officiant had pronounced them man and wife.

Sailing farther down the sea, they'd at least have something of a honeymoon.

The ship rocked slightly and he tightened his grip on the railing. The sea stirred more strongly than he was used to. Upon the new ship, the *Muriel*, everything felt different. This time, he and Amara were sailing toward an entirely new life. Behind them was their old life and that was exactly where he wanted it to stay. Far behind them.

Even his father. Among all the devil's other problems, Darren knew he'd have trouble getting his approval.

Amara, thankfully, had no idea how deeply his father resented hers now. It didn't matter that they had been the closest of friends. Darren didn't understand it himself. The so-called theft by omission in Darren's eyes was understandable. Amara's father was only staying true to his word, to his wife, no less. If Darren himself had made such a promise, he would have kept it too. Just as he had promised to stay mum about the caves' location. No matter how much his father might pressure him.

It was high time he defied his father, anyway.

So long as he had Amara's mother's approval, he didn't care about his father's. He would be returning to England a different man. An honest man.

He laughed grimly to himself. His father might have gotten his way after all. Once Darren got home, he had every intention of renewing his interest in the Order and claiming his birthright. Immediately. The only difference was that his father would be losing his.

He wasn't doing it all for him, though. He was doing it for the good of the Order and more importantly, for her.

The new position would make up for the fact that he wasn't a member of nobility. The Order would give Amara the kind of power and standing in the world that an earl never could. That not even a duke could.

Even if Amara had said she didn't care, he simply wanted her to have it all. Maybe even more than she had ever dreamed.

He hadn't been lying when he'd told her how seductive the Order and all its secrets could be. He had always felt that way about the Order. It had never been the Order he'd been trying to get away from. It was his father.

Behind him, he heard footfalls. He swung around to Amara, now dressed in more practical traveling clothes.

He smiled at her, bemused. He'd wanted to help her get undressed, but after undoing the buttons down her back, she had blushed and asked him to wait outside. Didn't she know what was coming for her as soon as the sun slipped below the horizon? What he'd get to see then?

After that, she didn't realize how quickly things would change between them. Just how comfortable they'd be with the things that made her uneasy now.

He only had to be patient a little while longer. Until tonight.

When Amara joined him at the railing, a sudden rush of déjà vu washed over him. They had done this before on the *Evangeline* too, only there were no longer any guards or lady's maids to interrupt them. It was just them now.

"You look so deep in thought." Amara placed her hands on the railing and leaned toward him. He savored the closeness. He wasn't used to this type of contact, especially since his mother had died.

"What were you thinking about?" she asked.

Was this what it would be like having her as his wife? Always having someone concerned about what he was thinking and his overall well-being? He supposed he liked it. Just not the part where he had to spill his guts. Now that they were married, he didn't dare lie to her. That wasn't the kind of marriage he wanted.

"My father," he admitted.

Amara chewed her lip, suddenly nervous, which was why he hadn't wanted to bring him up in the first place. "Are you afraid he won't approve?"

"I couldn't care less. It's what I'm going to have to do that concerns me."

With her at his side, he could no longer risk a major row. He needed to try to remove him from the Order peacefully. He just didn't know how or where to begin. What troubled him most was what awaited him back home might very well be more dangerous than what had come so far for them on their expedition. Would the violence ever end?

Amara was patient as she waited for him to expand. But he couldn't bring himself to say the words aloud just yet. That would make it all too real.

"You'll need to force him to retire and take the reins for yourself," Amara said for him. "Is that what you mean?"

Somehow, she made it sound so simple. "I should have done it ages ago. When my mother died."

She squeezed his hand. "You were grieving then too."

"You understand that we can't just leave?"

She nodded. "You love your father too much for that."

"I have a duty to my name as well." He tried to brush all that aside. He hadn't felt love for his father for some time. Yet it was still there.

"I'm just not looking forward to the fight. I'll have to lobby other men to my side. No doubt there will be those who turn against me." And all the while, he had to keep her safe.

"Are you so sure that it will be a fight? If you think your father has had issues with his temper, it's likely others have noticed too. Even himself."

God, he hoped so. Though part of him still expected his confrontation to turn into a total brawl. But he liked her optimism. It gave him the smallest breath of hope.

"Either way, you can't escape him. You can't just be rid of him," Amara said, perhaps a bit less optimistically. But it was true. He was his father. "You might have to compromise."

Darren huffed. "Easier said than done."

"Take it step by step. That's what I do when I feel overwhelmed. First, you'll need to try talking with him."

He shook his head. "As if he would listen."

"Perhaps if he knew how much his temper was affecting you—"

"Not to mention pushing me away from the Order. My birthright."

"Maybe if he knew that, he'd try to change. He'd calm down. You said this all began with your mother's death?"

Darren nodded.

"He may be a bit volatile at times," she said, "but he loves you, Darren. He just doesn't show it to you in the way you want or need. Just in the way he knows how."

"And how is that?" he asked sardonically. But he already knew. By sending him here on this trip in the first place, by trying to revive Darren's love of the Order. It had worked. Something for which his father was ironically to blame.

"Perhaps you need to remind him how your mother might feel regarding his behavior," Amara suggested.

It was good advice. Even when they'd been children, he'd always revered her intelligence. To preside over the Order, she'd need to have a good head on her shoulders. It had always mattered more to him than looks—though Amara had been blessed with both—because for the rest of his life, she'd always have his ear.

"That will be first on my to-do list when we get home." He took up her hand and kissed it. "Now let's try to put this behind us."

"I suppose we do have far bigger issues on hand."

"None of that is any of our concern at the moment," he said, his eyes on her lips.

They still had several days at sea. He didn't see the point in worrying themselves about what they'd do once they arrived in Manila. That was for the future.

She stayed near, though not quite as close as he'd like. She was still jittery around him, like a wild animal too afraid to step out of its cage even when it had been left open. He'd need to lure her out with the best of enticements. Soon enough, she'd be running free.

It was only a matter of time until they were back in bed, her head was resting on his bare chest, her long hair spread out over his arm. A comfort that couldn't come soon enough.

"Let's return to our rooms." Darren pulled her lightly at the waist. The type of touch only a husband could claim.

"Now?" She swallowed, seeming to know exactly what he intended. "I thought we could explore the ship. Don't you think—"

"I have something for you," he said, all innocence.

She raised her eyebrows, clearly intrigued.

Thanks to the Darbys' fast connections, they were able to book passage on the best ship the sea could offer. The *Muriel* was a passenger ship just like the *Evangeline*, though a bit more crowded with eager tourists. Their state rooms were much nicer too. Located not far from the captain's own quarters, they felt particularly safe. In a way, it was like they were starting their trip back at the beginning before all the trouble, when things had been much rosier. Even if they hadn't yet claimed their feelings for each other then, the sentiments had still been there. Only now, those feelings would get deeper, more intimate, more physical. He clenched his teeth to contain himself.

"Here it is." In their room, he broke away from her for the armoire, where he had unpacked his trunk. "I'm afraid it requires some ceremony."

"Oh?" Amara sat down on the bed, her back against the headboard. Her skirts and legs swept off to one side.

"I realize we had a rather short engagement, but it only seems fair… Hopefully, it's to your satisfaction."

He dropped down on the bed in front of her and showed her the box. For suspense purposes, he waited a beat, then opened it.

Amara bit her lip. As he had hoped, her whole face lit up.

Nestled in black velvet lay a large hall-of-mirrors-cut emerald on a band of gold. It was rather simple, allowing the rare stone to stand out most of all.

"How did you—"

"Darby managed it last minute. It may not be from Manila, but I hope it helps memorialize not just our union, but this amazing trip. I want to remember it always. When everything changed between us."

"If you're trying to seduce me"—she shifted on the bed—

"this is an awful good start."

This might prove easier than he'd thought. The look she gave him made his insides clench with desire. He'd expected to have to do more coaxing. Maybe he'd had to wait a few more nights like some new husbands had lamented. But he knew that look. She wanted him.

"Just a 'start'?" he questioned. In his eyes, she looked like she wanted nothing more.

"I thought that sort of thing waited until nighttime?" She pulled back slightly. "It's still early evening."

"Maybe for the nobs of the ton. Not me, I'm afraid. I'm different from them, remember?"

"Quite."

She still wanted him, he knew she did. She just wasn't going to be toward about it.

She reached out for the ring, but playfully, he tugged it back. "Like I said, it requires some ceremony. When it comes to the Order, I think you'll find that we are all about ceremony."

"I see." Her voice quavered, if only slightly.

He struggled to wipe the smirk from his face. He was done with all that serious talk. They were man and wife now, which he couldn't stop reminding himself. Especially because she was the only one he'd ever wanted. He had fought so hard for her. But at long last, he had her.

He thought again of her head on his chest, her hair spread out across his shoulder. He rather appreciated it loose around her shoulders, like how she'd had it on the *Marsala*. In Bombay, she had it pinned up again.

"Maybe you should take your hair down," he said. "It might help you relax."

Even if he didn't think he could contain himself a moment longer, every moment that he was forced to wait felt more delicious than the last.

She did as he'd asked. "What shall I do next?"

"Oh, right." Darren smiled. "Well, I thought that now that

I've confessed my noblest and purest feelings… I might be able to express my baser ones."

Amara blinked, taken aback, no doubt, by his bluntness.

"Are your feelings truly debauched?" she asked.

"Rather, they're more like demands." He leaned in an inch from her lips.

"Is this a trade?" She eyed him. "For the ring?"

"For everything. For me." He was enjoying this little game he was playing, brimming with so much mirth, he felt he might burst. But he reeled himself back in. He didn't dare break the spell he had started to weave.

"I can't promise that I won't refuse," she whispered.

It took him a moment to realize she was saying *yes*, just in a purposefully convoluted way. So much blood had rushed to his lower regions, he'd nearly thought she was saying *no*. But she wasn't. Thank heavens. He needed to get his deepest, darkest desires off his chest for once.

"I want to enjoy all of you, Amara. As deep and far as I can reach. Inch by inch. Like I said, it will take some ceremony. And time. Do you want to know where I'd like to begin?" He leaned in and began kissing her neck. He didn't stop until he felt the subtle nod of her chin. She was stiff at first, but he could feel her relaxing into him, completely at his whim.

"First I want a glimpse," he whispered in her ear. "How about it?"

She laughed, seeming to know exactly what he was saying. "For the ring?"

"For the sake of ceremony." Their wedding had been rushed enough; he wanted this to take some time. She had to know what he wanted. She just had no idea for how long. Ever since he had seen her, really seen her.

Just before she'd entered society, when they'd still run in the woods together. A sudden burst of fast and hard rain had hit, forcing her hair out of her braids. He'd watched, not caring how the rain drenched him as she'd pulled out her pins. Coated with moisture, her face had been shining, so sweet and pure. With a slight shake of her head, she had let her hair fall stingy and wet around her shoulders. Almost as if she had just walked out of a bath, naked.

"What do you say?" he asked.

She didn't nod at this; she simply began to undo her corset strings. Without a lady's maid at her disposal, the strings of her corset were thankfully positioned in the front so she could undo them herself. So could he.

He began tugging at them too. Beneath it was a sheer, white chemise. It was thin enough that he could almost see through it. If only her hair was pulled aside.

For a second, she seemed to have second thoughts. She went still. Darren was losing his patience; she was his wife, after all. He was allowed to see her. Even she had to know that. He wasn't going to just lift up her skirts and finish after a minute or two. He wanted all of her. He wanted her to know it.

So Darren finished the task for her, slowly and prepared for her to resist. He pinched her chemise at each shoulder and shimmied it down. Then with the other hand, he gathered up her hair, the black strands a wonderful contrast to her skin. He didn't let go, even when he had exposed her blushing nipples.

Catching his balance, he leaned back to fully take in what was his now. She was more beautiful than he had dared dream.

Darren grabbed her hair more tightly, pulling her into his mouth.

"Wait..." She held out her hand, breathless. "It's only fair if you..."

Darren obliged. Still staring, he placed down the ring and shrugged off his waistcoat.

She stared at him, bare-chested, as he worked to undo his trousers. She was practically drinking him in. She hadn't bothered to cover up, either.

Instead, she stood up and squeezed her hips out from her skirts, more unabashed than he'd thought possible. Something in her had shifted. Was she finally giving herself to him? She was a better gift than any ring he could ever offer her. Than all the jewels in the world combined. One he had waited for for so long.

☾

THE REMAINDER OF their sea passage was a haze of hot skin and silky sheets until they finally arrived in Manila. On deck, they watched as the ship pulled into port. Entangled with his wife, Darren rested his chin on her shoulder, taking in the intoxicating scent of her skin.

After what they had done that morning, in fact, *every* morning—and night, and afternoon—since they'd boarded, he didn't know how he'd muster the energy to push through the jungle. *I wish we could remain here forever*, he thought languidly.

But soon, they would need to pick up supplies. Next, they would be venturing into its depths.

Yes, it would be difficult, but he tried to think of it like this: the sooner they found the cave and healed Amara's mother, the sooner they could continue on the rest of their lives. It lit a new flame inside him. He was ready, he told himself. Even to take on his father.

He followed Amara through the crowded port, both of them searching for any sign of Miss Granger and his guards. But what were the chances? Neither of them spoke of it, though their eyes kept searching, their chins stretched up above the crowd. They both knew it was unlikely for their companions to show. Even if they believed they were still alive, Amara's maid and his friends wouldn't have the time nor energy to come to port every time a ship came in.

Amara cast him a shaky look. As if to say, *they're not here.* Of course they weren't. The sad truth was that they were on their way home.

Their only comfort was that Amara's maid had been accompanied by his guards. It would likely be weeks until his guards got his letter back in England. By then, it would be too late. He and Amara were on their own.

Darren tried to focus instead on the vibrant city. Its richly painted buildings had wide windows and endless balconies that wrapped entire buildings. Rather than being indoors, it seemed everyone preferred the outside.

"We should be able to get there on foot," Amara said, continuing to lead the way. Like the cave, she had directions to her family home memorized.

The more the pair walked, the busier the city became. Almost as busy as London.

"I think that's it up there." Amara pointed.

Quite stately and impressive in size, the house was a mix of gray stone and cedar. Certainly not everyone here lived like this. Amara and her family were among the elite, just as she was in England.

A woman of similar age to Amara answered the door. The two had never met before. But somehow, they recognized each other, perhaps by the sprinkle of freckles that covered both their faces. Or perhaps it was something more meaningful than that. Darren couldn't be sure.

"Selene, this is Mr. Darren Pierce, my husband," Amara said, beginning introductions. "Darren, this is my cousin Selene Reyes."

Selene squealed something in Tagalog.

Though Selene spoke English, she wasn't quite as fluent, resulting in much conversation in Tagalog that he didn't understand.

Darren didn't mind. Selene led them to an ornately carved table that matched the wood-paneled walls. Soon he was too busy eating. Servants kept bringing platter after platter of food. Mountains of rice, beef, pork, and noodles with vegetables. While he explored the vast array of sharp and savory flavors, Amara and Selene chatted excitedly, half in English. Almost like they had known each other for years.

Even though every window was open, the heat eventually forced Darren out of his jacket. He unbuttoned his collar, even, but was still covered in drips of sweat.

Amara, on the other hand, simply took on a slightly dewy look. She didn't have beads of sweat on her skin like he did. In fact, she appeared more relaxed than ever in her new surroundings. Like she quite belonged.

Selene handed him a heart-shaped fan made of straw and poured him another cup of water.

She laughed when he dipped his napkin into the water and dabbed it over his face.

"Don't worry," Selene said. "You'll get used to the heat."

He prayed she was right. The jungle would only be worse.

When they were all finished eating, Selene showed them to their room to freshen up. Farther away from the kitchen, it was much cooler with windows surrounding almost the entire room.

The moment Amara had closed the door, Darren decided they had had enough time apart, even if they really hadn't been apart at all. Her focus had merely been on Selene, not him. Now, he couldn't keep his hands off her. For just a little while, he wanted to linger here and forget about the journey awaiting them.

Even if the heat was just starting to become bearable, he didn't care. He was about to make it much worse.

CHAPTER TWENTY-NINE
Babaylan

AMARA COULDN'T BELIEVE she was finally in Manila. It was a place she'd thought about often growing up. She'd never expected that she'd actually get to see it.

But here she was, halfway across the world, feeling the humidity thick on her skin, just like she'd always heard her mother talk about. The vegetation here was nothing like it was back home. Here, the leaves spread out like fans. The fashion she saw on the streets was different too. And yet, even if it was home, in a way, it didn't entirely feel that way. She didn't know why.

Maybe it was because her mother wasn't here to show her around. Maybe it was because everything was still so new and unfamiliar.

In the morning, when there was a strong knock on the door. Her eyes snapped open, expecting for a moment for a servant to come in and tell her one of her friends was calling when she realized: she wasn't in London. She was thousands of miles away, in an entirely different country.

A few moments later, the doorbell chimed and there was an even harder knock. Not the polite kind, but a much wilder and more demanding rapping. Amara sat up. Next to her, Darren was still asleep and snoring softly. Ever since they'd wed, he'd slept so deeply. It seemed cruel to wake him, especially if the knock ended up being nothing at all. She still had to inquire after it, though.

Someone calling at this time of day was an unusual thing.

So she put on a dressing gown and stepped out into the hall. Selene had already been coming for her. She stood at the opposite end, her hair slightly disheveled. She had just gotten out of bed too.

"Word has gotten out about your arrival," Selene said in Tagalog. "A woman wants to see you. She says she was once friends with your mother. Would you mind?"

"Of course not." Amara tightened her dressing gown. She was happy to meet anyone friends with her mother.

When she got to the threshold, the visitor crossed herself and said what sounded like a little prayer. Not only was she similar in age to her mother, she looked similarly wan, her skin pale with dark circles under her eyes, as though she hadn't slept in weeks. Instantly, Amara was brought back to her mother's bedside, so abruptly, tears welled in her eyes.

"So it is true," the visitor said in heavily accented English. Before Amara could answer, the woman swept inside. "You must heal me."

"Heal you?"

"Yes, of course," she said, as though it were plainly obvious. "Your abilities are stronger. I can tell."

She thrust her arms out as if Amara had any idea what to do with them.

"Take my hands," the woman begged. She hadn't even introduced herself, hadn't even told her her name. The way she looked at her, it was as if Amara were some kind of saint.

"I don't even know where to begin. I don't have the skills my lola has for salves and remedies."

"Those don't work. Not even the ones Selene makes. I'm too sick." She began to cough, devolving into a fit.

"Grace." Selene stepped into view. "You know she can't help you. Not all things can be healed by touch. Only the most minor of illnesses."

"It couldn't hurt," the sickly woman argued back, her voice

straining. "Even if it were only a moment of temporary relief."

"May I ask what ails you?" Amara could practically smell the sickness on her. Was that part of her gift too, being able to sense illness? In this case, it was obvious.

"Pneumonia, I've been told," Grace mumbled.

Amara wasn't much familiar with it. As much as she wanted to, she couldn't recommend any remedies. "I'm sorry, but I don't think I can help you. I just don't know how."

"But you must at least try. Please."

Darren's footsteps echoed down the hall. "What's all this commotion?" His voice seemed to roar in the enclosed foyer.

"It's nothing you need be concerned with," Amara said, trying to reassure the worry in his voice. "This woman. She wants me to heal her."

"Maybe you should just try." Selene sighed. "It will only take a second, though I doubt it will do much." Selene shot Grace a look, a familiar yet exasperated one. "Or we'll never be rid of you, will we?"

"I won't bother you for another moment." Grace nodded excitedly. "In your presence, I can already feel a shift. I'm getting better, I swear it."

"I don't know how." Amara threw up her hands.

Grace grabbed at Amara's wrists quite aggressively, pulling at her sleeves until she heard a stitch pull.

"Wait…" Amara struggled to get away. "What are you—"

Darren wasted no time in intervening. He pulled Amara away from the woman and slid her behind him.

"I think you better leave," he said with authority.

"Please." Grace's eyes filled with tears. "Just one touch with your most focused attention."

"This is nonsense." Darren scoffed.

"Nonetheless, this is what the people here believe," Selene said, somewhat sharply. It might have sounded ridiculous, but to Grace, Selene, Lola and perhaps many others here, Amara's talent was as real as the sun.

"That's—That's not what I meant," Darren sputtered. "I—"

"It's fine." Amara placed a hand on Darren's shoulder. "I'll help her."

Darren stayed close as Amara approached Grace again. The poor woman had broken down into sobs by now. All the same, he watched over them both carefully.

"Very well, but one false move and I'll escort you off the premises myself," Darren said, clearly unaffected by the tears. She was too frail to actually do any harm. That was probably why Darren had allowed this in the first place. Now that he was more than just Amara's guard, he had become so protective, no matter how small the threat. Even Selene seemed amused by it.

"All I need to do is touch you?" Amara grabbed the woman's hands and closed her eyes. She tried to focus and concentrate like the woman wanted. She pictured her skin color brightening and her dark circles fading. She even thought of her blood clearing of impurities and sparkling anew. But for how long would she need to do this?

After half a minute, Grace pulled away. "Thank you."

"I hope it works." Amara returned a weak smile.

"But you don't think it will," Grace said as if she could read it on her face.

Amara nodded. "You see, my mother is sick. If I could heal with touch, then she'd be healed. I wouldn't be here."

"I heard. I am sorry for it. So sorry. I know she was a great healer."

Amara nodded, if only she had known that herself.

"Since you're here, it's true, then." Grace breathed. "About the emeralds."

"You know about them?"

"It is naught but legend," Selene said, shaking her head. "Say nothing more."

Amara bit her tongue, as if that might keep her from talking and saying such stupid things. She shouldn't have said so much. The emeralds needed to be protected, not just from the British, but from everyone. Because of their limited supply, it had been that way for generations. They were only to be used for the most desperate of circumstances. Even if she hadn't said the words "emerald cave," she had made it obvious enough what they were doing here.

"I'll not say a word." Grace crossed herself again. "I owe you that much. Thank you."

Maybe Amara was seeing things, but Grace seemed less wan. Some color had even returned to her cheeks.

Grace nodded her goodbyes and turned away.

"Did you see that?" Darren asked as Amara shut the door.

Her hand was still on the doorknob when he took up her hands. They were slightly warmer than she was used to, but she must have just warmed them on Grace's. And there was rarely a breeze that didn't feel like hot breath. The extra heat could have come in through the door or any one of the windows.

"She looked better," Darren said.

So it wasn't just in her head.

"Yes, she is likely feeling better too, but the pneumonia isn't healed." Selene looked down then up again. "Whether you want to believe it or not, your hands do have power. The emeralds make it stronger."

Amara had had weeks to accept this, but somehow, it still felt raw and unreal. "Why didn't my mother tell me? If I'd known, I would have held her hands more at night. I never would have let them go."

"But it still wouldn't have healed her," Selene said solemnly.

"I told you that whale came to us for a reason." Darren raised up her hands, making them cup his face. "It explains so much. Why I always feel better in your presence, why—"

"I think that might have to do with something else." Selene raised an eyebrow.

Amara smiled weakly. The way Darren looked at her was obvious not just to her, but everyone. She didn't care. It was a look she never wanted to fade. "Lola has this ability too?"

"And her lola before that too. Even I, to some degree...although I'll admit my gift is not as powerful as yours." Something flashed across Selene's eyes. Was it jealousy? Whatever it was, it only lasted for a moment. In a place where the people truly valued and believed in this ability, Amara could understand. She might have even felt a little jealous herself in her cousin's position.

"I'll explain it all over breakfast," Selene said. "Everything is prepared. Follow me."

They sat down at a shaded table outside, where they could best feel the breeze. A mango tree and its tempting fruit were all within reach.

Amara grasped one. She'd never seen a fresh one before. She had only ever had dried mangos imported from India.

Darren noticed her brief reverie and picked one of the fruits himself.

"Ah, mangos," he said. "I've heard of these before."

He took a hearty bite, pausing for a moment after the first few chews. Selene's eyes went wide. "You don't eat the rind."

Selene snatched it out of his hand and lifted a silver dome, revealing slices of fresh, *peeled* mango arranged in the shape of a fan.

"Wonderful, thank you," Darren said, his face slightly red.

Amara took up a few slices onto her plate. Dried mangos had always been so sweet, she wasn't sure what to expect from fresh ones. When she bit into a slice, it was just as sweet, but the texture was different, smooth and supple. Something akin to a nectarine, but sweeter and tarter.

"It's wonderful," Amara said.

Selene looked at her, blinking.

"I've never had one fresh," Amara explained.

Selene waved it away. "Of course you haven't. There's much you don't know. The true taste of a mango, not to mention what runs in your veins."

Amara bit her lip. It was her mother's fault, really, though she didn't want to say that. The dowager countess had hoped to keep her sheltered from all that. To somehow completely transform her into a pure English rose. To blend in, so to speak. No wonder there were days when she'd wanted that more than anything. Just not anymore.

"Our lola and her lola before her were once called the Babaylan." Selene poured them each a glass of pineapple juice mixed with something else she couldn't place. It was delicious and refreshing nonetheless. "Did your mother ever tell you that?"

Selene also offered eggs, rice, and dried fish, much more than they could ever possibly eat.

"No, I'm afraid," Amara admitted. "I don't think she saw a point."

"Couldn't have been easy. We've had English visitors come here. I know how they are. They like their rules. There's a strict and proper place for everything and, more importantly, everyone."

"That's exactly right." Darren snickered. "A rather fastidious bunch we are."

Selene looked down, apologetic, but quickly moved on.

"The Babaylan were the ones everyone came to for healing. Thousands of years ago, they were our doctors, the ones who were trained in all things healing. Not necessarily by choice, but because of their greater connection to the spiritual world."

"They had abilities like my touch."

Selene nodded. "Our ancestors' gift, however, was enhanced. A special blessing from the diwata, guardian of the sacred mountain. Legends say that in exchange, a great sacrifice was made. One of our ancestor's lovers. A most handsome one at that."

"You mean—"

"He was given up to the diwata and never seen again. Whether he was killed or taken to some other realm beyond our own as a slave…no one can say. It was a terrible thing, but your ancestor recognized the need for such a gift. People had fallen sick with plague and the remedies to heal them couldn't keep up. She wanted so badly to help."

Amara cringed at the idea. It was utilitarian, sacrificing one for many. But could she do it? Could she sacrifice Darren to save others? She couldn't bear seeing him suffer again. She didn't think she had loved anyone more in her life. No, of course she couldn't sacrifice him. She was far too selfish.

The distant *ping* of the doorbell came from inside the house, followed by anxious knocks so loud and fierce, they traveled through the halls and out to the patio. Selene rolled her eyes. "The housekeeper will turn them away. I expected this. Truth is, they're going to keep coming until you leave."

"Were they like this with my mother? With Lola?"

"They used to see them both. By appointment. But your mother has been gone for a long time. Now so has our lola."

"But they have you."

"Not enough. Your abilities are much stronger, like your mother's."

The knocks came again.

"Maybe I should consider seeing a few," Amara said softly. "One at a time, perhaps. If I can help them—"

"No!" Darren nearly shouted. "Didn't you see the look in that woman's eyes? She was desperate. Desperate people do desperate things. I don't care how weak of sickness they are, they could still hurt you. You could catch their sickness. If they don't get the result they like…"

"Just how sick are they?"

"I can't know," replied Selene.

"I wish I could help them all." Amara frowned, picking at her food.

"You can't," Darren said. "You'd only get hurt doing so."

"He's right, sadly," Selene said. "You came here to heal your mother. That's what you should do. We'll just have to ignore them."

Amara flinched at yet another set of knocking.

"We'll barricade the door with furniture if we have to," Darren said.

"Then we can't stay long. We'll leave for the cave first thing tomorrow," Amara concluded. More knocks erupted. She wasn't sure she could take this all day. She could only pray the door would hold. Even if it felt selfish. For her mother, she had to be.

Chapter Thirty

Touch

For the hike, Amara wore her most durable clothing. The Darbys had been most kind to provide a divided skirt of the deepest blue. At the moment, she kept the front panel buttoned, leaving it a regular, albeit narrow skirt, but if necessary, she could unbutton the panel and essentially turn them into wide-set trousers.

They were rather comfortable and very practical for climbing over rough terrain.

"What do you think?" She turned around to Darren. She didn't mind him watching her dress now. He had already seen her naked form and now so much more.

"Quite nice on you." He smiled with teeth.

"They're supposed to be the latest in fashion. For riding and cycling."

"A regular pair of trousers would have worked just the same."

She sniffed. A split skirt was enough of a deviance from her usual fashions as she could stand. This one was so much narrower and flatter than she was used to.

She flinched. Another wave of knocks snapped her out of her reverie.

"The people here are quite persistent." Darren sighed. "I can't believe I'm saying this, but I think I'm actually looking forward to some peace and quiet in the jungle."

Murmurs from the crowd echoed in the hall. It was impossible to ignore. She couldn't make out everything that was being said, but a few words rose above the roar.

"Just one touch!" someone cried out in Tagalog. "Please."

"Do you think that's all they want?" Amara asked Darren. "One touch?"

She approached the door, shaking from the weight of the crowd.

"Amara," Darren said sharply. He tugged on her wrist. "They could—"

"They wouldn't hurt me," she argued. "If all they want is a single touch, it shouldn't take much time at all. Perhaps I owe it to them."

As a powerful Babaylan, bestowed this enhanced gift from the diwata herself, Amara had a duty to these people. Her gift would always be needed. Even as modern hospitals made their way to the islands. But she couldn't stay. And she couldn't heal everyone. Maybe that was the part of her gift that actually made it a curse. There would always be those she didn't help.

"I'm just going to say *hello*."

But when Amara placed a hand on the doorknob, Darren clutched it.

"Against all those people, I might not be able to protect you," he warned, worry glossing his eyes.

"I'll be fine," Amara persisted. He was being over-protective. These people were kin. If they wanted her help, they wouldn't dare hurt her. Grace earlier had just gotten overly excited.

Still, Darren kept close, his arms out and his body stiffening as if to make himself an iron shield.

As she stepped out and down the walkway, the crowd parted with a collective gasp. Could she really be so revered? For a gift she still wasn't entirely sure she possessed? Sure, her hands had warmed with Grace, but what if it had been only temporary? For someone in the crowd, maybe that would be enough.

She blinked and the mass of people closed in again. Whether she wanted to or not, she had no choice but to get to work. She touched her hands to the faces of as many people as she could. Many closed their eyes, openly shedding tears. Others fell to their knees.

Was she actually healing them? Was she really doing it? What was she healing, exactly? She might never know, but that same warmth returned to her hands. How come she hadn't noticed it before, especially when she'd grasped her mother's hand? It truly troubled her.

While her mother had lain sick in her bed, Amara had held her hand so often. Maybe she'd just never noticed or maybe it was the island itself that was making her stronger. Something not just about the land, but the air that she breathed in. The scents. The closer angle of the Earth to the sun. Who knew?

She raised her chin and looked out down the street. A long trail of people extended down both sides of the sidewalk. The line just kept going. She couldn't even see where it ended. She was encountering far more people than she'd thought she would.

Darren grabbed her arm and pulled her back. "We have to go back in. It's dangerous."

His words did not go unnoticed. There were immediate shouts and whispers. People were telling others that he was trying to make her leave. The crowd continued to press in.

"I'll come back," Amara tried to promise them in Tagalog.

"When?" they demanded. "How long will you stay?"

"I have to return to London soon. I have to."

Darren started pulling her even harder then. "He's making her return to London," someone shouted.

There were immediate shouts and jeers, which only hastened Darren's tugs. Amara wanted to stay there and reassure them, but the crowd was getting out of hand. Soon, they would crush her, especially now that they were angered.

Though she wanted to follow Darren through the crowd, her delay widened the space between them. She was starting to get caught on other people. Their arms and fingers stretched out for the slightest graze. She turned and grasped one straining hand just for a second. When she turned back she couldn't see Darren any longer. The tight bodies blocked out everything ahead.

Panicked, she shouted his name, fully expecting him to shout back, but she heard nothing. She had lost him completely. Had he returned back to the house? He wouldn't have.

She was about to shout his name again when there was a scream. To Amara's relief, the crowd parted. She had no idea why. Not until she saw red.

Darren was lying in a pool of blood, his hands gripped to his side and gasping. She heard another scream, not realizing it was her own until a hand touched her shoulder.

Amara turned around to see Selene. She didn't have the words. She didn't even know what had happened. He'd had her hand one moment and the next…

Amara knelt down beside him.

"It's going to be all right," she said, trying to reassure not just him, but herself. She couldn't watch as Selene pulled his hand away and examined his wound. Someone had stabbed him. Someone had stabbed him. Amara repeated this over and over. She was waiting for it to make sense. But nothing did.

Worst of all, she couldn't heal this. She didn't know what it was, instinct, maybe, but something told her touch wouldn't be enough by a longshot. That he would die.

The crowd had fully disbanded then, running mostly in terror. She didn't know what they feared more: getting stabbed themselves or being accused of murder.

"I don't think the knife hit anything vital, but we have to stop the bleeding. We have to bring him inside." Selene nudged her. "Grab his legs."

It took a moment for Amara to register those words before doing as she'd been told. Yes, bringing him inside was the most sensible thing to do. But it was a struggle. Even half his weight would have been.

At the slightest movement, Darren jerked and groaned, especially as they went up the steps of the portico. She was surprised he didn't altogether scream. The way his face had gone pale, he was undoubtedly in great pain. Something she wished desperately to wash away. The pain must have been awful.

"We're almost there," she told him. This wasn't just Darren. This was her husband. She needed to care for him just as he had cared for her. He had tried to, anyway. Even if she didn't always listen. Now, she wished she had. For this, she'd have to make a thousand apologies. And that still might not be enough. He'd be so angry with her, he'd—

"Amara," Selene called out her name sharply. "Focus."

Amara nodded. She needed to stay positive. If she couldn't manage that, she needed to at least clear her mind. She tried to focus on the sound of their steps. One after the other until they placed him onto the cushioned settee. There was so much blood, it dripped down onto the rug. Fittingly almost, it, too, was red.

"What happened out there?" Selene demanded. She was already gathering up throw blankets and little pillows to press into the wound.

"I don't know. I told them I had to go. Darren was tugging me away. Then someone shouted something about me going back to London. I think they thought he was forcing me. Against my will."

Selene shook her head.

"They're not thinking rationally. Heaven knows they hold enough resentment for the British."

"Darren warned me it would be dangerous. I just never thought... I never thought it would be dangerous for *him*."

"Yes, what you did was very stupid. For both of you. Here." Selene directed her to the decorative pillows and blankets pressed over the wound. "Hold this. I'll be right back."

"I'm sorry," Amara said meekly. But she was hardly apologizing to the right person. It was Darren she should be apologizing to.

"I'm sorry to you too," she mumbled to Darren.

"It's fine." He opened his eyes briefly. "Not…your…fault…"

When Selene returned she began dressing the wound. Not daring to look at the open gash a second time, Amara kept her gaze on Darren's face. His eyes squeezed shut and his jaw clenched at the pain. Amara tried to hum a song for comfort, but it didn't seem to work. Nothing she did could.

"There." Selene pulled her hands away from the clean and well-fitted bandage. "I think he's stopped bleeding."

Finally, Darren went still.

"We must call a doctor," Amara said.

Selene turned up at her. "That's me."

"Then you can help him, can't you?" Her voice ached.

"So long as it doesn't get infected or open up again. I can't say either way."

"What are his odds? Please be honest."

"I have some herbs I think will help." She shrugged. "Fifty-fifty. The odds will be better with an emerald."

Amara chewed her lip. That too felt like a gamble. She still wasn't entirely convinced they would work. Not until she saw it with her own two eyes. And yet, hadn't she felt it already? The warming of her hands? That had to mean something was working. It had to.

She needed to venture into the jungle more than ever. Only now, she'd be alone. She grazed a finger down his face. His eyes were staring at her widely.

"Don't worry," she whispered. "You're going to be fine."

"It's not me I'm worried about. It's you. In the jungle. All by yourself," he said.

He could die and yet the fear in his eyes was only for her.

"I could come with," Selene offered.

"No," Amara said adamantly. "Someone needs to care for Darren. You're the only one here I trust."

Selene couldn't do both. Going alone was the only option.

"Amara—"

"I know the way by heart." She tried to shush Darren. "And it's not a far journey. I'll be back before you know it. Who knows, maybe the jungle will know me and help ease the way." Lola had said so herself.

It was a fanciful idea, but one to which she clung nonetheless.

CHAPTER THIRTY-ONE
Jungle Orchid

Unlike the grayscale colors of London, Manila was bursting with colors. The hackney she'd hired, or kalesa, as it was called here, was brightly colored in yellow and red and black trim, just like everything else. It helped make things a little more cheerful, but not by much.

She wore thin, long sleeves that were dosed with a ylang-ylang solution Selene promised would keep the bugs away. Most of all mosquitos. She had a tiny bottle of it reapply if needed, right alongside her water canister. She was as prepared as she would ever be.

The kalesa took Amara to the Laguna Province as far as the roads might allow, right to the base of the sacred mountain. The driver seemed worried for her, but Amara tried to seem unbothered. If not for the man's sake, then for herself.

She walked along the edges of the mountain, warm and humid air breathing out over her. It felt unpleasant on her skin, as if the jungle itself were warning her not to enter. *I'm not afraid*, she told herself. She just had to stay focused and find the official entrance Lola had told her about. She grew worried vegetation might have covered it over the years. Maybe it wouldn't look as Lola had described it. Maybe she'd missed it altogether and would need to retrace her steps.

She was close to turning around when something stopped

her. The small alcove surrounded entirely by mountains seemed to call out to her. She didn't need to see it so much as *feel* it. This was the intuition Lola had told her about, a thing she hadn't understood until now. The way it lit up her senses and drove away her doubts. She just seemed to know.

This was it.

Her ancestors had carved out the entrance generations ago. It was deep enough that the vegetation couldn't hide its inward curve. Still, passersby who didn't know what to look for would likely assume it was just some natural formation. Nature had indeed taken over again.

She pushed back branches and leaves at the far-right corner. A sculpted single wing shone in the bright sunshine. A brilliant, eye-catching white marble. At the other side, the tip of a sculpture just barely peeked out above a twisted column of leaves and vines.

At one point, the wings were connected in a beautiful arch-way, Lola told her. Bits of stone were still there, littered across the ground. She could almost picture it. Although the stone was covered in moss and rounded from age, it still held a certain majesty. A grandness that seemed to declare that there was something special about the jungle ahead. That this was the territory protected by the diwata. She could already feel the magic. A certain sparkle in the air. The same that gave the emeralds their healing power.

Thinking of them kept her moving forward. Amara took one cautious step at a time and entered the shaded canopy. Here the jungle wasn't dense. Just loud. There had to be millions of buzzing insects. Under the trees and loops of vines, it was surprisingly dark too but still as humid as ever. She repeated Lola's directions in her head.

She was lucky, supposedly. At this time of year, the jade orchid would still be in bloom. Once she found it, all she needed to do was follow its long vines and roots straight to a stairway. She expected the steps to be covered in tons of dead vegetation just like the winged archway and barely walkable. But it would still be a proper path and that was better than nothing.

She kept her eyes peeled for any hint of that strange blue color. Blue, her lola had told her, was the rarest color in the plant kingdom, but somehow the jade orchid had achieved it. The color was also far more vivid at night for the sake of the flower's pollinators: bats.

Amara shivered at the thought, even if it was the least of her worries. The mountain was home to all sorts of creatures, particularly supernatural ones. If she were to cross one, she was to pretend they didn't exist. Walk past them no matter what they said or however they tried to lure her. No matter what they promised, they couldn't be trusted. It was best not to engage, she repeated to herself. She just prayed they didn't follow her home like Lola had said they might.

Whether or not she believed Lola's tales, she couldn't ease the fear that tightened around her heart. It was instinctual, a memory from a forgotten past that didn't belong to her.

She knew better than to fear the venomous snakes and bugs. Not when the diwata was here, watching over this land and now over her. Lola had cautioned her not to damage the plants and other wildlife for a reason. She could only take home the emeralds and nothing else. No matter how much the orchids tempted her. Her ancestor had faced the consequences of doing so once. Though Lola hadn't told her what those consequences had been, Amara wouldn't dare risk it.

She already had a terrible feeling of what was to come. When Darren got hurt, the pain that twisted her heart was stronger than she had ever known. Rivaled only by her mother's worsening illness. Only something supernatural could save him. This jungle, the way it smelled, rich and almost sweet… Perhaps the air alone could heal.

To think it was just outside of the islands' busiest city, entirely untouched. But how long would that last? Part of her feared for the jungle and the diwata that watched over it.

Not more than she feared for Darren, however. That was who mattered to her now. Aside from her mother and once, her father, no one had ever meant so much to her. A feeling she was now certain had been there for years.

She'd just never imagined he'd actually marry her. Now that he had, he was slipping through her fingers. She couldn't allow it. Though she was tempted to get her knife, she pushed aside an entanglement of vines and pulled her way through. She would only break the vegetation if she really had to.

According to Lola, she didn't need to go more than twenty to thirty paces inside to find the flower.

But she was already thirty paces in. Other orchids began to encroach her path. Dangling from moss-covered tree trunks, the speckled yellows and magentas were almost mesmerizing. With long, ruffled petals, these were different from the Phalaenopsis orchids she had seen in London exhibitions. Dewdrops clung to its petals, making them glisten and sparkle.

How much might they be worth if she brought them home? Orchids this rare could be worth exorbitant amounts. But as much as she was tempted, she couldn't even think of it. Not with Darren waiting. She was looking for the jade orchid. Nothing else.

The problem was that the orchid was meant to be seen at night, not during the day. She wouldn't dare consider coming here at night, though. The jungle was far more dangerous then.

She was beginning to panic. What if the plant Lola had relied on was long dead? *"It holds too much magic,"* Lola had responded simply to the question back in London. More than anything else, it was faith that Amara needed. That was the only thing that could possibly keep her going.

She closed her eyes and tried to believe. Maybe with fresher, calmer eyes, she'd find it. When she opened them and gazed around, a streak of blue crossed her vision. The color was so subtle, she almost missed it. On the jungle floor, the spent, bluish-purple flowers confirmed it. Her lola had been right: the color was unusual for the plant kingdom, most unusual.

She tilted her head up to get a better look. Between a tangle of vines, a sudden sliver of sunlight lit it up like a blue electric bulb. She pushed away the vegetation and revealed the rest of it: a cylindrical clump of blue flowers, its petals curved like claws pointing to the sky.

Perhaps she was imagining it, but when she reached out, they seemed to lean into her touch. The flower's petals blossomed a half inch, as if to take her in. *It's just a trick of the light*, she told herself. *An illusion caused by the light bouncing from the dew.*

She paused to drink from her canteen. In a show of offering, Amara shared, pouring the water over the vines just as Lola had told her to do. Instantly, they changed color. Not just that, they expanded. Only that didn't seem a sufficient enough word. They *grew*. The once-silver root plumped and flashed green, not just where she poured the water, but northward, spiraling along the tree and jungle floor. This wasn't natural. Amara stared wide-eyed. This was the enchanted part of the jungle she almost didn't believe.

At last when the jungle's magic was confirmed, Amara became intrepid. In utter awe, she ran, following along its vines downward into a ravine. Each step took her deeper and deeper into the jungle. She was totally at its mercy. Whatever it threw at her, she only had a blade with which to defend herself. And yet she didn't feel afraid.

She was nearly out of breath when she came upon a glittering stream. It was just what she needed. She splashed the water over her face, grateful for the cool refreshment. Unlike the jungle all around her, it wasn't the least bit warm. It probably came from deep within the mountains. She filled from her canteen too, fully catching her breath before continuing on.

As harsh as the jungle seemed, it was nurturing too. She could think of worse places, especially in London. She began to walk with ease, maybe even a bit of confidence. But she couldn't let herself get too carried away. At every turn, there were still threats.

She looked up at the dense and varied tree canopy, her eyes searching for monkeys that Lola said would sometimes stalk humans. But in this part of the jungle, it seemed quiet, too quiet. Maybe this was the part of the jungle the supernatural claimed. Monkeys knew better than to venture here.

Her eyes were still skyward when her toe hit something hard. She stumbled forward, her hand landing on a flat surface of rock. This had to have been it. The most important piece of the journey her lola had described. Finding it meant she was near the end. It had almost felt too easy.

She dropped fully to her knees and peeled back the dead, rotting leaves. Wet stone cooled her fingers, making her shiver. What could only be a step. Jagged and worn in some places, it had to have been carved out of the mountain itself centuries ago.

She mounted the steps. She was almost there. The stairs would lead her straight into the cave, straight to salvation. Not just for her and her mother, but for Darren. If it wasn't so hot and humid, she probably wouldn't even have broken a sweat. Climbing the steps was that easy. Her whole life she had been destined to come here, to find the emeralds. There was nothing stopping her. Nothing except a shadow.

Foreboding darkness swept over the path first, then over her head.

She went still, but vegetation continued to crinkle under the weight of someone's steps. Just like her lola had warned, something supernatural had indeed followed her.

Whoever or whatever it was closed in. Suddenly, the trees and insects seemed to go even more quiet. As if the jungle itself were trying to warn her. But what good was a warning when it was already too late?

CHAPTER THIRTY-TWO
Wounded

IN THE CROWD, Darren thought he had been seeing things. It had just been a flash for a split second, but now, he was sure he had been there. Julius. He'd recognize his ugly mug anywhere.

He had tried to convince himself he was mistaken. But now that he was regaining his senses, he knew for certain. And now it was too late. All he could think of was Amara. Had his mind been clearer, he would have warned her. He had fallen asleep before he could put all the dots together. And by the time he'd woken up, she was gone.

"I have to help her, warn her." Darren tried to get up from the sofa. "It's not too late."

He was halfway up when Selene came running. "Don't you dare," she warned him crossly. "I'll tie you to the bed if I have to."

"But the man who stabbed me..." He tried to explain between breaths. "He'll be after her too."

"Don't worry about that. The jungle will protect her. She's deep in it by now. Don't you understand? There's no turning back."

The only thing that made Darren feel slightly better was that Julius didn't want to hurt her. He wanted to take her for himself, which wasn't much better. Darren uselessly gripped the blanket and threw it aside. He couldn't allow it. Not a second time. Not when she was finally his. He couldn't fail this time.

"Don't!" Selene barked again, her voice so fierce, his immediate instinct was to back down. He could have laughed. No one stood in his way. Especially when it came to something he truly wanted. And Amara was everything he wanted. Frankly, he had never wanted anything more in his life. Not even if he could bring his mother back or his father to the way he used to be. It all just felt like fate bringing him exactly where he needed to be alongside Amara.

He stumbled onto the floor, barely able to stand again. A battle raged within him: between his desperation to find and warn her and the pain that screamed throughout his entire body.

"What do you suggest I do?" he demanded of Selene. "Sit here and do nothing?"

"Yes. And pray that wound doesn't get infected. If not for yourself, then for Amara."

"You don't understand. If I don't get out there and fight off Julius—"

"'Fight off'? You're in no condition." She shook her head, frowning.

"I have a pistol."

Selene rolled her eyes and shut the door. "Just try to get some sleep."

As he lay there, all he could do was sweat. The heat was getting to him. The fans offered little relief.

"Hello," Amara's follower said.

Instantly, she knew. This was no supernatural being. She might have begged for that instead. No, this was worse.

"For how long?" Amara froze. She didn't dare turn around.

"The moment you arrived on the island," Julius replied calmly. "I must say, it is lovely to see you."

He spoke with such refinement, it was as if they were speaking in any London ballroom, not here in the wild jungle. As if she didn't have dirt smeared on her clothing. She took a breath and drank from her canteen, trying to pretend like his presence didn't bother her. In truth, every bone in her body shook with terror. Perhaps it was the sudden rush of blood that brought her clarity and understanding. Suddenly, she knew.

"You were the one." Amara swept around to confront him. "You were the one in the crowd who stabbed him."

It was all part of some plan, she realized now.

"I tried to get you on my side," he said, his face drenched with sweat. "I thought you'd relish in the destruction of the Order. I told you what they do and still… Why won't you listen?"

"All I want is for my mother to get well." And now Darren. But he already knew that, didn't he? For all he knew, Darren was dead.

"You took advantage of me, you know." He slicked his hair back. "Encouraging me to drink. Taking me to my room. Very unladylike." He clucked his tongue.

"As if I'd have to get you drunk to get you to bed." She sneered.

"No, you were after the key." His voice hardened. "I know that now. Tell me, if I hadn't passed out, how far would you have gone? What would you have done? Did Pierce know you would have done so much more?"

She shook her head, cringing at the possibility. She would have knocked him over the head with a lamp, anything. "What difference does that make? He's dead," she lied.

What more did he want? He had his revenge. He'd claimed he didn't want the emeralds. Maybe he really did.

"Isn't that enough payment for his family's wrongs?" she asked of him, as if he might ever see reason.

"Of course not."

"You want the emeralds, don't you? You're a hypocrite." Amara spit. "You're no different than the Silver Order."

"I am simply claiming my due. If it weren't for me, Pierce

would have taken those emeralds. I am only taking the same."

Amara didn't know what got into her. She suddenly forgot her fear and laughed. After all his talk about how wrong it was, that the Order was nothing but thieves. As much as he was trying to convince himself otherwise, he was just like everyone else. More than that, he was a fool.

"I'm owed this," he barked over her laughter. "My family is owed this."

"From the Order, not from me. Nor from the jungle. Or the one who guards it."

"It would be no different than if Pierces took the emeralds and I stole it out of the headquarters myself."

"They didn't take an emerald from you, they took a sapphire. That's what you should steal back. Not—"

"Damn it, woman, don't you think I've tried?" He covered his eyes with his hand. "It's a secret too well kept. This, yes, this is the only way the debt can be repaid."

He started walking past her toward the cave opening where it was nestled within the side of the mountain. Using a blade, he sliced through vines that covered the entrance like a curtain. Amara winced at the unnecessary violence. He could have simply pushed the vines aside. The diwata wouldn't like this.

She waited for some reaction. A branch or even a tree to fall. Something. For a long moment, Amara couldn't move. She could only watch.

"I daresay you have plenty to spare!" Julius shouted back at her.

Her best option at the moment was to run. But she couldn't leave without the emeralds. For all she knew, Darren was close to death. So was her own mother.

Instead, she stepped inside. Julius lit a small electric torch that looked almost like a whiskey flask. It gave out a weak but sufficient glow. The cave was small, no larger than a broom closet. And yet it shimmered all around. Shards of emeralds covered every inch of the cave. They both stared up, equally stunned.

"It's unbelievable," Julius said. "I never imagined there would be so many. Damn the healing properties. If we were to mine these, we'd have millions."

The diwata had to shudder at that.

He didn't need it, not with his private yacht and self-proclaimed resources. But this wasn't about need—it was revenge.

"You don't care about money," Amara said matter-of-factly. "This is about vengeance. Over what, something that happened generations ago?" It was ridiculous.

His mouth twisted, fury building inside him. "If the Order hadn't taken our sapphire, we could have had power and influence just like the Order had."

"You think a single sapphire could give you the power the Order has?"

"You know not what it does. My grandfather had plans. Great plans."

Amara scoffed.

"They were better men," he said. "You think just because you've gotten to know Darren Pierce, you know them all? You don't know them as I know them. They are far crueler than you think, each generation worse than the last."

Amara refused to believe it. Darren was an improvement, a vast one.

"What will you do with them?" Amara asked as she gazed upon the irregular and glistening facets. Each one of them precious to her.

"I told you knowledge is meant to be shared." He threw his arms out.

"It is not *yours* to share," she snapped. He really was like everyone in the Order, only worse.

"Don't be selfish. I think it's a gift your ancestors have held secret long enough." He touched one of the stones that clung to the stonewall. Even that felt like a violation. She couldn't stop herself. Instinct demanded that she yank his arm away.

When she did, she felt a power that was more than just her own, but perhaps that of the diwata herself.

Julius was, of course, unaffected. "I would stab my own mother just to see their magic."

Amara stared at him, confused and disgusted.

"Why do you think I stabbed Pierce merely once? I knew how it would drive you to find the emeralds at once." He looked up to the ceiling. "Oh, how I craved to do it so much more."

He was going to follow her out of here. Back to a defenseless Darren and Selene.

"You want me to show you how the crystals work? Then what? Then you're going to kill him, anyway..." Amara breathed out. "In that stupid twisted way you call justice."

Amara grit her teeth, her outrage devolving into anger. Was there no persuading him away from this madness?

"How can you actually believe you're doing the world good and at the same time commit murder?" she demanded to know.

"I won't deny it." He pushed out his lower lip and shrugged. Perhaps there is a bit of vengeance involved. Perhaps a bit of jealousy too."

He eyed her. Did he still harbor feelings for her? He should have been angry with her for her tricking him on the *New Dawn*. And yet he was oddly calm.

"We're married," Amara said stiffly. "There's no undoing that."

Julius laughed. But behind it was deep bitterness that could only result, not from a broken heart, but from a damaged ego.

"Unfortunately, I refuse to allow Pierce to ride off into the sunset with you. Not when he's denied me and my family so much."

That was what he grieved most, Amara realized. Power.

"How sweet will it be to give it to him with these stones then take his life away."

Amara could have crumpled at the thought. Looking down on the ground, she steeled herself. It was made of emeralds too, as if the entire cave were a giant, beautiful geode. But unlike the jagged cave walls that surrounded her, the floor was less jagged. In fact, it was perfectly smooth. How many thousands of years ago had this place been discovered? The floor with long stretches of cut lines seemed to have been manmade. This was more than just a cave, she realized with a rush of blood to her head. It was a temple.

This place was sacred, more than she could possibly know. She could sense a sort of pious aura, much like electricity buzzing through the air. She felt it on the tip of her finger when she touched any part of the cave. Something she was sure no one else, least of all Julius, could channel. Only she and her ancestors for many, many years.

"Go on." Julius handed her a small chisel. "Take what you need."

His words brought her back to reality. Regardless of Julius and his plans, she had to remember her own plans. She had to survive. More than just her mother depended on her—Darren did too. She'd figure out something after she saved him. She had to.

Even though she had one strapped to her waist, Amara snatched the chisel from Julius and jabbed it into the stone. He handed her a hammer too. With one whack, the crystal shard broke off into her hand. Like a lightbulb, something inside her ignited. Her hands warmed just like they had when she'd touched all those people who had gathered at her cousin's house. For a second, the gem glowed too, lighting up the rest of the emeralds around her.

Julius stepped back, intimidated by the sudden show of power. Clearly, he hadn't expected it to be so great. Neither had she. Until now.

"Give me that." Julius took the emerald into his own hands. He squeezed and opened his hand again. But it didn't glow. Of course not.

She snatched it back. Her eyebrow quirked as if to say: *did you really think you, of all people, could get it to work?* She had rather hoped it might burn his hand.

He huffed and took up the small chisel, roughly breaking off a piece of the cave himself. She winced. The diwata wouldn't like this at all. She had another urge to push him away. *But all in good time*, she told herself. *All in good time.* She didn't know how he might react or just how uncontrollable his anger was.

Just shoving her in this cave could have dire consequences. The shards of crystals pointed out at least six inches deep at every angle. For all she knew, they were sharp enough to cut. Maybe even puncture if she fell against them hard enough.

Julius closed his fingers around three emeralds. Each of them dull and dark. The one in her hand, however, continued to shimmer.

Julius was captured again by its radiance.

"What gives this cave its power?" he demanded to know.

Amara shrugged. He might as well ask what gave the jungle its life. What she really wondered was how many other crystals out there existed like this one or his mystical sapphire. Were there other gems with strange, albeit powerful properties? Maybe people wore them as rings and bracelets without truly knowing their properties, thinking of them as nothing more than lucky charms.

Thanks to the diwata, her ancestors were the only ones to discover the power of these stones. Them and the Order, she supposed. She could understand the Order's urge to explore and go on expeditions like this one. If she had heard of a similar gem elsewhere, wouldn't she want to search for it too? *No*, she told herself. It was just a wild, careless thought. She would never claim what wasn't hers. She certainly wouldn't hurt others for it.

They both gathered a few more emeralds, Amara cringing every time Julius chipped at the cave. She used her own set of tools now, slipping seven large stones into a small satchel that hung at her waist.

Dropping to her feet as if to lace up her boot, she placed three others in a pocket sewn into the ankle of her split skirts. She was glad she had requested it in Bombay. She had first thought of it on the *Evangeline*. At the time, she'd thought she'd have to protect the gems from Darren. How foolish she'd been. How could she not have seen the love in his eyes from the very beginning? How could she not have felt it radiating from his very skin like she had just a few days ago?

"Shall we?" Julius motioned her out of the cave.

What choice did she have but to move forward? It didn't matter how fast she ran. He'd always be behind her. There was nowhere to go but straight to Darren. He was dead either way.

CHAPTER THIRTY-THREE
Mudslide

"**I** KNOW YOU were after my keys. But tell me, did you at least enjoy yourself?" He kept close behind her as she walked, nearly breathing down her neck. Every time she picked up her pace, he seemed to match it.

"I might ask the same of you. You know how Darren felt for me. Were your efforts to seduce me your own or merely an act of revenge?"

"'Seduce' you?" He wrinkled his nose. "That's a funny way to put it. If you fell in love with me, that's one thing, but I made no effort—"

"That glittering yacht, the food, the clothes, not to mention the ball in Alexandria?" Amara raged. "Don't play with me, Mr. Julius."

"It hardly matters now," Julius said, unaffected. "When you left my ship with Pierce, you sealed your fate. You chose your side. Unfortunately, it was the wrong one."

The cool, unfeeling determination in his voice chilled Amara right down her spine. The tone alone seemed to tell her of all that was to come. Maybe she did have the gift of premonition, because for a moment, she glimpsed her own death.

She'd never known fear like this. But she was determined not to show it. If she was going to get through this, she needed to try to at least feign courage. This was her home, after all. That cave, this jungle—it was in her blood. Somehow, she could use it against him. The jungle was teeming with venomous insects and dangerous animals. It was also riddled with sharp cliffs, valleys, and uneven terrain. One wrong step and he could go careening off the side of the mountain.

The stairway was particularly steep. Built straight into the mountain, there was only about a foot to the edge. From age, erosion—whatever the reason—the steps were unstable. Bits of soil tumbled down the side of the mountain with each of their steps. At times, small rocks rattled down too.

Julius, so sure he'd already won, didn't seem to notice, let alone care.

Amara tested the theory, dropping her feet down harder on the steps. She wasn't sure if it would have any effect, but she prayed that with Julius's heavier steps, it would create something of a disturbance and eventually a landslide. Lola had warned her of them the night before she'd left home. It was one of the jungle's many dangers, especially given her path up the side of it. If it had rained too much in the days before, she'd advised Amara to wait if she could or to proceed, at the very least, with caution.

Amara ran a hand across her forehead. The thick curtain of humidity persisted. Only a sip from her canteen seemed to break it, even if just for a moment. Maybe it was her fear too, but she was dripping sweat now. She couldn't allow Julius to follow her out of this jungle to Darren.

Even if she did manage to create a landslide, it was a risk too. There was a chance neither of them would make it out. She could only hope that enough of the mountain—at least the part on her side—stayed intact. Even then, she would only have a second's warning to jump back and grab a vine, tree branch, or whatever she could. She'd have to stay on her toes.

"Stop!" Julius suddenly grabbed her arm.

She twisted around, fearful he was onto her plan.

Julius went completely still, as if listening for a soon-to-come quake. As much as Amara held her breath, hoping it would come, it didn't.

"These steps are ancient," he whispered gently. "You must step lightly."

Amara yanked her arm away, annoyed the mountain hadn't even budged. How much more stomping would it take?

She had to get rid of him. His presence, knowing what he would do to Darren, had become unbearable. Even his footfalls began to irritate her, most of all his voice.

The worst part was they were getting closer to the jungle floor. By now, they had reached the halfway point. She didn't have much time left. She pounded her feet down harder.

A few steps more and Julius grabbed her arm again. "What are you trying to do?"

She felt the step beneath her crack and tilt. *Please*, she begged the mountain. She couldn't hide her plan from him much longer. She had to take action now before he threw her over his back and carried her or worse, tied her up.

In answer to Julius's question, she stomped down again and again. First with one foot then with both. She jumped down as hard as she could until she felt like she might break her legs. Terror filled Julius's eyes. She relished it. It was just the encouragement she needed to stomp again. She couldn't stop until the mountain crumbled altogether. She pictured it in her mind, a rush of hope sending her foot down even harder. She needed to invoke the diwata herself.

"Stop!" Julius screamed. He squeezed her arm so hard, her knees buckled.

The shout certainly didn't help matters. The vibrations shook free the last remaining dirt from beneath the steps. The mountainside was beginning to break apart, but Julius still had her arm. She couldn't let him take her down with him.

She yanked her arm back and forth as hard and fast as she could. In the struggle, he fell to his knees, loosening his grip. Amara jumped back.

Julius watched frozen in horror, but only for a moment before he was taken down the side of the cliff in a flurry of dust, dirt, and vegetation.

Amara had barely managed to jump back. As the mountain-side continued to rattle, she realized she wasn't far enough. On her back, she tried her best to scurry away, her limbs not moving nearly fast enough. Right in front of her, the dirt continued to peel away. It was right on her heels.

She had expected the landslide to weaken by now, but it only strengthened. Every slip of rocks and dirt led to another. Entire trees and their roots were pulled down. One after the other, they cracked like twigs, only louder. The whole cliffside was tumbling free in a quake Selene and Darren could likely hear too. Amara couldn't believe what she had done. It had to have been more than just her footfalls that had done it. Rather, it had been the diwata herself, protecting her mountain, taking revenge for what Julius had stolen.

Her palms clutched on to a sharp rock. Though everything finally went still, the mountain continued to roar beneath her. She pulled herself up, but the ground was shaking too unsteadily to gain her footing. She needed to make one last-ditch effort to leap for the nearest tree branch. But before she could jump, the earth disappeared beneath her. For a split second, she hung midair. Then the mountain sucked her downward.

☾

AMARA WOKE UP half-covered in dirt. She was still alive. The only saving grace was that she hadn't been completely buried. Julius, she hoped, hadn't been as lucky. She wasn't about to wait around and find out. She took off, whipping between trees back toward Darren. The farther she ran, the more she could make out the sounds of the civilization. The faint shouts of a distant market-place and horse hooves had never been more welcome. The trees began to clear away, farther and farther apart, until she reached the winged archway.

Her head was pounding, begging her for a break. But the slightest chance that Julius might be close behind her kept her going. She didn't let herself think of it. Legs aching, she continued to run toward the city.

Even though part of her just wanted to keep running, she forced herself to stop and hail a kalesa. She brushed herself off the best she could, but with twigs, leaves, and dirt all over her and probably in her hair, the driver still gave her a look.

"Here." She offered him extra money. "Fly as fast as your horse allows."

Before she could sit down, the kalesa took off with a jerk. The wooden seat, as hard and un-cushioned as it was, was an immense relief. She enjoyed the breeze as they picked up speed, but she still felt anxious, constantly looking over her shoulder. Even if Julius had died back there, she'd likely never let go of this fear of being followed. She'd feel it for the rest of her life. Only when she could see his lifeless body with her own two eyes would she ever be able to relax.

But she couldn't think about that now. She needed to get to Darren. She planned it all in her head. First, she would heal him, then they would immediately leave to book passage. They'd pack their trunks as fast as they could and kiss Selene goodbye.

They'd get on the first boat they could—it didn't matter where it took them. When they sailed away, she could tell him all that had happened. But they couldn't stop until then. They had to keep running.

The problem was she didn't know how long the emeralds would take to fully heal him. She knew how to do it thanks to Lola, but whether or not he'd be able to walk was another thing entirely. Everyone was different, Lola had said. Amara just hoped Darren could heal fast. She'd get one of those wheelchairs if she had to.

She placed a hand over her heart as if that could calm its steady beat. *Breathe,* she commanded herself. *In and out.* She couldn't do anything until she relaxed at least a little bit. The kalesa ride offered her plenty of time. But it was painfully long when all she wanted was to get to Darren.

"Faster," she pleaded with the driver.

When she was almost home, her heart picked up again. She needed to conceal herself. The last thing she wanted was a crowd to gather, not now.

There wasn't much she could do but change her hair. She pulled out her long, tight braids Selene had fashioned and pushed her hair forward until it hung out over her face. Her hair was such a tangled mess, no one would recognize her in a thousand years.

The moment the carriage had stopped, she descended and walked up the steps of her lola's palatial home, one she wished she could have called her own. Maybe someday in the future, she could stay here, if only for the summers.

She and Darren could put all of this behind them. They might not have boarded the ship together, but they had certainly disembarked together. All she needed to do was heal him.

But as soon as she got within five feet of the door, something felt off. She rushed to grip the doorknob. Her heart dropped. It was unlocked. The door swung open. For a moment, she just stood there, going over the possibilities and letting the silence consume her, too scared to go in. All of it weighed down on her mind, overtaking her. "You just needed to take a step forward!" she shouted at herself. *Just one step.*

"Selene?" Amara's voice echoed strangely in the foyer.

If he was dead, how could she endure it? She gathered her courage. She couldn't hesitate anymore. She ran straight to the guest room she and Darren had shared. The door was shut. She knocked, barely able to stand still.

Of course there was no answer. She sucked in a breath and threw the door open. He was right there in bed. Asleep, apparently. His form tucked tightly under the sheets, even his head.

"Darren?"

He was still, too still.

"Darren?" she repeated.

Her heart raced faster. All she needed to do was pull the covers off him and make sure he was still breathing. But something stopped her, keeping her three feet from the bed.

"Darren—" she screamed when the blankets whipped into the air. She was wrong. God, she was so wrong. The person lying under the sheets wasn't Darren. She stumbled backward, collapsing onto the floor.

CHAPTER THIRTY-FOUR

Gone

SITTING UP IN the bed, Julius laughed. A storm seemed to shake the entire room. It didn't make sense—he couldn't have been here already. Unless… Unless he had woken up first. As fast as she had worked to get here, it had already been too late.

"Where is he?" she demanded while he continued his shrill laugh. She was close to smacking him, punching him. But what good would that do? She needed to reason with Julius.

If only he would stop laughing. The longer he went on, the more she began to wonder if he'd have any sense left in him at all.

"You said you wanted to see how the emeralds work," she reminded him when he'd settled momentarily. He needed to let her heal Darren. If nothing else, he needed to do that.

"No need." He cleared his throat. "I decided to skip that component of my plan."

"Where is he?" Amara grit out. She was done with his games. "Just tell me where he is."

"Right back where he belongs. Prison. For your murder."

Amara gaped. She didn't know what to say. "That's impossible." She shouted again for Selene, but there was no response.

"A public execution by your own people couldn't be more fitting, if you think about it. It is fate."

"But how. What did you do? Pay them off?"

"There were witnesses. Those in the crowd yesterday. They

saw how Pierce forcibly pulled you away. You stabbed him in self-defense. Naturally, he retaliated."

Her heart twisted at the idea of Darren imprisoned yet again. There was no knowing his condition. He could very well be dead before the execution.

"Then all I need to do is show them I'm still alive." She would save him. No matter what she had to do or whom she had to bribe.

"You really think I'd allow that?" Julius got up from the bed, all humor gone from his face. He loomed over her, his tall frame imposing. How was she going to defeat him now? She didn't have the advantages of the jungle. Without even Selene to help her, she felt so very alone.

"What are you going to do? Keep me as your prisoner?"

"For a short time. Pierce must face justice here for what he's done. I'm only sorry we won't be able to stay for the execution."

Amara felt ice in her veins. She'd have to kill him herself. No more hoping that he'd die by some other means. It had to be her own hand. And she had to watch the life drain from his eyes. It was the only way she could be sure. A certainty that chilled her through and through.

It was all too foreign and off-putting. Like something out of a nightmare. She wasn't a violent person. Murder wasn't something she had ever thought she'd have the capacity to do. Until now. Until she'd seen the determination Julius had to kill Darren and eventually her too.

In fact, she wanted to strangle him right then and there. But he would no doubt overpower her. She needed to gain the upper hand first. She needed a weapon.

"Give me that." Julius came close and snatched her canteen. He drank greedily. "Lord knows I can't eat anything in this house. No knowing what's poisoned."

Poisoning him wasn't a bad idea, if only she could figure out how.

"Selene!" Amara made one more effort to find her. She had to have been somewhere in this house.

"She's upstairs…" Julius drawled. "That's where she'll stay unless you agree to come with me back to London."

A trip that would likely take weeks, perhaps over a month. She couldn't endure that. Not with Julius, not knowing she'd left Darren here to die.

"I'm not going with you," Amara said stiffly.

"You'd let your own cousin die?"

"You wouldn't," she grit out. Just how far was she willing to go to call his bluff? What might he do?

"You can take the emeralds," she said, trying to persuade him. "Take them and go. You've had your revenge. No matter what I do, Darren will die."

Her heart sank as she realized this was true. In a dank prison, possibly worse than the one on the ship, his odds of survival were low.

"You should be glad I'm not asking for more." Julius took a step closer, eying her up and down. "I should demand you finish what you started."

She winced with disgust. She needed help.

"I want to see Selene. Take me to her first." Amara listened for sounds of struggle coming from above but heard nothing. If Selene was anything like herself or anyone else in her family, she wouldn't have given up so easily. She'd still be fighting.

Julius threw up his hands. "But of course. After you."

He followed closely behind as she made her way into the foyer toward the stairs. Her eyes were glued to the door. Everything in her wanted to bolt, out the door to jail in the heart of the city. They had passed the large compound when she'd first arrived. She knew exactly how to get there.

But she needed to make sure Selene was all right. Even Julius knew Amara wouldn't leave without that reassurance. The stairs creaked under their weight. Selene couldn't be up there—it was too quiet.

"I think somewhere along our trip, while we're enjoying our

first-class accommodations—endless champagne and walks on the promenade—you'll be glad you left with me."

Amara huffed. "You think I'm going to just become your mistress? For what? The champagne? I'll run every chance I get, even if I have to swim."

As she said the words, no matter how intense their meaning, she knew she meant them.

"Then swim you must." He clasped his hands together. "Once we get far enough from shore, I think you'll reconsider."

As they closed in on Selene's room, Amara pushed ahead, shouldering the door open. But just as she feared, the room was empty.

Julius cursed loud enough that she knew it was genuine. "Where is she?"

Amara already knew. The sheets were in disarray. The blanket had been tossed aside and the mattress was exposed. The window was wide open, as they usually were. Nonetheless, it was all too obvious what Selene had done. She'd escaped.

Julius really was a fool. Once more, Amara considered doing the same. Before she could move, Julius took her up by the arm.

"We're leaving now," he barked.

Amara struggled, but it was no use. He pulled her across his torso then began swinging her around, almost as if they were waltzing again. He even began to hum. He was absolutely mad.

"If you were wise, you'd let me go," she pleaded, tears streaming now. What else might she be forced to do? "You've gotten your revenge, haven't you?"

He paused at this. "The best revenge would be *you*."

"What are you going to do? Force me the entire way? Sir, you haven't thought this through."

He smiled, showing off his rather large, grayish teeth. Perhaps he *had* thought this through.

"You'd truly prefer life with Pierce after all he's done? In time, you'll change your mind."

A sudden commotion outside stole both their attention. The

sound of carriage wheels groaning to a stop and a horse nickering. Had one of the locals seen she had returned and already spread word? Before Julius could stop her, she rushed to the window.

Her heart leapt. Mr. Drake descended the carriage and Granger was not far behind.

CHAPTER THIRTY-FIVE
Sacrifice

BEFORE AMARA COULD open her mouth to shout and bang against the window, Julius gripped a hand over her mouth and yanked her backward.

"How could you marry with him?" he demanded quickly, knowing his time was coming to an end. "After what he's done to your parents, you—"

"No," Amara said flatly. "My father's death was his own fault."

As difficult as it was to admit, it was true. She didn't have room in her heart for hatred anymore, not when Darren could fill her so completely.

"Not your father, your mother. The Order is the reason she is sick. A little convenient, this whole voyage, don't you think? Pierce showing up to 'escort' you?"

Amara froze. For a second, she thought she'd gone mad. She couldn't breathe. Her knees went weak. All the fight in her dissipated. Julius seemed to sense this, releasing his grip on her, she crumbled to the floor.

It didn't make sense.

"She's been sick for over a year," she whispered on the cold, tile floor.

"The Order has been planning for some time. Ever since your father returned from Manila emptyhanded." Julius knelt down beside her, gracing a hand along her chin. "I was waiting for the perfect moment to tell you. At sunset, perhaps, when its colors reflected off the ocean before us."

"How, though? She has tuberculosis. How is it—"

"They are alchemists. They have just as many poisons as they do cures and remedies, I assure you." He sneered. "The Silver Order is willing to stop at nothing. Do you really think Pierce would let you get in the way? You'd sooner be dead. Why do you think he married you? What does it matter if you're dead?"

Darren didn't need her to hand over the emeralds anymore. He practically owned them now. All he'd needed to do was marry her.

Suddenly, she questioned everything. How could she have allowed it? How could she have just handed over everything her family had fought to protect for generations? Lola had made the importance of secrecy clear enough. Others had already made sacrifices. She would have to make hers too. Just like her ancestor had done all those years ago with the diwata.

Footfalls sounded down the hall. They woke her from her reverie. Though Julius kept a tight grip, she still struggled, their feet shuffling loud enough Drake and the others were sure to hear.

On her next breath, they were thumping up the stairs. The moment Miller caught sight of Amara, he rushed ahead.

"Countess!"

Mr. Drake and Granger were close behind. Selene too. But no Darren. Of course not. She wouldn't know what to say to him if he were here. She wasn't sure if she could even speak.

Julius pulled Amara to her feet.

"Good day." Julius tipped his head nonchalantly. Mr. Miller and Mr. Drake already had their weapons drawn.

Julius merely smiled at them.

"No need for weapons here. The countess has complete control of whether she stays or leaves. Now that I've informed her of all truths."

And yet Julius still kept a tight grip.

Mr. Drake and Mr. Miller looked at each other. "What truths?" Mr. Miller demanded.

Julius sighed, surprised they didn't already know. "I told her it was the Order who poisoned her mother and made her sick."

"Shit." Mr. Drake guffawed, looking at Miller.

Amara's knees buckled again. Julius held her firm. So it was true.

"No, Darren didn't it do it," Miller waved his hand back and forth, trying to get Amara's attention.

But if it hadn't been him, then it'd been his father. It'd been the Order.

"I have it on good authority he did," said Julius.

"She doesn't believe you," Mr. Miller said. "Do you, my lady?"

"What about his father?" she demanded to know. "The elder Mr. Pierce. Did he—"

"There's an explanation," Mr. Miller answered, his voice sharp.

"Who?" Selene suddenly demanded too. "Who would do such a thing?"

"The Order." Mr. Drake looked down at his feet, finally admitting it. "But not Darren."

"Mr. Pierce is *part* of the Order." Granger raised her voice.

"My lady," Mr. Miller called out to Amara, dropping his weapon slightly. Worry crinkled his brow, as if to silently beg her. "Let us explain."

"How could you go along with it?" Amara eyed both of them. "Did you administer the poison? Or whatever it was? Who did?" She didn't know why it mattered, but she needed to know every detail.

"Marx." Mr. Miller looked to Drake, as if they were just realizing. "That's why the elder Pierce got rid of him."

Mr. Drake nodded. "It has to be. Darren knew nothing about it. Neither did we. We only knew the elder Pierce sacked him.

We just didn't know why."

"But this Marx works for the Order, does he not?" Amara spit.

"He *did*…for Theo Pierce specifically." Mr. Miller lowered his gaze.

"Then *he* gave the directive," Granger put in.

"No, not directly," Mr. Drake said defensively. "You don't know how he's been since his wife's death. He's been distracted and negligent. He must have told Marx to find a way to reclaim the emeralds. He didn't know what he'd do. When he found out, he sacked him. I'm sure of it."

Amara wasn't sure if she believed him.

"If you did end up going to the islands, Theo Pierce wanted to be sure you were protected," Mr. Miller added. "That's why he sent Darren after you."

Amara shook her head, tears filling her eyes.

"You could have stopped him." Even if she didn't know how.

"My lady!" Granger reached out to her. "Please." In utter disbelief, Amara didn't immediately run to them. She no longer fought Julius, either. She just stood there.

"Pierce is dying in a cell," Mr. Drake said stiffly. "We saw it ourselves. Are you going to just let him die?"

An idea that nearly paralyzed her. That was when she knew. What had she been thinking? Of course she couldn't give into Julius. She needed to take the emerald to Darren. Now.

He should not pay for the mistakes of his grieving father, nor the crimes of his ancestors. She had already let go of the hatred that had lingered for generations. To let Darren in, she had to.

"Please," Mr. Drake pleaded. "It will be days until we can reach his father and get him out."

Julius gripped her arm tighter. "That is his due."

"You two had a deal!" Mr. Drake shouted. The argument seemed his last and final hope.

He was right. Darren had risked his life to protect her. All he'd wanted was one emerald. Now he needed it. Not just that, she loved him. Darren was her husband. She had made a vow.

Amara finally stepped ahead and broke her arm free from Julius. But sure enough, Julius grabbed her again.

"Damn woman." Julius wrestled her close. "You'll never see reason!"

He didn't care for justice. All he wanted was suffering. The Order might have been wrong for what they did, but so was Julius. She couldn't forget that.

Mr. Drake and Mr. Miller raised their weapons again, but Julius held her over him like a shield. There was no possibility of getting a shot in at him. She couldn't continue to put at risk the lives of the guards, least of all Selene and Granger. They were both innocent in all this.

"I'll go," she muttered, pulling away from him. "I'll go!"

"No," Selene responded. "Shoot him!"

Selene grabbed Mr. Miller's gun. It went off, loud and piercing, shattering the window behind Amara. The powerful sound startled and reset her senses. In the melee, her anger came back to her. Julius was coming too close to hurting more of who she loved. She needed to fight.

Amara pulled back from Julius's grip, veering left, then right. A far enough distance away that Mr. Drake took his shot, the blast radiating smoke and heat through the room.

Not more than a foot away from her, Julius grabbed his chest. Blood oozed between his fingers. She'd almost expected it to be black. She lurched back. His eyes were still set on her, determined. Instead of coming for her, he crumpled to the floor. He reached out in one useless plea to take her hand.

She couldn't believe she had considered anything he had to say.

"I'm sorry." She looked up at the others. Her vision seemed to clear and come into focus, like she was coming out of a daze.

"You have nothing to apologize for," Mr. Miller said.

"He preyed on your emotions," Mr. Drake said.

"How could the elder Mr. Pierce allow such a thing...?" Granger stuttered, grabbing her throat. She had seen the dowager countess suffer too.

"It's why we want Darren to take over the Order," Mr. Drake tried to explain.

He fell silent when Amara took Granger into her arms. Amara didn't want to think of any of that anymore, only the relief that Granger was safe and well. She clutched Selene next. With a shaky exhale, she released the fear her mind had been holding on to with a death grip.

"They helped me escape," Selene said.

For that, Amara hugged Mr. Miller and Mr. Drake too.

"How—" she began.

"We reached Manila two days ago," Mr. Miller explained. "It took some time and asking around before we found your home. When we did, the police were taking Darren away." He looked down.

"How bad was it?" Amara asked.

"The whole city came out to watch. As much as we wanted to, we couldn't do anything. We made the choice to stand by. T'wasn't easy."

Amara could only imagine. She doubted the police had carried him away with any kind of concern for his wounds. Judging by the look in Mr. Miller's eye, they'd probably dragged him.

"We at least learned where he was going," Mr. Drake said somewhat optimistically. "The Old Bilibid Prison not far from here."

Mr. Miller nodded. "We went there as soon as we could. We had just returned to see if you were back when we saw the door was open. Perhaps we shouldn't have gone. We should have made sure—"

"Don't think of it," Amara said. "Of course I'm glad you went to Darren first. But—but where is he?"

Mr. Miller's face turned even more grave.

For a long moment, no one said a word. But she needed to know. Only no one wanted to deliver the bad news. They exchanged troubled glances. Amara was getting fed up.

"He's still there?" Amara gasped. "Didn't you talk to anyone? What about the Americans?"

"Julius has some kind of connection with them," Mr. Miller said. "They refused to help. They are the ones with the ultimate authority. Not even the British embassy could help us."

"Can't they at least delay the execution?" Amara asked.

"Julius must have paid them handsomely."

"Did you see him? Just tell me," she demanded. "How is Darren?"

"We tried," Mr. Drake said. "They wouldn't let us."

"But he's alive." Her heart picked up. "Isn't he?"

"As of a few hours ago, yes. Right now? I couldn't say. The place was filthy, Countess. But they're willing to accept bribes. It just has to be more than whatever Julius provided."

"But we don't have enough," Mr. Miller cut in, as if to prevent Amara from getting her hopes up. "Not without getting in touch with Pierce's father first. We've sent a wireless message, but—"

"Forget money. I have something better." Amara didn't waste any time. She moved down the hall and went straight out to the street to hire another kalesa.

Everyone followed without argument. She was willing to do anything for Darren, even if that meant offering a limb. She hated that she had ever doubted that. Especially when she had accepted that Darren's father's mistakes were not his own. They were mistakes that had been borne out of negligence, a sadness that had swelled in the elder Mr. Pierce since his wife's death. Ultimately, Darren's father had even tried to protect her during her inevitable trip. The Order needed change was all. Change that she was certain Darren would initiate at once. The news had just been so shocking and unexpected, she hadn't known what to do.

Behind her, Selene struggled to keep up. "You have them, don't you?" she shouted in Tagalog.

Amara nodded.

"Can you trust them?" Selene asked.

Amara gave her a look.

"Emphatically?"

"Yes!" Amara almost shouted. She had risked all of their lives. She at least owed them her trust.

"They came back for me," Amara told her in Tagalog. "They all could have gone home. Granger to her mother in London and Mr. Drake and Mr. Miller back to the Order. Instead, they returned for us."

"Good." Selene seemed to believe her. "But it will do little good now. You and you alone can help Mr. Pierce now."

"I need only give them one stone."

"That is if they believe. Manila has become a modern, forward-thinking city, Amara. Not everyone subscribes to the old ways."

"Then I will give them *all* the stones if I have to. All but the one needed to heal Darren and the one to heal my mother."

"Just...remember, nothing is ever guaranteed." Selene was trying to prepare her for disappointment.

"I'll pray, then," Amara said.

Since Darren had been stabbed, she hadn't stopped.

CHAPTER THIRTY-SIX

Green

THE NEAR-CONSTANT DRIP of water was beginning to drive Darren mad. In this heat, his shirt was soaked in sweat and nearly black with grime. And that was the least of his worries. With the moisture and mold came any number of bugs, spiders, lice, and bedbugs, not to mention kitten-sized rats.

They made the ache at his sides seem like a gift and the thin jute rug that was his mattress seem like a comfort. Like in England, one could pay for nicer accommodations. He had enough for his own cell and better portions of food, just not enough to get himself out of here.

He simply needed access to his funds. And a lot of it. The general dislike the people here had for the British ran deeper than he'd expected. He'd be lucky if they didn't execute him first. Or if his wound didn't open up again.

He was beginning to wonder if this had been his father's plan all along. To send him on a suicide mission before he could question his reign. If only Amara had opened his eyes sooner. He could have... It didn't matter. Not when she was on his mind again.

If someone could just get him word that Amara was safe, that would be enough. The constant drip of water was nothing. It was the worrying that he could endure no longer. He had long given up on the idea that he'd be able to help her. He had to hope and pray that she could retrieve the emeralds on her own. She was strong, stronger than any countess had a right to be. She might not be able to out-muscle Julius, but she could certainly outwit him. She had managed it with those ruffians once, and she could do it again. The thought at least was one small comfort.

But as night fell, it was getting harder to keep his faith. The other prisoners all had thin and drawn bodies with the same tortured expression on their faces. Some would be impossible to forget. What had they done? He had plenty of time to think of the possibilities. Did they truly deserve this kind of punishment?

He was reminded all too well that there was much suffering in the world. Any time life offered its few pleasures like Amara, he had to grasp on to it and never let go. If he had any courage, he would have been more blunt about his true feelings from the start. Why had the words been so caught in his throat that day he'd seen her in the rain?

As the seasons had worn on, he'd been too fearful of hearing 'no.' He'd felt certain that without noble blood running his veins, his money alone wouldn't be enough. He'd been a damn fool. They might have been married for years, getting to know each other carnally and spiritually for years.

Now that he'd lost her, he wouldn't get a second chance. It was too late. In the blink of an eye, it seemed, his life had come and gone. The pain radiating from his wound had grown so constant, he was starting to believe it had always been there. Until death claimed him, it always would be.

Whatever Selene had been giving him, that strange paste and pulpy drink might not have fully healed him, but it had done something just as valuable: it had taken the pain away. Now the pain was so great, he was getting delusional. What he wouldn't pay for those tinctures. Her family did indeed have a gift.

Nothing else could have taken away this kind of pain. Nothing that wasn't some sort of narcotic like morphine. Unlike those drugs, her botanical came without fog. If Selene's gift was considered weak, then just how strong was Amara's?

No matter how far-fetched his father's stories about her family had gotten, Darren had always believed her family was special in some way. His father wouldn't have paid them so much attention otherwise. But it was different seeing it all play out before his eyes. Hell, Darren had felt the power in his own flesh. He had held a newfound reverence for them.

Now all he felt was desperation. For the worst possible thing: death. He couldn't endure this pain any longer. He'd always thought he was stronger than that. He had too much honor. He was always so determined to see things through, no matter how bad things got. No matter how violent his father became.

Discomfited by the thought, he jerked his head from side to side. Movement, no matter how insignificant, caused him pain. He groaned, but at least it was enough to temper the emotional hell bubbling deep within him. He didn't want to be reminded of things he hadn't resolved. There was so much he needed to say. So much he needed to do.

The first was to tell Amara the truth. As one last blow before Darren had been taken away by the police, Julius told him something he'd thought at first had been a lie.

The Order had poisoned Amara's mother. The more he thought of it, the more it made sense. His father hadn't known at first. He was sure of that. He'd been too distracted, too overcome with anger at his wife's death to plan something so elaborate. But nonetheless, his neglect had allowed it to happen. Darren had no doubt about who had done it. Marx. That was why he'd been sacked. His father must have found out what Marx had done and had kept it to himself. He'd lied.

In a way, Darren had been just like his father. Rather than deal with whatever was going on in his head, he'd run away to drinks and society parties, chasing after Amara.

He should have taken over the moment he sensed his father was losing control to men like Marx. And yet, he hadn't.

If he lived, he'd have to take charge and clean house. More importantly, he had to tell Amara. A thought that stabbed his gut but felt so necessary nonetheless.

So he couldn't embrace death. He needed to hold on so Amara could know the truth and his father didn't inadvertently end up hurting anyone else. Even if that meant Amara might leave him.

The thought made him ache even more, but what were the chances of any of it happening, no matter how much he dreaded it? How unlikely was it that she'd rescue him a second time when he was the last person who deserved it? He was ashamed to think that he had once been willing to trade her protection for a single precious gem. It was something he should have been willing to do for nothing. Not even a kiss. In the end, he was just like everyone else in the Silver Order. He just wanted to take, take, take.

Somewhere in these thoughts, he drifted off, returning to them only when he saw her face again. That was when the pain stabbed at him the worst. When it wouldn't let him go. Not even for a second. Sleep was his only respite. A task that was getting harder and harder to achieve, no matter how long he closed his eyes. Even at night.

He didn't know how long he had held his eyes closed. Time was starting to lose meaning. But when he opened them it was day. Early morning, given the pale light and dewy scent to the air. So early, the guard hadn't even shouted for the other prisoners to wake. And yet there was a commotion and shouting.

Darren was still exhausted—he always was—and Lord knew it hurt like hell to move, but he forced himself to sit up. The commotion picked up. From his solitary cell, he could only see the other prisoners through the opening at the end of a narrow hall. They rarely came into view. But pressed up against the bars, every single one of them had their arms stretched out, trying to reach something. They were piled on top of each other, chests tight against the bars, their fingers as far out as they could get them. They got like this for food sometimes, even water. But with their shouts and pleas, this was different somehow.

Whatever it was, it was traveling down the hall now, getting closer. Like the others, he pressed himself hard against the bars too, eager for a look. It was useless to hope, but he had a feeling.

A large mass shadowed the doorway. A group of figures.

One of them was stopping every few paces. They weren't pulling away. They were actually reaching out toward the prisoners. The image didn't make sense. This person was holding the prisoners' hands. A squeeze that lasted a couple of seconds each. Every time, it calmed and silenced them. The prisoners closed their eyes and dropped to their knees as if in prayer. They wouldn't do this for just anyone, least of all their American oppressors. Was it someone from their rebel government? It had to be someone they respected. Silhouetted against the light, the person was only a figure. He couldn't make them out until they were close enough to touch.

Just like the other prisoners, he reached out too. It was everyone in the world whom he wished most to see, the people he would have given life and limb for.

The bars were wide enough that he could press his forehead against hers as she grabbed his arms. Already, he felt better. It was more than her gift of healing that seemed to cure him from the inside out. It was her presence alone.

Darren held on to her even as one of the guards opened the door to his cell. Even when Miller stepped inside, he didn't want to break away.

"How?" he whispered with his eyes closed, pretending for a moment that no one else was there. At the same time, he was terrified to death that this was just a dream.

He half-jumped when Drake answered. It wasn't exactly the soft and gentle voice he wanted to hear, but it was still welcome all the same.

"The guards here are a bit more superstitious than we could have imagined. They recognized Amara at once. At least one of them did."

"It's not superstition at all, then," Darren replied somewhat tersely. The enchanted warmth that he held in his hands was quite real. He thought about staying there in Amara's arms, perhaps forever, when the guard barked something in Tagalog.

"We should go," Amara said in soft tones that could have lulled him to sleep.

He held back a groan. Just the thought of walking already had him wincing. He had gone unconscious from the pain when they'd brought him here. They'd barely supported him, almost as if they'd hoped he might die on the way. What did they care? If he died, at least then they wouldn't have to feed him. They hadn't cared until he'd offered them money.

Like that day, death was still calling out to him. The relief Amara had brought back to him could only be temporary. Like Selene's paste, her gift could only provide relief, not actual healing. There was simply too much that ailed him. Unless...

Was it possible that she was able to do more than defeat Julius? What if she'd gotten emeralds?

Between the fingers that clutched his side, something hot oozed. His wound was open again. Merely standing for a few moments had been enough to do that.

Inside the cell, Miller caught him under the arms just as he was about to fall. "The stones," Miller whispered. "Can't we...?"

Stones? Did he mean the emeralds? He had to. For a moment, it gave Darren hope and with that, strength. Enough that he was unable to brace a foot against the floor and push himself up. Miller positioned Darren's arm over his shoulder and pulled him forward.

"The stones, my lady," Miller pressed.

"We can't, not here," Amara whispered harshly. "It's not safe."

"His wound is dripping blood." Drake came to Darren's side, pressing his hand hard against the wound, what felt like a soldering iron.

"Then we have to hurry." Amara cupped his face with her hand.

Darren had no more energy left. Miller and Drake had to take his full weight, struggling to bring him forward. They'd only taken four steps when Darren stumbled. He broke free of Miller and Drake and would have hit the floor if not for Amara. She caught him on her shoulder, halfway to the ground, nearly falling to the floor herself.

"No," Darren groaned, using every last bit of his energy to protest. "Julius is right. I won't… I won't have you regret this or anything else."

"Darling, no." Amara tried to soothe him. "Let him haunt you no more. He's—"

His spirits lifted. "Is he dead?" If Amara was still alive, he had to be.

"Then he didn't tell you."

"We don't have time for this." Drake tried to help him the rest of the way up. But Darren only shoved him away.

"He's delusional," Miller said.

"I'm not!" Darren barked, suddenly speaking clear. Where the energy came from, he hadn't a clue. "She needs to know. Julius told me something, Amara."

He held her still with his intense gaze. "Something that I've been dreading to relay to you. But if I lived, I promised myself I would. Especially if you came for me."

Tears began to swell in his eyes.

"I already know." Tears swelled in Amara's eyes too.

"You do?"

She nodded. "He told me what the Order did to my mother."

"My father, he… He's been struggling, but I know that's no excuse. I should have taken over years ago. I should have done something."

He waited for a look of horror or anger, but her face didn't shift. Instead, she looked concerned. Of all people, for him. Was he hallucinating again? He had to have been. He didn't know how she could stand him, let alone help him. She should have let him die here. Julius was right. It would have been true justice.

"It wasn't your fault," she finally said. "If it had been, I wouldn't have come. I wouldn't be here with you right now."

"You'd be forgiven that."

"We all should have tried to help your father," Drake put in. "The anger that overtook him forced everyone else away. We shouldn't have let it force us away too."

"We could have found a replacement." Miller nodded.

"Treason or not."

"Now's hardly the time for guilt." Amara looked back at Drake and Miller then suddenly gripped both sides of Darren's face. The feeling of her nails digging into his skin woke him the rest of the way up and out of his daze.

"You've told me," she said. "Now it's time to go."

Why wasn't she more angry?

"Don't you understand?" he said. "My father hired that man, Marx. He gave him free rein to do his dirty work. Who knows what else he could have just let happen."

When he'd first boarded that ship, Darren had had every intention of giving his father at least one emerald, even if he'd known what it might lead to. Just so he could have time with Amara.

"But you don't want what your father wants, do you?" Amara asked. "And you're going to change things."

"How do you know?" he asked as Drake and Miller tried to pull him up again.

"Because you love me."

"I will back you." Drake grunted as he took Darren's weight.

"And so will I," Miller added. "Together and perhaps with a few more friends, we're practically an army."

"Just swear to me you'll do it." Amara gripped his shoulder.

"Yes, I swear it. Of course." Solemn promises were usually reserved for temples or altars, but this rank jail cell will have to do. "I promise to overthrow my father and punish every single person who had a hand in this."

The membership needed him to do it. Amara too.

"Come, then." Darren volleyed all his strength to take a single step. Each one was utter agony.

There was no keeping in groans any longer or trying to seem strong. He was well past that. As they turned a corner, he even let out a few shouts, but soon the pain pushed him in and out of consciousness.

During the brief moments his eyes were open, the prisoners were still on their knees. They let them pass unencumbered, with reverence, even. But it wasn't him they bowed their heads for.

It was far more likely they wished him dead, but because Amara thought him worthy enough to live, so did they. Perhaps that was enough.

His back thumped against the hard seat of the carriage. Above him, the bright and brilliant blue sky was on fire. The clouds were shifting fast.

"Amara?" he called out, worried.

She touched a hand to his face just as the carriage took off at a jarringly fast rate of speed. These bumps were even harder on his body. He was nearly numb from the pain, but not completely.

"No." Amara's face appeared above him. His head, he realized, was cradled in her lap. "You have to stay awake. Sit him up."

As his body shifted upward, he felt more blood spill out of him.

"Hurry!" Drake shouted. "He's gone white."

A cup was forced to his lips. Instinctively, he opened his mouth to drink. Whatever it was, it was sparkling, a translucent green. The most beautiful green he'd ever seen.

WHEN DARREN WOKE, the pain was gone. He'd almost forgotten everything that had happened. Those two miserable nights in jail. It was like waking up in the past before anything terrible had ever happened to him. But that feeling lasted only for a moment. Soon enough, he remembered.

"You're awake."

He sat up to see Amara, washing him with a sponge. Except for a towel over his waist, he was completely naked. There was only one thing he wanted to do. He pulled Amara against him until they were chest to chest. With the contact, everything came crashing back to him in one big jolt. She had saved him.

"Julius, what—"

"He's gone, finished." Amara placed a hand over his chest delicately.

"I wanted to warn you. Out there in the jungle, I knew he was coming after you. Oh, God, how it tortured me. Never again." He closed his eyes a moment. "I'll never allow you to be so vulnerable again. Did he—"

"I handled Julius fine. The jungle too. I felt so strange there," she began in rapid succession, as if to say all the things she'd been holding in while he'd been asleep.

"I can't explain it," she continued. "It was like I was connected to it, to the trees, bugs, everything. I was protected there, Darren. Nothing could have happened. I was safe. But you..." She rested her forehead against his. "What happened to you was far worse. I don't care how much you think you deserved it."

Until he changed things, or rather *they* changed things, he still did. He owed Amara that much, at least. He was more than fine living in her debt. There was so much to say, but all that felt exhausting at the moment. For now, he just wanted to make sure she was still his. At the moment, that was all that mattered to him.

She spoke again. "I wish I could show you everything I saw: the jungle, the archway... But my mother...we'll have to book the first ship out."

"Of course—wait, what do you mean, *show me everything?* Does that include...?"

"The cave? Yes, of course, it's magnificent. More like a giant geode, really. That's the best way I can describe it."

"You would show it to me?" Darren sat up straighter but kept her close in his arms. He was done with all the distance between them these last few days. Certainly nothing good had happened. If he hadn't been sure before, he was sure of it now. They needed each other.

"Indeed."

"But then that means I'd know where it is. I could tell my father or anyone else in the Order, for that matter."

Amara smiled slightly. "I know you won't."

"You do?"

"I *know*."

He smiled. "You trust me, eh?"

"Not because of your past, but because of who you're going to be."

"A premonition? Are you saying you have gifts beyond just healing?"

"It's no premonition, Darren. It's just faith."

"Where was your faith that night at that dinner party? Do you remember it?"

Amara smirked. They both knew how different things had been between them then. The unfair animosity she had placed onto him. It was just anger from her grief. All that time, it had been misdirected.

Darren closed in and kissed her. He had gotten just what he'd wanted, more than what he'd ever hoped for. He turned so Amara fell under him. He felt more than capable, remarkable, really. "Now I shall take you home. As my bride."

Amara laughed. "I see you're well on the mend."

"We have to make sure your mother is too," he said much more seriously, frowning. "You have more, don't you?"

She nodded. "It will be hard to leave. But Mr. Miller and Mr. Drake have insisted we do so first thing tomorrow morning. In case there are those who object to your freedom."

"As long as you're around, I don't think I'll have anything to worry about. But I am eager to be home."

With Amara, London wouldn't quite be the same. Rather, it

was going to seem completely new.

"And Julius," he began. "I'm sure the police—"

"Selene has already reported him to the authorities. As an intruder. It wouldn't be the first time a tourist has tried to steal from us."

Darren gave her a gentle nudge. "No, it isn't. But I imagine news of his death will spread like wildfire. Our membership shall be impressed. Enough that my place as chair will be all the more secure."

"You mean *our* place as chair?" Amara asked coyly. She wasn't about to let him forget. He had a feeling she'd be a very formidable leader, indeed.

"Of course I do. In due time, things are going to be different with us in charge. Very different."

And he wasn't just saying that. He was making a promise.

EPILOGUE

THE GUARDS YELLED and protested, but Darren didn't care. He swept through the doors. His father was behind his desk, sleeping. A small, framed photo—what he knew had to be of his mother—on his chest. It was hard for him too, he wanted to say. But his father had never considered Darren's grief. He had only been consumed with his own.

"Father!" he shouted, startling the old man.

He blinked and smacked his lips together. "I was just having the most pleasant dream. And you woke me from it? For what?"

Had he forgotten about his trip entirely? The fact that he had been gone for months?

"How about a *hello*?"

"Hello." Theodore Pierce grumbled and jerked a hand through his tangled mess of hair. He never bothered to comb it back anymore.

"I'm assuming you've heard? At the very least have you skimmed my letters?"

"For the love of God, be direct, Darren."

"I've married, Father."

He stared back at him, not looking disappointed, per se, as Darren had expected. He just didn't care. Despite her desire to, Darren was glad Amara had agreed not to come.

"To the countess," Darren clarified.

"It's your life." His father waved it away. "Do with it what you will. If you want pain like this in your life one day. So be it."

Darren rolled his eyes. "Would you really have preferred never to know her? Would you really prefer a life in which I'd never been born?"

"Would I—" he started as though he'd never even considered such an idea. "Just tell me one thing. Have you found the blasted emeralds or not?"

"I have not." Darren clenched his hands behind his back, not bothering to take a seat just yet.

His father clenched his jaw. "Then you have failed me greatly."

"If I had discovered them, what would you have done with them, Father? It has nothing to do with building our knowledge or the Silver Order—which you have a duty to, need I remind you?"

His father clasped his hands and leaned over his desk. His face fell, pulled down by exhaustion and the heavy weight of grief.

"You think it does more than just heal," Darren said. His father had told him as much just before he'd left on the *Evangeline*.

His father widened his eyes. "Yes, it can resurrect. It's true, isn't it?"

"No, of course not. Even if it could, do you really think Mother would want that? She's passed on," he said firmly. He could accept it—why couldn't he? "She wouldn't want to be brought back."

"Her death was so sudden, there's nothing anyone can say for certain. She had not time to…" His father looked off.

"It's time, Father."

"Time for what?" He snapped his gaze back up.

"You need to retire and hand the chairmanship to me."

His face twisted, confused. "Excuse me?"

"If you make me explain, you shall not like what you hear."

"And yet, I shall have to hear it nonetheless," he bit out, teeth clenched.

"One of your own men poisoned a woman. Do you even remember?"

"I remember perfectly well. I'm not overtaken with drink as you are, am I?"

"You are the one who has failed, Father. You have failed all of us."

"I? It was Marx who took that course of action. And he has been dealt with." His father pointed a finger down on his desk.

Darren was unaffected.

"You should have seen his plans coming a thousand miles away. Of course he resorted to those sorts of means. I've met the man all but once and would expect little less."

"I had you follow Lady Webb. I made sure she had good protection. You even got a wife out of the ordeal."

"You didn't send me after Amara to protect her!" Darren started to yell. "You wanted the emeralds and nothing more. And for your own selfish purposes."

Panic was starting to build in his father's eyes.

"If you don't agree, I'll make a case." Darren went very still. "I'll expose everything you've done."

His father said nothing, just glared back at him.

"You know you've been distracted. At best."

"Is that why you've come here? To threaten me?" He pounded a fist against the desk.

"There are those who are already on my side, if you must know. Julius came after us. And now he's dead. It's the kind of tale everyone just loves to hear. The sort that precedes a great leader."

His father stood and Darren straightened. "I've never raised a fist to you, Father. But those days are long past."

"Then go."

"Retire, Father, or it's civil war we'll have."

For a moment, they stared back at each other. This was going nowhere.

Without another word, Darren turned to the door.

"Goodbye, Father," he grumbled as he left.

☽

AMARA PULLED THE hood up over her head as she snuck out into the night. Her heels clicked over cobblestone with only dim street lanterns to light her way. She hated any secrecy between herself and Darren. But she knew he'd never allow her to meet with his father alone. As angry as Darren was with his father, she was convinced he wasn't so bad. She often wondered if, without him, she would have ever found her way into Darren's arms. A most wonderful end through the most awful of means.

Though their lives were still far from perfect. They needed ten guards now, five times what they'd had on their expedition. And their lives were more than twice as dangerous.

Especially now that his father had refused to retire and give up his position as chair. Ever since, stability of the Order spun wildly out of control.

The membership had split into two factions. All regular meetings and research had ceased. It was no way to start her position as co-chair. Sacrifices, she realized, would need to be made. She had a suspicion that something else was at play too, not just the elder Pierce's relentless need for power.

Alone and completely vulnerable, she found the hired hack at the end of the street just where she'd told the driver to be. Even he sensed her nervousness.

"Are you all right, miss?" he asked.

She was leaving behind a warm bed and her sleeping husband at the witching hour so she could travel alone to one of the less-savory parts of London. Of course she wasn't all right. But she told him she was fine nonetheless.

If she simplified it, all she was really going to do was have a little chat with her father-in-law. But deep down, she couldn't brush aside the importance of meeting. How so much hinged on this, namely whether or not an all-out civil war would erupt within the Order.

She couldn't stomach it. She couldn't allow so much chaos to take over her new life with Darren, but that was exactly where they were heading.

The roar of the White Stag tavern reached the hack well before it came to a halt. *Thank God.* Deep into the night, the tavern was crowded, just as she'd hoped it might be. The lower classes and even the gentry ventured there. It was easy to tell them apart by cleanliness and dress. But when it came to ill-intentions, they all had much in common.

She kept her gaze down, though most were too deep into their cups to notice her, let alone appreciate the importance of a meeting that was about to happen at another one of the tavern's many tables and benches. Whispering her pardons, she shifted through the bodies entirely unseen.

It wasn't difficult to spot Pierce. He was at the only table where everyone sat up straight and relatively still. At this hour, most patrons were hunched over their mugs, some even passed out at their tables.

Pierce's table, on the other hand, was filled with his best men. Ten, to be precise. How amusing that he thought her such a threat. So he'd heard the rumors, then. She smiled at that. Members were rumored to call her 'the Emerald Enchantress,' a woman who supposedly had abilities well beyond just healing.

She dropped her hood and sat down at the table's one open seat. He more than slightly resembled Darren. This alone helped warm her to him. Even if he looked angry.

"Father," she began boldly.

He raised one corner of his mouth. "You are brave for a woman," he said even and without emotion. "My wife was brave too."

"It takes much courage to marry into a family like yours."

Pierce nodded. "True words."

"How long ago did she die?" she asked.

"Seven years in July," he half-whispered.

"I understand what you're going through, you know."

She could hear it in his voice—the grief she knew all too well that had once forced her to do so many irrational things like hate the man she now loved.

She could see it on her father-in-law's face and feel it like Lola once had—as an aura all around her. She could practically smell it. He had been filled with not just darkness but great pain. The grief and anger feeding into each other like a snake eating its tail.

Darren had told her the real reason his father wanted the emeralds was to bring back Darren's mother. Amara didn't want to believe it, but maybe it was true.

Even though the elder Pierce seemed beyond skeptical of her, she didn't hesitate. There could be no more of that. She reached out and before he could move away, Amara gripped his hands. Pierce flinched for a moment but eventually went still. So still, in fact, that he closed his eyes. Whatever relief she brought to him, he was clearly savoring. He must have been in more pain than she'd thought. Seven years had done little to lessen his grief.

It must not have all been on the surface. There was more buried deep inside him. The kind of grief he wouldn't let anyone see, that he hid all too well. When her father had died, she had tried to hide it too.

It explained his temper, even his violence. She was finally beginning to understand just how bad it had gotten for him.

Almost a full minute passed before he opened his eyes again.

"So your power is real?"

The guards around him shifted and whispered to each other. If she was capable of this, what else was she capable of? She'd come alone, but maybe it wasn't just because she was brave. It was because she had the ability to fight them off as easily as taking a breath. They would think twice about strong-arming her.

She had considered the worst-case scenario too. The possibility of them taking her against her will and holding her for ransom, demanding whatever they wanted from Darren. Lord knew he would pay whatever they wanted. She had gambled on something else: Pierce needed her.

"I haven't felt that good in years," he whispered.

"It's only temporary, I'm afraid."

In other words, he'd never feel that good again. His lip quivered at the thought.

"But I do have a more permanent solution."

"The emeralds," he breathed, leaning forward. "Tell me you have them. I merely want to see one."

"They can't bring your wife back."

Pierce narrowed his eyes. "You're certain."

Amara lifted her chin.

"Of course." He raised his hands, looking more than a little defeated. "I should have known that part was only legend."

"But they can lessen your grief. They can soothe the pain from your heart."

Pierce looked down, considering, then barely above a whisper, he said, "Please."

"I'm not just going to hand them over, sir. I have terms."

He crossed his arms. "Yes, I imagine you do."

"I want you to step down."

At this, Pierce made a face.

"But you may continue to serve as an advisor to your son."

"Like Drake and Miller now? Am I to have the same standing as a couple of impoverished orphans?"

"Those *orphans* helped keep your son alive while he was out correcting the Order's wrongdoings. Just like these men keep you alive." Amara looked at the men briefly then back at Pierce. A few of them nodded ever so slightly. While they had chosen the wrong side in these matters, she could at least appreciate their loyalty.

"How is your mother?" Pierce asked.

"Well now."

"I do apologize for that ordeal."

"Thank you." She smiled, the apology more surprising to her than if he had reached out and hugged her. He had been sick with grief was all. He just needed help. "When you feel well, you'll be able to focus better."

"On the Order?"

"As an advisor."

"I'll feel better?" His voice grumbled without cheer. He was still hesitant to believe any of it. "Do you swear it?"

She nodded.

Before complete relief could pass over his features, he continued to look skeptical.

"You're sure Darren will agree to this? He's lied to me from the start. Told me he never even found the emeralds. I knew he was lying. I'm his father. I could tell before the words even passed his lips."

Amara sank down a little. She'd never wanted him to lie, but he had nonetheless. To protect her.

"He feared what you might do with them. But I have far more faith than he does. And I know what you want for him."

More than that, she knew what the elder Pierce wanted for himself and it wasn't just the emeralds. It was relief from his persistent grief. A difficult task that would require his retirement.

"He'll be angry," Pierce said. "After what I've done, he won't think it's fair."

"It isn't fair. But that doesn't matter and neither do Darren's wishes in this case. These stones are mine to give out as I please."

Not to mention that she and Darren now had the same footing. In the end, it would all be for the best. He would forgive her, just as he would forgive his father for his negligence. One day, maybe even she would.

She reached into the deep pockets of her cloak. "As it is, you shall only receive one."

"Then what?" He let out a long breath. Fighting this civil war had been just as exhausting for him as she'd expected.

"Then we shall be a family again. As difficult as that may be."

She had faced many challenges recently. Forgiveness might very well be the hardest.

"Will you allow them to be studied?" He steepled his hands,

his eyes alight with all the possibilities.

"No, I don't think I will. Not in your lifetime, anyway."

"But why?" He started to raise his voice.

"Because you'll never understand them." She raised her voice back. Wasn't it perfectly obvious? "But they will soothe your grief so you can become a proper grandfather." She placed a hand over her stomach though she wasn't quite showing yet. "After all, our child will only have one. A role that is far more important than Chair in my mind."

Though he tried to keep his expression straight, his eyes wavered a little. For a moment, she could actually see some warmth in them. It was still there, no matter how deeply buried.

"A promotion." He lifted his chin, his eyes slightly glazed.

"A child born into all of this will have much to learn," Amara pointed out. Maybe by retiring, he was afraid that he'd be bored, that he'd sink deeper into the depression that had seized him since his wife's death. But Amara wanted to promise him that he wouldn't.

"Very well," Pierce finally agreed with surprising swiftness. "I shall retire and the infighting will end. You have my word."

He stretched out his hand.

When Amara dropped the emerald in his palm, even the guards who had clearly been listening in on the conversation sagged an inch or two into their seats, complete and utter relief overtaking their faces. With a drop of a stone, she had essentially ended a civil war.

They had too many enemies like Julius to allow infighting. And the emeralds they had in their arsenal were sure to attract even more. But so long as the rumors about her kept circulating, Amara wasn't much fazed. Not when she could see the fear that still lingered on the faces of Pierce's guards. They were right to be afraid. Everyone should be. The Order and their enemies had no idea what was coming for them.

THE END

About the Author

Ella Leon writes historical romance with a twist of magic and suspense.

During her 9–5 career, she has delved into many different styles of writing: journalism, public relations and marketing. Fiction, however, is where she finds the most freedom to transform the page. Like the Victorians she writes about, she loves all things gothic and supernatural. Unlike the Victorians, she is a feminist who enjoys exploring the precolonial past.

When she's not writing, you can find her spending time with her family or tending to her rose garden. She lives in the Chicago area.

Links:
Website: ellaleon.weebly.com
Facebook: facebook.com/ella.leon.author
Tiktok: tiktok.com/@ella_leon
Threads: threads.net/@e.k.toth
X: @Stoeverit

9 781967 169481